# Never Apart

# Never Apart

## ROMILY BERNARD

Copyright © 2017 by Romily Bernard. All rights reserved, including the right to reproduce, distribute, or transmit in any form or by any means. For information regarding subsidiary rights, please contact the Publisher.

Entangled Publishing, LLC
2614 South Timberline Road
Suite 109
Fort Collins, CO 80525

Entangled Teen is an imprint of Entangled Publishing, LLC.

Visit our website at www.entangledpublishing.com.

Edited by Heather Howland
Cover design by Fiona Jayde
Interior design by Toni Kerr

ISBN: 978-1-63375-822-3
Ebook ISBN: 978-1-63375-823-0

Manufactured in the United States of America

First Edition October 2017

10 9 8 7 6 5 4 3 2 1

entangled teen
an imprint of Entangled Publishing LLC

*For my one and only Alodie.*

# chapter one

*I'm going to die again.*

Ander's hand tightens around mine like he can hear my thoughts. Or maybe it's just because he can hear my breathing: too fast, too ragged. We're running and running, and I can't go much farther. My lungs are burning. My knees are buckling.

"C'mon!" Ander tugs me closer and I slip, lose my shoe in a puddle. The rain's coming harder now, the grass turning to mud, but we don't stop. We can't.

Finn is drawing closer.

"Don't look back," Ander says.

I do. I can't help it. I can *hear* him.

Finn's breathing's gone ragged, too. He sounds like a dragon in the dark. He's driving us into the swamp, hunting us.

*I'm going to die again.*

Low tree branches whip my face, rip hair from my head. Ander grunts and staggers sideways, rights himself. I squeeze his hand, pump my shaking knees harder. He matches me stride for stride. We splash through a pocket of swamp water, and Ander shoves me left, toward a tangle of dead cypresses.

*One…two…three…four…*

Finn splashes in four seconds behind us and Ander twists sideways, hauls me to the ground. Mud, thick and rotten-smelling, cushions our fall. Ander rolls left, tucks us close to a thicket of overgrown briars. It's a hot summer night, but the swamp water's cold. I can't stop shivering. I clutch Ander's arm with one hand, my knife with the other, and for the first time I'm glad there's no moonlight. Finn will never see my blade coming.

Ander crouches over me as Finn draws closer…closer…

Away from us.

Finn slogs deeper into the water and stops, listening. Ander holds me tighter, and I crush my mouth against his T-shirt.

*He's going to hear you. He's going to hear you.*

Finn turns right, splashes farther into the swamp. His footsteps drift right and then left and then right again, and I swallow a sob, taste the rain running down my face. He's looking for our hiding spot.

*I'm going to die again.*

"Don't be afraid," Ander whispers. "If we Fall again, I will find you."

This is what Ander always says: *I will find you.*

This is what Ander never says: *so will Finn.*

Because Finn always finds us. Always. It's in my head like a mantra, like there are *rules*—and there are no rules or, at least, there aren't any rules that I know beyond this:

It's always the three of us.

We always find each other.

Ander and I can run, but Finn always follows, and we always die.

"Not this time," I whisper, which means this time I can't

miss. This time I have to kill Finn first. I lean forward even as Ander tries to press me back. He's afraid for me. He should be afraid *of* me. When did I become capable of murder? When Finn killed Ander the tenth time? The twentieth?

He always finds us—and he'll find us *soon*, even if we stay hidden. He knows we're here.

Another sob wobbles in my throat, and I chew it down, fingers tightening around the wet knife handle. I place my free hand against Ander's chest. For a heartbeat, he resists.

"You promised," I breathe, and somewhere in the dark, Finn stops. He hears us. "You promised," I repeat, lifting my voice a little louder because it will bring Finn closer and force Ander to keep his word.

In every lifetime, he has died and I have watched. In every lifetime, he has fought Finn and we have lost. This time? This time I will fight and Ander will watch and maybe the pattern will finally break.

And maybe we will live.

My heart swings like a pendant on a string. We will *live*.

Finn sloshes closer, and I force myself to stand. He's a shadow against the trees, liquid dark churning through the shallow water. I manage three steps sideways and then three more, drawing Finn away from Ander. He follows until I pause.

I fight like total crap, but I'm good at being Finn's lure. He's given me lots of practice. I wait and wait and he studies me and studies me and then—

"Grace," Finn breathes.

And I charge. I hit him low, ramming my shoulder into his chest as his fingernails dig into my arms. Finn plows me into the mud, and I jam the knife in deep. Deeper. Finn swears. I stagger.

My hand slips. I lose the knife as Finn tips sideways. He seizes my wrist and I kick him, grabbing for the blade handle and missing.

No, I didn't miss. I can't *find* it.

We're grappling in the mud, then hands dig under my arms, yank me to my feet.

"Run!" Ander drags me forward and I stagger, feel Finn's fingers snatch at my bare leg, hear him hiss my name.

"Go!" Ander shoves us deeper into the swamp. We push past thicker trees and into colder water. This far in, it's even darker and the mud is deeper and Finn is cursing. He's to our right? Our left? I twist and trip, crash against a tree coated in wet moss.

"I can't," I gasp, and Ander doesn't argue. He presses his face into my neck and breathes me in like I'm not covered in sweat and tears and mud, like we're on a date and I am what he's always wanted. "You know how this ends," he whispers into my rain-soaked skin.

I don't answer. I can't. Won't.

My eyes search the shadows as my hands search for Ander. I find his fingers and knot them in mine. "It's like he didn't even *feel* it! Maybe I missed? How could I have *missed*?"

"Because we always miss and Finn never does. Grace" — Ander gives me the tiniest shake — "*you know how this ends*."

I dig my fingers into his T-shirt, and tears leak down my cheeks. They're even warmer than the rain.

There's a splash to our right, and a shadow moves closer. Finn.

"When I jump him," Ander whispers, "I want you to run. Do you understand?"

Of course I do. We've done this over forty times. I understand how it works, how it ends, how much I love the boy I'm about to watch die.

"I love you," he whispers.

"I love you, too."

Ander pushes away from me in one smooth, silent

movement. We've gotten good at that, but Finn still tenses. He heard us. He's gotten good at this, too.

I shrink against a rotting tree trunk, taste mud when I swallow. Once upon a time, we were all friends and now… now…

"Go, Grace," Ander says as Finn swings around. "Don't look back. *Go*."

Ander rushes him. One stride. Two strides. Connect. They go down with a splash and I'm ready to run, but running would mean leaving Ander to die, and I can't. I can't do it anymore. I can't *watch* this anymore.

Ander spins Finn around and there's the horrible smack of flesh on flesh. Finn staggers and I'm moving before I even realize it. I smash my fist into Finn's face and he tilts sideways, stumbles.

Ander lunges. Finn twists. The knife lifts.

Ander drops.

His knees hit the water. His head rolls back. I cannot catch him as he falls.

"Ander—"

Finn grabs for me and I stumble away, my bare foot plunging into a hole. Pain spikes up my leg. I yank sideways. More pain. I falter, color spraying behind my eyes, and when I open them again, I'm on my knees.

*Get up! Get—*

I feel him.

Ander.

His chest under my palm. His T-shirt twisted in my fingers. I struggle to turn, shivering from the cold mud and the colder water, as Finn limps toward me. It makes tiny waves lap at my forearms and thighs. I shove up and we look at each other— really look at each other.

I see a boy barely past seventeen with Ander's blood on

his shirt. Again.

He sees a girl barely past seventeen with Ander's blood on her hands. Again.

I'm coated with mud and drenched with rain. I look like I crawled from a grave, and it's so damn fitting I want to laugh.

"Please," I force through cracked lips. "Please don't do this."

"So many lifetimes," Finn says, drawing closer. "So many Graces and yet you all cause so much damage. How is that possible?"

I don't understand. I swallow, swallow again. All I taste is blood and all I smell is rot. "Please," I try again. "I don't understand! We used to be *friends*! Why does this keep happening? Why do you keep *doing* this?"

Finn shakes his head like he hates it when I lie, only I'm *not* lying.

"I don't understand," I whisper.

Finn lifts my dirty knife. "We all have to pay for what we did."

# chapter two

I wake up screaming in a voice that isn't mine, grabbing for a knife that's no longer there. I blink, blink again. Something's beeping, and I can't tell where it's coming from. My vision won't clear. I shake my head hard. A mistake. My stomach threatens to heave into my mouth.

I open my eyes to white tiles under my knees...white towels above me...white—oh. I'm in a bathroom. I Fell.

*I'm going to die again.*

*If only it would work.*

I slide a trembling hand under me and push myself up. There's club music thumping hard enough to vibrate the floor, and outside the door, someone's calling someone else an asshole.

Oh, wait. The guy's calling *me* an asshole.

"Hurry up!" he bellows.

"Out"—I cough—"out in a minute."

The guy grabs the door handle, rattles it. He thumps his weight against the wood, and I freeze because for a terrible moment I think it isn't just some random person out there.

It's Finn, and he's here to kill me again. The handle rattles and rattles and I can't drag my eyes from it.

*He's never found me this fast before. We've always had five days. He's never been this quick.*

The door handle jerks once more, stops. I suck in a breath, blow it out, suck in another. In, out, no pause—even though I should because I'm already light-headed. I'm *always* light-headed after I Fall, but this feels different. It feels…off, way worse than usual. I try to stand and topple to my knees.

This isn't the Fall. I'm *drunk*. Or, rather, *this* Grace is drunk. I lurch up again and have to grab the sink edge for support. My legs are numb.

*How long was the other me on the floor?*

I crank the faucets as high as they'll go and splash my face with water. Still dripping, I grope for a hand towel and press it to my skin. Better. I feel better. I still press the towel a little tighter though, because I know what comes next.

*Just do it already. C'mon. You've done it*—I squint against the rough terry cloth—*forty-two times now. Just look at yourself.*

I snap up my head and flinch. The face in the mirror is mine, but the details are never right, and maybe by the time I get to Fall 142 I'll be used to it.

My fingers wrap around the sink's edge as I lean in. This Grace has my brown eyes and my pointed chin, but she wears her eyebrows heavier and her hair curlier.

"My name is Grace," I whisper. My voice is raspy, vibrating inside my head like a stranger.

Which I guess is fitting, since this Grace kind of is.

"My name is Grace," I repeat, forcing my voice to lift because I could go on. I could say I've died forty-one times and now woken up forty-two times and every time I wake up, I'm me—only I'm a different me in a different timeline.

I take another breath, smelling vomit and perfume—roses? Whatever. Doesn't matter. I'm stalling, and I know the drill. These are the other rules Ander and I know: get your stuff, get oriented, get *going* because we only have five days until Finn finds us again.

My stomach rolls, and I hold my breath until the nausea passes.

*Bam! Bam!* "Hey!"

"One second!" I toss the hand towel in the laundry basket by the tub and smooth down my dress, spotting a heavy brown purse sprawled on the floor by the door.

*Get your stuff.* Considering the huge purse is on the bathroom floor, it's probably mine. I paw through the contents, fingers brushing something plastic. Phone. I check the screen. It's Saturday night, almost eleven, and the battery's dying. The beep I heard earlier now sounds more like a bleat.

*Saturday night means you have until Wednesday.* I toss the cell back in my purse and consider myself in the mirror again.

*Get oriented. Where are you?*

Clearly, I'm in someone's bathroom—I don't think it's mine, though. For some reason, it feels like this is someone else's house. This Grace is at a party, a big one from the sounds of it. Is she happy about being at the party? Too soon to tell.

I look down, noticing my clothes again: silky purple sundress whispering against my full hips, white platform sandals with a neon green grass stain on the right toe, a tangle of mismatched gold necklaces. I touch one nail-chewed fingertip to a tiny pendant shaped like a coin.

*Get going.* You can handle this.

Except when I readjust my purse strap, I wobble again. I press one hand to the glossy white wall. Is it the beer or the shock?

"Get a grip," I whisper and then almost laugh when I

realize that should be another rule. I tug the door once and it flies open, nearly smashing me in the face.

"What the—"

"Sorry!" I shove past the boy on the other side, gagging again because he reeks of sweat and pot.

The hallway's crowded, and the music is even louder. I have no idea which way to go. To my left, a bunch of people. To my right, a bunch more people. So much for getting oriented. A brunette with a fraying braid and a pine-green dress staggers into me. I shrink against the wall.

"Grace?"

I pivot, searching for the voice. Eyes meet mine, but no one holds my gaze.

"Grace!" A blond girl bounces to my side, ponytail swinging. She's smiling at me like we're best friends.

Maybe we are?

"Where've you been?" she yells. "We've been looking for you everywhere."

"Bathroom," I yell. She links her arm through mine and I'm grateful. I'm nowhere near steady. I have to concentrate on every step even though my new friend weaves us easily through the crowd.

Or maybe it's just that the crowd parts for her. The blonde's like Moses in a miniskirt; people just skitter out of the way.

The hallway widens into a massive white living room. The couches are white. The walls are white. The cavernous ceiling above is white except for the far corners, which are dusky with shadows. Two girls are dancing on a coffee table, and at least four guys are watching. Someone's strung white lights across the rafters. They dribble down the columns and into twinkling pools by people's feet.

*Never seen a party this big.*

Only as soon as I think it, I realize I'm wrong. The night of my first Fall, I was at a party like this. In fact, the house almost feels familiar—like Ander should be kneeling in the bathroom to my left and Finn should be waiting for me by the door on my right, like we're back in our real lives again.

Even though Finn isn't there, my heart still lurches. My blond friend squeezes us between a beer pong game and a couple making out against the wall.

"Becca!" A guy in a baseball cap grins at her and she—Becca—marches straight past him. His smile crumples and unease curls through me. I know what it feels like to be blown off.

"Sorry," I mouth, and his face slackens. He's surprised. Why is he surprised?

I look at my feet and concentrate on the grass stain smudge. *Get oriented*: he's surprised because this Grace doesn't apologize.

Becca tugs my hand hard. "How much have you had to drink?" she shouts.

"Um…" I can't find an answer. Everywhere I look, people are watching us, and chills creep across my skin. It's not my imagination. Almost everyone is sliding sideways glances in our direction. They look…nervous, maybe even a little scared. They watch us, but they don't come any closer. It's like they're in awe.

Becca tugs me again and I stumble. Are these girls popular? Am *I* popular? The idea is like bubbles on my brain. I've never been popular before. I wonder if I'll like it.

"Who're you looking for?" Becca asks.

*Ander. Finn.* "Nobody."

I follow her through smudged glass doors, and humid summer air hits me like a wall. I smell freshly mowed grass and honeysuckle and water and…

Blood.

*I'm going to die again.* I suddenly can't breathe, and I have to shake myself. *Stop it.*

Becca releases my hand and joins a long-legged brunette lounging on a porch swing. "Found her," Becca says, taking a blue Solo cup from the other girl.

"God, Grace." The brunette plays with the tips of her hair as she studies me. "Did you get lost or what?"

"Sorry," I say, shifting from foot to foot. No matter what lifetime I am ever in, girls like these make me nervous. They keep staring, and I try not to wince.

"Is it your asthma again?" the brunette asks.

I shake my head hard, curls bouncing. "Guess these parties aren't my thing."

Only as soon as I say it, I know these parties *are* my thing. This Grace, the Grace I'm supposed to be now, loves these parties, and that's partly why everyone's here. They look at me like I've lost my mind, and I look everywhere else.

The wraparound porch sits above a wide sweep of manicured lawn. The grass slopes down, down, down to a hard edge of shadows. Trees.

Swamp.

I turn, putting my back to it, which is stupid because the smell doesn't go away. The porch lights cast our reflections against the darkened windows, and I catch a glimpse of myself again.

As far as Ander and I can tell, every time we Fall, we surface with different lives. It's not time travel—we don't end up in the past or the future—it's more like we end up in parallel universes, timelines that belong to other versions of ourselves.

Sometimes the new timelines are like ones we've lived before. Sometimes they're not. I'm always *me,* though. My soul or whatever is the same. Give or take some cosmetic decisions, my bodies are always the same, but my *lives* are the products of parents and grandparents who made different decisions.

Like Fall number 4, when my dad didn't even know I was alive because my mom had gotten pregnant during a one-night stand. Or Fall number 14, when both of my parents hated me.

Or Falls number 1-41, where my twin brother didn't exist.

I don't know why my name is always the same. I don't know why Finn—who used to be my friend—hunts me. I don't know why I recognize some people, why sometimes I instinctively know things I shouldn't. It's an infinite universe with infinite possibilities and yet these things have always been mine.

Becca makes a joke, and everyone laughs. Except for me. I'm too busy cataloging: these are my new clothes. These are my new friends. This is my new life.

I'm not cold, but my skin stands up with goose bumps.

*This is my new life. For the next five days.*

# chapter three

*then...*

Our grandfather died when Jem and I were six. He'd been sick for as long as we'd been alive, but the phone call still knocked the knees out from under our mother. She sat down hard on the kitchen floor, staring at something we couldn't see.

"Mama?" I didn't think she heard me, so I said it again. "Mama?"

"I need you two to be good. Do not leave the house."

I was too scared to ask why. She didn't sound like my mom. The words were rusted, like she resurrected them from some part of her I didn't even know existed.

"Do not leave the house," she said again, hauling herself toward her bedroom. "I need a minute."

Jem stood beside me. He studied her, and then he studied me. "C'mon," he said at last, and I followed because I always followed Jem. He was my second heartbeat.

We watched television. We ate dry cereal. We made a fort out of couch cushions even though we knew we weren't supposed to.

Our mother didn't come out. She was there, but she wasn't *there*, and when our dad came home four hours later, he looked at the kitchen and living room and then at us.

"What's going on?"

Jem peeked over the wall of couch cushions. "Grandpa died."

Our dad jerked straight, eyes widening like he'd stumbled on a step. "*When?*"

"This morning," I said.

Dad nodded and nodded. He passed one hand through his hair. "Are you hungry?"

I held up the pink cereal box. "No."

He turned to my brother. "Jem?"

"No."

"Okay...okay..." Dad rubbed the back of his head again. He retreated down the hallway, toward their room. The bedroom door shut with the softest *snick*, and he didn't return until the living room was lit only by the television's blue light. Jem and I waited for him to yell about the mess. He didn't, though. He sat on the floor with us, his long legs pushed in front him. He looked boneless, like one of the rag dolls I was supposed to be interested in playing with.

"Is Mama better?" I asked.

Dad shook his head, and I nuzzled into his side, forcing myself to fit into the hollow under his arm. "Will she be better tomorrow?" I asked.

"No."

"Because she's sad?"

He stared at the wall and nodded. "Your mom didn't get along so well with your grandfather. She never had with her dad what you two have with me."

I didn't fit under Dad's arm like I used to, but he pulled me tighter against him like he didn't notice.

"She didn't have a good dad," Jem said. "He wasn't like you."

It made sense and didn't make sense. How could Mama be sad about something that never existed? How could you miss something that wasn't there?

I picked at the carpet by my toes, picked at the wrinkled hem of Dad's pants. "Why will she be sad then?" I asked him.

He still wouldn't look at me. "Because the past wants to be heard and sometimes you have to wait until it's done with you."

My funeral dress was scratchy, and Jem's jacket was too small in the shoulders. He had a hard time swinging his arms.

"You're not supposed to swing your arms," Mama said. Her eyes were pink and puffy, and her hands were cracked and chapped. She couldn't stop washing them. "It's a funeral. You're supposed to sit quietly and reflect."

Jem said he couldn't reflect on anything when he felt like he was in a straitjacket. Mama stopped dead at that one. She even looked like she might laugh, then the laugh was swallowed.

"It's not a straitjacket," Mama said at last. I thought she was trying for mad and missing the mark. She was amazed at what Jem knew. We all were.

Maybe that was why the relatives always asked him what he was doing in school. They never asked me things like that—mostly they complimented my dresses, which had nothing to do with me because my mother picked out all my clothes.

"You look very nice, Grace," my great aunt said when I

came by with cookies. She took two even though we both knew she'd never eat them. "Your dress is so pretty."

*It's making my armpits itch,* I wanted to say, but didn't because people had been saying it all afternoon. They seemed awfully glad about it, too. Gave them something else to talk about. Grown-ups drifted from huddled group to huddled group, reciting the same lines like my teacher's pet parrot.

"So sad."

"He's in a better place."

"At least she has the children to comfort her."

I sat in the corner closest to the kitchen and watched. Jem went…somewhere and didn't invite me. I finished my fourth cookie and started on my fifth when I heard the screen door slap. I bolted for the kitchen.

A blond boy stood on cracked linoleum floor. We blinked at each other.

"Who're you?" I asked.

"He's our neighbor. Dad said he just moved here." Jem was getting flashlights from the junk drawer and didn't bother looking up as he explained. "His name is Ander."

"It's short for Alexander," Ander added.

"Oh." I wanted to know why he was here. I wanted to know even more why my brother was so interested in him.

"Here." Jem passed a green metal flashlight to Ander. They turned them on, splashing around yellow circles of light.

"I want to come, too," I said.

My twin sighed. "You don't even know where we're going."

"I want to come anyway."

"You can't," Jem said. Ander didn't say anything. He watched the kitchen door like he was afraid a grown-up was coming. Jem glared at me, his mouth screwed up in the way I hated most. It meant he was going to say I couldn't come because I was a girl or I couldn't come because it was only for boys, which I especially hated because I didn't have any way to pay him back. I couldn't say, whatever I was doing was only for girls. Everything I wanted to do, I wanted to do with him.

"Let her come," Ander said, still not looking at either of us.

"Fine." Jem sighed. "But you're not going to like it."

He was right, of course. They had decided to explore the space under our house. I followed them through the brittle pikes of grass and stood by the air conditioner while they tugged at the crawl space's door.

"We're not supposed to go under there," I told Jem. Jem ignored me. He broke the latch on the plywood door, and Ander held it open.

"Better in here than out there," Ander said, and suddenly I knew I agreed. I didn't want to go back inside with the adults and their whispers that sounded more like a beehive hum—didn't mean I wanted to go under there with the spiders and the dirt and the snakes, either.

Then the boys ducked into the dark, leaving me. I scrambled after them. Under the house, it smelled like wet earth, and the farther we crawled, the worse it got. We paused next to a column of cinder blocks, listening to the adults' footsteps overhead as Ander pointed the flashlight toward every corner.

"Why are we doing this?" I whispered.

Jem leaned so close his whisper poured into my ear. "Because I didn't want to."

Funny. It sounded like he was saying "Because I'm scared," and Jem was never scared. Ever. Then Ander crawled on and Jem followed Ander and I followed Jem until the darkness had a weight and I thought I was going to suffocate.

We crawled all the way to the far end and sat with our backs to the concrete walls. The footsteps were lighter over here, but the shadows were worse.

"Are you okay?" Jem whispered, and that's when I knew I was wheezing.

I shook my head. "I'm afraid of the dark."

"Why?"

My heart wobbled. Our mom would've said I was too old to be scared. Our dad would've agreed with her. Jem never said stuff like that to me, though. Even when our parents said he should.

I took a deep breath. "It's where monsters live."

The boys thought about this. The silence stretched and stretched until Ander said, "Then we'll be monsters, too."

"What?"

"That way they won't recognize us." His hand found mine, twining around my icy fingers. Until then, I hadn't realized I was cold.

"We'll look the same as them," Ander told me, and in the dark we made our scariest faces.

Later, I couldn't drag my eyes from him.

# chapter four

*now...*

A warm breeze pushes through the swamp, and suddenly everything smells like rain. I take a deep breath, pulling it into my lungs, my stomach. I concentrate on my feet, my toes. The nails are painted the softest baby pink.

"This is lame," one girl says. "Let's go."

"Where?" another asks.

"We're staying," Becca snaps. She takes a blue Solo cup from the rail and swirls the contents around. I sneak a glance at the others. They're all dressed like me...or maybe I'm dressed like them? Everyone's wearing sandals and sundresses, and two brunettes flank me like gargoyles.

*That's not nice.* They're not flanking me like gargoyles. They're flanking me like guards, like I won't have to be alone anymore.

I don't know if I'll like being popular, but I do know I like that. It's breathtakingly lonely Falling like we do. You're walking around in skin that's yours and isn't yours, with friends that know you and don't know you. You don't have your own life anymore. Everything is temporary.

Except for Ander.

And Finn.

"Where's your drink, Grace?" Becca asks. "Did you leave it inside?"

I cast a glance around me. Maybe? I could have left it inside. I don't think I left it in the bathroom.

At least, I don't remember leaving it there.

I heave a sigh. I'll need to get another, and I don't want it. I'm finally filling out this body. The world's stopped swaying. I can feel my feet press evenly against the porch flooring, and I open my mouth to say I don't want one…then notice how their eyes keep straying over and over me. They think I'm being weird.

"I'll get another," I say.

"Dude." Becca smirks. "You are *way* off tonight. Are you about to be sick? Because I told you not to drink anything the baseball players offer you."

I force my face into a smile. "No, I'm fine. Really. Sorry."

"You should be." Becca scowls and checks her phone. The screen splashes white light across the angles of her face. "Did you call your brother? Jem says he's here. He wants to know why you haven't answered his texts."

For two whole seconds, I am not standing on some stranger's porch. I'm fishing with Jem. I'm having my thirteenth birthday with Jem. I can hear *Jem*. His laugh. His voice. The way he said my name.

In all my Falls, through all my variations, he's been missing.

"Grace!"

I blink, back on the porch again.

Becca waves her cell at me. "Why'd you call him?"

I have no idea.

"Okay, now you really do look like you're going to barf." Becca takes a step back. That's probably smart. I might be.

We have a word for losing parents: orphan. We have a word for losing spouses: widow. There is no word for losing a twin.

Will Jem be my twin again? Or some other half-formed version? I touch my fingers to the hem of my new-to-me dress and catch myself.

"C'mon." Becca hops to her feet and links her arm through mine. Our skin sticks. "I'll walk you."

She steers us down the porch steps, our sandals sounding like hooves, and we're almost to the grass when someone shouts at us.

"Becca!" A guy in a dirty white visor trots out of the shadows. He gathers Becca to him in a lingering hug. She lets him, and for some reason that surprises me. I've known her less than fifteen minutes and somehow I don't think that usually happens.

Cars file down the street below us, and headlights suddenly bounce across the lawn. Someone shouts again, but this time I barely notice because even though we must be forty yards away, I would know that knocking engine anywhere.

That's *Jem's* truck. Someone's low-rider Honda pulls away from the curb, and I spot it. In the dark, the Ford looks black instead of storm-cloud grey. Just like before. Just like it's *supposed to*.

"Seriously, Grace." Becca cranes her head around Visor's thick shoulder. "Are you damaged? Why are you just standing there?"

*Because I can't move.*

Becca jams one finger in the opposite direction, toward the lawn below us, past the flower beds and badly parked cars, to Jem's grumbling truck. There's a sharp honk, and then the headlights flash.

"What are you trying to do?" she asks. "Get the killjoy to come up here?"

I wrench myself forward and run down the lawn on rubber

legs. "See ya," I call over my shoulder.

"Bye!" the other girls chorus. I don't hear Becca's voice in them. Is she angry? Part of me cringes about that. I've botched another Fall. This much practice and I'm still not graceful—irony, *har, har*.

Here's one even better: What kind of irony is it that I lost *my* life, but I didn't lose any of my awkwardness?

I step off the grass and my stomach flips, churning on something I haven't named in so long I've almost forgotten it.

Hope.

Is that really Jem waiting for me? Is that really my brother? My sandals crunch across the dirt and somewhere in the dark, I hear giggles. My eyes strain against the shadows, searching…searching…nothing. I squeeze between two Ford Rangers double-parked against the curb and step onto the street, squinting into Jem's headlights.

"Would you hurry up?"

My feet do funny half steps, and then I plunge forward again, running around to the side of the truck and flinging open the door. The cab smells like gasoline and grass, and Jem is draped against the wide, worn steering wheel. He stares at me like I am the most irritating person on the planet.

It really *is* him—his long limbs and oversize hands and hair that always needs cutting. Like me, his curls are darker and his eyebrows are heavier, but it's *Jem*. Every Fall has the same rhythm, the same players, but this? This is new. This is *wonderful*.

"Took you long enough."

I grin. "You have no idea."

He rolls his eyes as I hop onto the bench seat. I slam the door behind me and tuck both hands under my thighs to keep from grabbing him. I want to tackle-hug him like we did when we were kids. Can we do hugs? Is that something this Grace and this Jem do? He's scowling at me like it isn't, but I can't stop my smile.

*I have missed you more than you will ever know. More than I can ever say.*

And that's more than just explaining how I'm his sister from another timeline, it's me. It's my problem because the words are too big and I don't know how I would ever say them properly.

The truck lurches as Jem puts it into first, and I nearly giggle. Apparently, my brother has crappy taste in trucks in this lifetime, too.

"What are you so happy about?" he asks.

"Thanks for coming to get me."

"Like I have a choice."

I deflate, feel my smile hitch. *Get oriented. This is not my Jem.*

The truck rumbles along, and the passing scenery looks familiar…ish. Hard to tell in the dark. I think that's the turnoff for Ander's house coming up on our right, and that should be the grocery store at the corner. Jem shifts into third and we pass the low brick building.

*Yep, that's the grocery store.* I sit up, feeling my chest unwind by a hair. Landmarks are excellent for getting oriented. Fall to Fall, the town shifts—once the courthouse had been burned down and another time it didn't exist at all—but mostly returning to Boone and its surrounding swamp is like listening to an old song: concentrate hard enough and the words begin to reemerge.

The sooner I know where I'm supposed to go and how I'm supposed to act, the better. I watch for Ander's usual street—he's been living on Advent Lane for the past four timelines. We roll past it, and I strain to see anything in the dark.

*Is he down there?* Impossible to tell. Only something inside me struggles like it feels him, reaches for him like I did the very first time we Fell.

Ander and I had been fighting, but when he said my name…

The memory is so vivid, even now I shiver. Ander said my name, and I turned. He offered his hand, and I took it.

And we Fell.

The first time was like a blink. It was a mercy.

Unlike the others.

Jem shifts, and exhaustion hits me in a wave. My eyes go gritty. How many more Falls? Will we do this another forty times? Fifty? A *thousand*?

The idea used to make me vomit. From Falls 6 to 23, I was obsessed with finding the end, but according to string theory and quantum mechanics and parallel universe possibilities, there is no end. The universe is infinite. Every single configuration of every single particle can take place multiple times. That means there isn't just a *thousand* more Graces for me to inhabit, a thousand other versions of me, it means there are billions upon billions.

It means Finn could keep chasing us until…forever.

Once I understood that, research lost its bloom for me. I haven't picked it up since.

Something else I know? Right now, Finn is slouching through the dark, searching for us.

Jem drives us on and on. I don't say anything, and he doesn't seem too worried by it. Silence between us must be normal, and that's so sad tears threaten the corners of my eyes. This Grace is missing out. Jem's amazing. He's funny and kind and smart and just sitting next to him again makes my chest feel overstuffed. I thought I had lost him forever, and the reminder wedges a wild laugh underneath my tears.

I cram one fist against my mouth. If I start laughing now, I might shriek.

# chapter five

*then...*

For our seventeenth birthday, Jem wanted to go fishing, and he said it like fishing was some sort of a surprise. "You mean like we did for our twelfth birthday?" I asked. Jem glared at me.

I stroked our Labrador's knobby black head and pretended I was thinking super hard. "You mean, fishing like we did on our thirteenth?"

"And your fifteenth?" Ander added, smiling into his second cup of coffee. He'd stayed the night again, crashing on the couch that always smelled like our dog no matter how many times we tried to clean it. Last night made the third time Ander had stayed over this week, and I kept expecting my parents to say something, but they didn't, and I kept expecting Jem to ask, but he didn't. Maybe it was because we already knew? Something bad was going on at home, except Ander never said a word.

He just showed up with old movies to watch (like he always did) and we opened the back door (like we always did) and the evening bumped on. Last night, we'd watched old horror movies until the moon set below the trees. Ander had made fun of the terrible special effects. I had maintained that the terrible special effects were the best part. Jem fell asleep somewhere around midnight, and that was typical. My brother could pass out anywhere. Ander and I never could. We were crappy at sleeping, so we stayed up.

Jem yawned, stretching his arms behind him until his spine popped. "Fishing," he repeated, and our dog, Visa, whined. "I want to go today, and I want you to come. You haven't been out of the house in days. People are going to wonder if we buried you in the basement."

"We don't have a basement," I said, and people weren't going to wonder. Jem was the Outgoing One, the Funny One, and frequently the Manwhore. I was the Quiet One. Always. Only.

We were twins—fraternal, of course—but so close in resemblance you could easily see Jem's sharp chin in mine, my dark brown eyes suspended in his face. It made people think we were the same in everything.

I shrugged. "Fine, birthday boy. We're going fishing."

"Really?" Jem tilted his chair backward, one hand pinned to the table because we both remembered the time I flipped him. "It's going to be that easy? You're not going to give me some speech about how you have to read ahead for school?"

"Probably because she's already finished the summer reading list," Ander said, eyes still on his coffee.

Jem tipped his chair back to the floor. "You're going to grow up to be a shut-in, Grace."

"Not before you catch an STD."

Jem glared at me, and I slurped my remaining cereal because I knew it would annoy him. The puffs were soggy, splintering apart in my mouth. Visa whined again. He had been hoping I would share. "Staring me down doesn't work,"

I told my brother—and my dog.

Jem scowled. Ander smirked. He found it funny when I stood up to Jem but never said anything about it—although that could have been my fault. Lately every time Ander looked at me, I found an excuse to look away. Stupid, really, because I would still feel his eyes on me. They trailed something very close to heat across my collarbone, my shoulders, my jaw.

It was one thing to laugh about fake blood under the television's glow, but lately…when we were sitting in the sunshine…I was beginning to feel stupid.

And awkward.

And *furious* because I always felt stupid and awkward. I had just never felt stupid and awkward around *him*.

It wasn't supposed to be like this.

*W*e took Ander's boat to our favorite fishing inlet— Jem's favorite because of the overhanging trees and shade, Ander's favorite because it was the farthest away, my favorite because of the quiet. No one was ever around.

Ander picked up speed once the river widened. He slouched low against the metal seat, and next to him, Jem slouched lower, his feet propped on the cooler, a beer already in his hand. As usual, I sat up front. I liked the wind, the spray. About twenty minutes after the river widened, it narrowed again, the trees and vegetation pressing in closer. Everything smelled like water and heat and wet ground. It was way hot, too bright, and absolutely perfect.

Then I realized it wasn't perfect at all—not anymore— because we rounded the river bend and I saw the other boat.

It was maybe fifty feet ahead of us—a small dinghy, not

much bigger than ours. A guy was studying the motor as two girls sunbathed near the prow. As we drew closer, their heads turned in unison, watching us.

Ander cut our engine, and we drifted under the shadow of a knobby cypress, scraping over an underwater log. Even in the shade, the air was warm and steamy.

Ander focused on gathering the fishing rods. Jem and I focused on the others. I'd never seen the guy before. He had the kind of face that belonged to vampires on television—all sharp cheekbones and almost too-full lips and eyes that were searching anywhere and everywhere but here. The blonde wasn't familiar, either. I'd had chemistry with the brunette, though. What was her name? Amanda?

My stomach squeezed. Summers were my time to get away from everyone. I didn't have to be Jem's Twin. I didn't have to be the Quiet Girl. I didn't have to smile and smile until my cheeks hurt. I was supposed to have another five weeks.

Amanda stood and eased to the back of the boat. The dark-haired guy was doing something with the outboard motor—or rather, he was *trying* to do something with the outboard motor. Nothing was actually happening. Amanda gestured at the blonde, and she rose slowly to her feet. Now all three of them were studying the motor, and still nothing was happening.

"You think their engine died?" Jem's eyes stuck to the girls.

I kicked off one sandal and then the other. He was going over there. I could see it in the lines of his shoulders, in how his spine had straightened.

People never made Jem anxious. For a heartbeat, I hated him.

He pivoted, grinning. "Anyone up for a swim?"

He jumped overboard before I could answer, landing in a huge crash that sloshed water everywhere. I held on as the boat tilted and Jem surfaced a few yards away, tossing wet hair from his eyes.

"C'mon!" he yelled. "It's not bad after you freeze your balls off."

"No."

"Please? It's my birthday!"

I laughed. "No!"

Jem grinned again and began to backstroke away from us. Across the inlet, the guy ignored us, but the girls faced Jem, shielding their eyes against the sun with their hands.

"Ten bucks says he comes away with both their phone numbers," Ander said. His smile turned the words to butter, made the vowels slide.

"Ha!" I flipped around, stretching out on Jem's seat and tilting my face toward the sun. It turned the darkness behind my eyelids a hazy pink. "I don't take bets I would lose."

Ander's laugh was a hard puff, and it made me smile. I trailed my hand in the cold water and listened to the girls squeal. They sounded thrilled with Jem. Per usual.

School would begin in a few weeks. Odds were really good he would probably date both girls (and dump them) before we started class.

"You're going to lose your fingers to the snapping turtles," Ander said. He was closer now. I hadn't even felt him move.

I smiled wider. "You always say that."

I plunged my hand in deeper, up to the bend in my elbow where sweat had begun to slide. Across the pond, the girls laughed and the boy stayed quiet and Jem shouted… something. Was he trying to get us to come over?

I sat up, lifting my sunglasses again. Jem and the girls had abandoned the engine and were flopping around in the water now. The waves lapped our boat.

"C'mon!" Jem called, and there was something hard

simmering underneath. He was aggravated. I was supposed to play along and I wasn't.

"You don't have to go," Ander said. He wouldn't look at me. He opened a beer, and for the first time, I noticed the two empty cans already at his feet.

"I know." But I really wanted to say: Why do I always have to be Jem's project?

"He's trying to help," Ander said.

I paused, ever so briefly wondering if I *had* asked why I was always Jem's project. This was Ander, though, and he knew everything. I slumped lower, dipping my hand into the water again.

*It's my birthday, too*. Only as soon as I thought it, I felt like maybe I *was* still six and Jem could still convince me to do anything.

"He thinks it'll make you happy," Ander added, and the whisper was so low I could've pretended I didn't hear him.

"I know," I said again, and I also knew I should let this go. "But I don't think I can be the sister he wants."

*Then who will you be?* The unspoken thought lingered in the silence between us. I turned onto my hip and Ander's hand found mine under the water. I froze. He froze. As soon as Jem swam closer, Ander let go.

# chapter six

*now...*

"So what'd you do tonight?" I ask. I have the overwhelming feeling that I shouldn't, but I can't help myself. Jem hasn't been this close since the night we first Fell. "Anything fun?"

He doesn't answer. We make another turn and the truck lurches, rights itself. I tangle both hands in my lap and stare into the night, recognizing nothing.

In the beginning, the Falls were terrifying. I kept waking up in bodies that were mine and weren't mine. Sometimes I had friends. Sometimes I didn't. It was hard being lonely. It was harder saying good-bye.

All those people, all those possibilities, and they just disappeared. Or maybe they didn't. Maybe the Grace that belonged to the other timelines woke up after I left and went, "What the hell?" Maybe she has to deal with Ander's loss and whatever screw ups I committed.

It makes my skin crawl to think about how she might have to clean up after me, how I might have damaged things she will never be able to fix.

Then again, she might not ever come back at all, and that's *worse*. So much worse. Maybe I eliminate her? Or Finn does. I still don't know how this works. Finn kills me again and again and I wake up in other Graces again and again. Am *I* killing them?

I wish I could talk to another Grace. I want to share my loss with someone, have someone understand what I understand: that Jem is our other half and losing Ander guts us every time.

Jem makes a right onto a gravel driveway, winding us away from the road and toward a sprawling Victorian. Guess this is home. I've lived in it twice before—well, I've lived in variations of it twice before.

In this timeline, the old house has gingerbread trim and Queen Anne's lace, like a fat, aged grandmother fanning herself against the heat. It's tidy, well-kept—*better* kept—than most of the other homes we've lived in. This is different, too. Do we have money this go-round?

I slide out of the truck and follow Jem up the slate sidewalk. Ahead of us, a dog barks and I stop, wavering, because I couldn't be this lucky twice…could I?

Another bark, and now the scrabble of nails on hardwood. My heart lurches into my throat as one hundred pounds of black Lab plows into me at a dead run.

He smells the same.

He feels the same.

He greets me like he recognizes me and has missed me, and the force of his hard, fuzzy body takes me to the ground.

"Visa," I breathe into his scruff. "Visa, Visa, Visa."

Visa kisses me like he knows.

"God, dog, she's only been gone for a few hours." Jem sounds exasperated, but he's smiling. In our real lives, he had called Visa a "farting doorstop." It was an insult (and a little true), but Visa had slept on Jem's bed as frequently as he slept on mine. He loved our dog—even if he wouldn't say it.

We climb the front steps into the dimly lit kitchen. Jem tosses his keys to the counter and drops his baseball hat on top of them. Under the yellow kitchen light, he looks younger. Or maybe it's just because I can see his eyes better now. We match.

Just like we did before.

Visa dashes off, and Jem glances at me. "Why are you being so weird? Stop smiling like you're stoned."

"Sorry." I'm not sorry. I'm giddy.

He kicks off his boots, and I leave on my sandals, following Jem past the mismatched table and chairs to the narrow back stairs. They're still uneven and chipped, but the hallway paint is different. This Grace's mom—now *my* mom—went gold instead of green. The walls are butter-colored and dotted with black-framed family pictures.

In one, Jem is smiling and holding up a fish as big as he is. He can't be more than four. I remember when he lost that front tooth in my original life. I had been so jealous—and a little panicked because we weren't the same anymore. For the first time, I could tell the difference between us.

I had tried to take pliers to my own tooth and our mom had freaked. I think I spent half a year in time-out.

In the picture next to it, this Grace is probably eight. She's wearing a sugar-white tutu and is covered in mud. She's grinning at the camera, and Jem's grinning at her.

When did that stop?

I touch my fingertips to the frame. I wish I had been there. I wish I had that memory.

At the top of the stairs, Jem goes right and shuts himself in the bathroom. The shower cranks on, and pipes thump behind the walls. I pause. Okay, so that's new, too. Bathroom's on the right. I peer down the narrow hallway. There are three more doors. Wonder which one is mine.

I shuffle past the bathroom and try the first, stick my head inside. Unslept-in bed, no clothes on the floor, nothing really personal on the walls. Guest room? I bump the door closed and reach for the next one.

"What are you doing?"

I tremble as I turn. He's never used that tone with me, and it stings. Jem stands in the middle of the hall, arms crossed over his chest. "Are you drunk?" he asks.

"N-no. Just…"

Confused? Disoriented? Hysterical? Nah, scratch the last one. I'm getting on top of this Fall. Sort of. If I can figure out where my bedroom is.

"Look," Jem says, stomping toward me. "If you want to drink with your cool friends, fine, I don't care, but stay out of my room."

His room? Jem brushes past me, and briefly, I can't breathe. Maybe the only thing worse than losing your twin is getting him back when he hates you.

I shake myself. No way. Having Jem back is way better than not having him at all. I can win him back. Whatever happened between them can't be *that* bad. Grace called Jem when she needed him, and because she needed him, he came. I can fix this.

In five days?

I shove the thought away and push through the last door, closing it behind me. I slump against the wood and listen to him reemerge and disappear into the bathroom again. Everything's quiet now except for my breathing. I grope against the wall with one hand, searching for the light switch.

There.

The bedroom goes bright. *Really* bright. This Grace is not

a fan of shadows. Awesome. Neither am I. I push away from the door and bump my hip into a dark wood vanity. I run my palm along the glossy top. No dust. Super polished.

Huh. Either this Grace is really into taking care of her stuff or she's a crazy neat freak. I drop onto the bed. It's already been made up, which makes the whole room feel a little like a hotel. Probably fitting, since I've never been able to shake that feeling of being an uninvited guest.

I dig my toes into the rag rug on the floor and study my surroundings—two vanities, a huge armoire, a battered trunk. The whole room feels overstuffed, like a suitcase crammed to bursting.

There's a dresser across from the bed, the top crowded with more black-framed pictures. I dig my toes deeper into the rug, studying them. The back of my skull prickles. Is that…?

I kick to my feet. Down the hallway, the shower cranks off and the pipes clang, but I can't take my eyes from the picture frames. Becca and Grace are in almost all of them. I recognize the girls from the party, the boys who said hi to us, and…Finn.

Stomach sinking, I force myself to pick up the picture. It couldn't be—it *shouldn't* be—but it is. Forty-two timelines and Finn always has that crooked smile, that mess of dark hair. He's sitting between Becca and me, one arm around my shoulders. I'm leaning into him, and he's looking at me in a way he *never* looked at me in our original lives.

I shudder, scrubbing one hand over my face and closing my eyes. Doesn't matter, though. Behind my eyelids, the second Fall surges past: I was calling Ander's name, and when I shoved through the warped wooden side door, everything smelled like car exhaust and there was Finn. Ander's blood was all over the concrete.

All over *Finn*.

I think I screamed—I know I Fell.

Five days later, I walked in to find Finn standing over Ander's body. We Fell again, and when we woke up for a third time, Ander remembered what happened. He remembered Finn's knife. He remembered *dying*.

It made him half crazy. Ander kept my hand clutched in his and said he could barely breathe anymore. "I know what's coming," he said. "I know *who's* coming."

And he was right. On the fifth day, Finn hit Ander with a truck. There was no time for questioning. No time for reason. We knew the pattern now, and when we woke up again, we knew to fear Finn.

The next four Falls, Ander and I told our parents what would happen to us. They didn't believe a word of it. They thought we were crazy, but the Falls kept happening. Every five days. Finn was like clockwork.

We told our teachers. They didn't believe us. We told the police. Same deal. We told anyone who would listen.

*Everyone* thought we were crazy.

That's when Ander decided to fight back. Only fighting never helped, because we always lost.

"It's like destiny," I told Ander during Fall 10. He hadn't answered me. Maybe he couldn't. After that, we started running. It hasn't worked.

Yet.

I turn the picture face down on the dresser. I know what Becca and this Grace see in Finn. He's all pale eyes and moody swagger, a walking, talking angst-filled question that girls always, *always* want to answer.

The way he's looking at me in that picture, though? It means we're *friends* again. I almost laugh. Being friends this go-round will be even more impossible than becoming friends the first time.

I check the other pictures and catch my reflection in the vanity mirror.

I stop.

Stare.

*Is that…?* I clatter across the pockmarked hardwood and tug the collar of my dress to one side. There's a tattoo below my collarbone.

*My* tattoo below *this* Grace's collarbone.

My fingertips trace the tiny pale ridges. It looks exactly like the one Ander drew for me in our fourth Fall—before I began to worry about the consequences we might be leaving behind. I trail one finger up the sweeping lines. It was the first and last time I changed one of the Graces, and this tattoo is identical.

That has to be a coincidence. Has to be. I get a new body every time I Fall. I keep my memories, but I never get the same body. It doesn't work that way.

Which means I'm back to the infinite number of possibilities stuff, and in all those possibilities, this Grace is into tattoos.

Except it's in the same place mine was.

Chills spray across my skin. The tattoo feels like mine. I have Visa again. I have *Jem* again. Everything is different… everything is the same.

How is that even *possible*?

Dread settles low in my stomach. Answer: it's not.

# chapter seven

## *then...*

There were advantages to having a twin. Jem was always around for company. He always stood up for me. If he was...*pushy* sometimes about getting me to branch out, it was from love.

Not aggravation.

Not because I wasn't enough.

We were twins. My thoughts appeared in his mouth. I finished his sentences. I could be myself...until other people were around.

Like that Saturday afternoon when Jem's latest girlfriend twined around him while we waited for Ander to finish work. Sunshine slanted sideways through the trees. We were parked in the shade, but the heat still clung to everything, like we were breathing through a warm, wet washcloth.

"How much longer do we have to wait?" Callie was straddling Jem, wedged between my brother and the truck's steering wheel. "I thought we were going swimming."

Jem gave her a lazy smile. "Just give him a minute."

"I don't want to."

"You have to."

"Don't. Want. To." Her voice was singsong, the kind of tone you'd use to offer little kids crayons, and I was going to have to listen to it for the rest of the evening.

"I'll go look for him," I said, sliding off the seat and slamming the door behind me. I scuffed across the gravel drive toward Mr. Farley's massive two-story barn. The heavy doors were propped open, throwing a wide wedge of sunlight across the sawdust floor.

"Ander?" I hovered at the edge, feeling like a trespasser. As a rule, I hated bothering him at work—especially at this work. The barn smelled like sawdust and dirt and *birds*. There must have been hundreds of quail crammed into wire mesh cages that lined the barn walls. They watched me draw closer and hid from my shadow.

*When you smell something, you're actually tasting it*, I thought, fighting the urge to breathe through my T-shirt.

It was Ander's job to look after the quail and, sometimes, the hunters, taking out wealthy visitors to shoot. According to most of the people in town, Farley was a pretty decent guy to work for. According to Ander, he was better than decent, but he would never elaborate on why.

There was a scrape above me. Dirt rained down as Ander stuck his head over the side of the hayloft. "Grace?"

I grinned. "Hurry up before Callie pitches a fit."

A smile walked up one corner of his mouth and lingered. "She still around?"

"Unfortunately."

"Step back, okay?"

I did, and a sixty-pound hay bale crashed to the floor, flinging more dust into the air. I looked up again, squinting against the sunlight. It turned the dust motes gold.

I coughed and waved one hand in front of my face. "Do

y'all ever wash this place out? I think this is how you catch bird flu."

"Says the future science major." Ander scaled down the ladder, kicking up an explosion of gold when he landed. We were almost toe-to-toe, and it was too close. I dropped my eyes—still no good, though, because now I had to watch his throat slide as he swallowed.

"Hey," Ander whispered.

"Hey." I lifted my chin, then lifted it higher. "Are you almost done?"

I hoped he couldn't hear the prayer in my voice. I stuck both hands in my jeans pockets. It felt awkward. I took them out. It felt worse.

Ander's attention shifted, pinned to something behind me. "Hey, man."

A dark-haired boy was carrying in another set of cages, and when he turned, the lowering sun cast him into a tower of shadows.

Ander gave me another smile—a real one. "Grace, this is Finn. Farley just hired him. Finn, this is Grace."

"Nice to meet you," I said, noticing how Finn hesitated ever so slightly before joining us. I knew that hesitation. I did it myself when meeting new people.

"Hey." Finn took my offered hand in his, and I had the briefest feeling of his fingers—long enough to brush my heartbeat through my wrist—before he pulled away.

"You were on the boat last week, right?" I asked, slowly recognizing him. He was the guy struggling with the motor. "You were with Amanda and Callie?"

Finn nodded. "Amanda's my cousin."

Ander tugged at his work gloves. "He'll be a senior with us."

"That's great," I said. "It's a nice school. I hope you like it."

Finn's smile was slow and deliberate and promised that he was counting on it. Honestly, so was I. Finn was half a head taller than Jem and Ander, and had the kind of face that would incite girl fights.

And maybe boy fights.

That smile set off the bronze to his skin, made his eyes stand out even more. They were the lightest brown I'd ever seen, like whiskey in sunlight in one moment, then turning summer-moon yellow in the next. Finn was going to be the only thing Boone High talked about. Would he be okay with that? I wouldn't be.

"Ten more minutes?" Ander asked, and I nodded. He bumped his chin toward Finn. "We're going down to the hollow for a swim. You want to come?"

My mouth opened on a silent puff. Ander never invited anyone else to hang out with us. Why now?

Finn made a noncommittal noise. "Not really my thing. I only went that one time because Amanda asked."

Poor guy. I scuffed the toe of my tennis shoe in the dirt. I knew how that went.

"Trust me," Ander said, heaving one hay bale onto its side. "Swimming is everyone's thing around here. It's the only way to cool down."

Another hesitation—only this time it stretched and stretched. I glanced at Finn and realized he was looking at me. His gaze dipped to his feet. Quick.

Not quick enough to stop the heat that surged up my neck.

"Maybe next time," Finn said at last. "That big hunt's coming through, and Farley's riding my ass. I'll see y'all around."

Funny how Finn didn't look like anyone from Boone, but he sure talked like us. Ander dumped the hay bales near the cages as Finn ducked out of the barn. I watched as Ander checked the locks, the water. He ran one hand along the chicken wire, and the birds fluttered away from him. They clawed the walls.

"Why aren't you helping Farley with the hunt?" I asked.

Ander's shoulders went tight. "I wanted to be taken off. I couldn't do it anymore. I—you ever feel bad about this?"

"About the birds? Yeah." Farley made his money off hunting, bringing in groups to use his land. The prey varied depending on the time of year, but quail were always popular even if they weren't always legal.

Ander hooked two fingers around the wire and tugged until it bent. "I remember when Farley had only about twenty of them."

That was a *long* time ago. Probably when we were ten? Eleven?

"He has way more now," I said, my eyes going from cage to cage. There were so many, all pressed together, all staggering over one another.

Ander released his grip on the wire. "Most of these birds never see outside these cages until we drop them in the woods. They get to see the world for a few hours until I kick them up and they get shot."

"Or not." I nudged him with my elbow and smiled. "You said those guys were more likely to hit you than the birds."

He didn't respond. Probably meant I didn't say the right thing, which was typical. I never said the right thing. Or maybe it was because there was nothing right, nothing that could be right when Ander got like this. You had to just wait it out.

*Or wait until he drinks enough.* The thought was small and hard and *right*. We were supposed to go swimming, and I already knew Ander would ask us to stop at the gas station that never checks ID.

I already knew. Did he?

Maybe it was just another unsaid thing between us—unsaid because it didn't need to be said. We knew everything about each other.

"I feed them," he said quietly. "I keep them safe, keep them caged until they don't even know how to function without me." His eyes swung toward mine, stuck. "If I let them go, they'd die anyway."

There was an edge to his words, and I couldn't tell what worried me more: that I couldn't name what Ander was feeling or that he was somewhere I couldn't reach. "It's just a job."

He didn't say anything. The birds fluttered in their cages, and when I swallowed, I was convinced I could taste them on my teeth. "That's their purpose, isn't it? They were born to be hunted."

"Terrible reason to be here."

It was. And usually I would agree with him, because we were always honest with each other and he was right, only there was something living behind his eyes that warned me off.

And then I did something that felt stupid and unstoppable and...necessary? Yeah, it felt necessary. I touched one finger to Ander's forearm. His breath caught.

*If I do this, there is no going back.*

Only as soon as I thought it, I realized there was never any going back. This was inevitable. I traced the ridge of muscle where his shirt met skin, and he swallowed.

"You take good care of them," I said, pushing out the words because my tongue was suddenly too thick. "It's better to be born and live a little than to never exist at all, right?"

Ander spun around, eyes huge and haunted. "Is it? Because I don't know anymore, Grace. I really don't know."

I wanted to step back, and I couldn't. I wanted to press into him, and I didn't dare. "Ander...what's going on?"

He shook his head. Hard. "Nothing. Just...home. Don't

worry about it."

Impossible. I nodded anyway, like I could forget it, like I would do exactly as he asked. Sometimes you have to be the friend that someone needs you to be, right?

I cleared my throat. "You ready to go?"

"Yeah."

But he wasn't moving. I took an uneven breath and turned, retracing my footsteps. There was the briefest pause, and then I heard him behind me. He caught up and together we tugged the sliding doors shut. Under the half-dead oak, Jem's truck was rocking.

I stopped. "Gross."

"Are they going to be like this all night?"

"Seriously?"

"Yeah, yeah, stupid question." Ander trotted ahead, then turned so he was walking backward toward Jem's truck and I could see nothing but him. "Guess that makes me yours."

# chapter eight

*now...*

I wake up curled in a ball, still sleeping in last night's clothes. This Grace's room is painted the faintest lavender, the ceiling encircled with white-frosting molding. Dawn light turns everything pale gray and paler pink.

*Second day*, I think, stretching my legs until my knees and ankles pop. I didn't kick off my shoes, and I've left small dirt clumps on the bedspread. Some of that was exhaustion. More of it was fear.

You can't run when you're barefoot—I mean, you can, but not for long, and I don't let my mind follow that reasoning any further or I'll end up reliving Falls 10 and 14.

And 3. Sweat pops up between my shoulder blades, and suddenly I smell dirt and blood.

I'm alone, but I can hear Ander's begging in my ears, feel hot breath against the back of my neck.

"Run," he had pleaded. It was only our third Fall, and I didn't understand why Finn was doing this.

"He's not a monster," I had said, trying to tug Ander back to me. "He's our friend. I don't know what's going on. We have to think this through."

Only Ander wouldn't listen. He dragged me after him. "You have to trust me, Grace. He's coming, and when he gets here, I'm going to die again."

And then Finn found us and we Fell.

Welcome to number four and the Quail Hollow Trailer Park.

I shake myself. No good, though. I still can't jar myself out of the panic. I stick my head between my knees, suck air.

There. Better.

I sit up, and the floor of my stomach lurches. Better-ish.

*Get going. Find Ander.*

I flip off one sandal and then the other, brush the dirt off the bedspread, and scowl when I realize I just managed to get it all over Grace's rug. She'd probably have a fit.

Whatever. I'll vacuum later.

I tug off my dress and rifle through the dresser. I can wear pastel, pastel, and—wait for it—more pastel. I end up picking a white polo and khaki shorts. Why do I have a feeling this Grace pops her collar?

I grab a hair tie from the vanity and try to untangle my curls. The face looking back at me from the mirror is a little pale, a white scar by her mouth a little more visible. I wonder how she got it.

A few minutes later, I give up and tug the whole mess into a ponytail. There. I'm presentable In fact, I'm almost...me.

The realization curls something behind my heart. Does it make up for all those Falls? I'm awfully close to me again and Jem's back and that's...better, right?

Ander will think so. It'll have to be. In my life—lives?—you take what you can get.

I open Grace's purse and dump the contents onto her bed. Two lipsticks...a wallet...an inhaler...my *cell phone.*

It's completely dead, but I find a charger by the bed and a few minutes later the phone has enough juice to power back on. I scroll through the contacts, half hoping I'll find Ander's name. No luck, though. From the looks of it, Grace has every contact in Boone except Ander.

There are her parents, Jem, *Finn*, two numbers for Becca, two numbers for a guy named Ben, and dozens of others. I exit the phone list and try to pull up Grace's internet, but the cell keeps stalling out. No big deal. There are other ways of finding Ander.

I ease my bedroom door open and hover, listening. Doesn't seem like anyone's up. I shift from foot to foot, wondering if this is normal. Probably. It *is* Sunday. I creep down the hallway and touch my fingertips to Jem's door. No sound behind it. He used to be an early riser.

I force myself back a step—and then another. I have to stop thinking about Jem like that. Yes, he's Grace's twin. Yes, he's Jem. But he's not *my* twin. He's not *my* Jem.

Except, I really want him to be.

I don't look at the pictures as I pad down the stairs. I focus on the house instead. Atmosphere-blue kitchen…a tawny-colored living room that was probably meant to look neutral and instead reminds me of dusty country roads…forest-green den. The flowers in the vase by the hall are plastic, and the potpourri is rose-scented. I linger by the kitchen door for a moment, knowing what I need to do next and hating myself for it.

If Ander and I are going to run, we're going to need cash to do it.

*Not that it'll help.*

The voice in my head is little and mean and quite possibly right, so I ignore it and focus on the kitchen instead.

If I were this Grace's mom, would I leave an emergency

stash hidden somewhere in the house?

I study the pale gray cabinets...the polished drawer handles...if there *is* a stash, I need to find it. I take a steadying breath, and then another, and it *still* doesn't loosen the cramp in my chest. Guilt. This many Falls and I *always* feel guilty.

*Get going.* I pick the closest drawer and go through it, move on to the next, and then the next. There are pans and pots in the cabinets, pencils, receipts, and silverware in the drawers, another bowl of flowery potpourri on the counter. The smell turns my stomach.

I move on to the small kitchen desk, and there's a folder tucked next to the house phone. There's a page of emergency numbers, a few takeout menus, and a single soft plastic pouch with almost two hundred in twenties folded inside.

I brush the tip of my finger over and over them. Not much, but it'll do.

I put the money back in the pouch and put the folder back by the phone, listening for any sounds of life upstairs. So far, though, there's nothing. I wander through the living room again and hit the jackpot: a computer.

I drop into the desk chair and power up the computer, then wait for the search page to load. When it finally does, I do a tiny victory dance in my seat. Sad how happy that makes me, but whatever. I'm all about the small wins these days.

I search Ander first and wonder if I'll get lucky. In some Falls, he's harder to find, but this Fall is stupid easy. Alexander Hale must have twenty different write-ups on him. I study a newspaper picture, trying to separate this version of Ander from the past versions. He's still tall, still has eyes so light they're almost colorless. Ander's hair is sun-bleached and shaggy again in a way I haven't seen since our original lives.

He's a painter again, too, but this time, he's an award winner. The article practically hails him as the next coming of

Michelangelo, which kinda proves that no matter the timeline, the town of Boone knows only a couple of painting references. The reporter goes on and on about how design schools are already noticing his talent. It makes me grin.

He'll love that. In our real lives, we'd both loved painting. I was okay. Ander, though? He had been brilliant—sketching, painting, whatever. He was good at all of it, and seeing him get his art back this time squeezes me breathless. Art was his thing. Math was mine, which my dad loved about me.

"Math's the key to the universe," he always said. "Or at least the key to job security."

Which might've been a bigger deal than the universe. Jobs weren't the easiest to come by in Boone. Most people worked at the mill. When cutbacks happened, everyone's eyes got a little wilder. Drinking at the local bar got rowdier. The police were called out to people's homes more often.

Jem and I were lucky, though. Our parents didn't fight that way. Or maybe they just found a way around it. I could have as many used paperbacks as I wanted—Dad loved to read, too—but spending money on art stuff was "frivolous." He thought I should be memorizing theorems or whatever in my free time, so Mom sneaked my art supplies.

According to the article, Ander attends the local high school. Good. That's helpful. I open another browser window and go to the school's website. There's a student log-in, and when I click on the username, Grace's username and password automatically fill.

Awesome. I settle deeper into the chair, relief making my head go a little light. I surf around a bit and finally find the student directory. Ander doesn't have a cell number listed. There's a school-based email for him, though. I click the link, and it connects to my account and opens a blank email. I type:

Where are you? I'm at that same old house—the one from 19 and 33. Jem's back and Finn's my friend again. Can't wait to see you. Miss you.

There's nothing else left to say, but I reread the words twice, feeling like there's something else I *should* say and have forgotten. I check my phone, add the cell number below "miss you," and hit send.

Something bumps upstairs. Footsteps? I lean back in the chair, listening. Nothing. I face the screen again, blow out a sigh, and search Grace's parents next. Looks like this timeline's dad is a college professor—literature—and the mom works for a nonprofit. I scroll through listings, reading about how her company raises money for cancer research.

There are only a few pictures of her. She has dark hair… darker eyes…she looks so much like *my* mom it kicks all the breath from my lungs.

Then I try Jem. There are no real mentions of him other than as "the son of noted professor Dr. Freeman" or, once, as "the winner of the Boone County Spelling Bee."

Upstairs, there's another *thud*, and I pause. Someone's up. I doubt the computer's forbidden, but I shut it down anyway, leaving it like I found it.

Not before I clear the history, of course. I'm good at that part; practice makes perfect and all.

I shove to my feet just as this timeline's mom comes down the steps. I don't know this Grace very well, yet I do know this: she's popular, she's mean, and she learned it from somewhere. This mom? This family? I put one hand on the chair back and tell myself it's nerves when the mom turns the corner and sees me.

"Honey! You're up!" Mom's smile is the kind that belongs to lingering hugs and whispers of "I love you." She doesn't move to touch me, though. Is that this family's normal? I'm guessing so.

I smile back and her expression twitches. Surprise? Worry? "I couldn't sleep," I say finally. "Seems like such a nice day, I wanted to get up."

"I'm going to have coffee and sit outside, want to come?"

I don't, but my feet have already stutter-stepped forward. "Yeah. Sure."

She makes coffee while I lean against the counter, watching—okay, *staring*. We're almost the same height and build, and her burgundy cardigan looks baby-animal soft. She has my mom's short dark hair and quiet way of moving.

She also isn't talking, and I know I should take my cues from her, play like this is normal and I'm her daughter and I won't disappear, but I really want to ask how she's feeling.

What she's thinking.

How she's been.

Except those are questions for my mom, not this mom. I'm about to *steal* from this mom.

"Grace? Is your asthma bothering you?"

I nod, shrug. "Sort of. I'll be fine."

She passes me a mug with kittens on it. "Don't tell your father. You know how he is about giving you caffeine."

"I won't." I follow her to the screened porch off the back of the kitchen. She takes a wooden swing piled with pillows and I take the closest rocking chair. I tuck my feet under me. She tucks her feet under her. We look so alike right now it starts my wheezing all over again.

I put my feet back on the acorn-colored floorboards and concentrate on the yard beyond us. It's a little shaggy and unkempt. The grass sticks up in thick tufts, and there are wildflowers at the edges, just as the lawn pushes into woods filled with Medusa-hair vines. Unlike the carefully curated house, the yard doesn't seem intentional. I like it.

*I want to remember this. I* hope *I remember this.* And it's funny how that realization flips my stomach low. It feels dangerously close to sad, and it shouldn't. If anything, I should be more panicked, but for some reason that feels like someone else's problem, as if I'm watching some other Grace from a very tall height.

"How was last night?" Mom asks.

*Horrible.* I string up a smile. "Good. Thanks."

"Did you see Becca?"

I nod. "What did you do last night?"

Her eyes linger on me for a heartbeat longer than they should. I guess Grace doesn't ask these questions. "Stayed in. Read."

She goes quiet again, and we sit in a silence that should be all kinds of uncomfortable and instead it doesn't feel strained, doesn't feel overstuffed, doesn't feel filled with things left unsaid.

If this Grace wanted to, she could have this every day.

Every. Damn. Day.

And I can't stay. I'll have to give it up no later than tomorrow. My chest burns, and my whole body feels tight. I'm confused for all of five seconds and then suddenly I know: I'm jealous.

Holy crap, I'm *jealous* of this Grace, of the life she has and I lost, of the people she's just thrown away. I can't afford to be jealous. It makes you stupid, sloppy.

Desperate.

It also makes you hold on, and I can't hold on. It hurts too much when I have to let go. We only get five days.

I shoot to my feet, sloshing untouched coffee onto my white polo. In the distance, guns fire and birds erupt through the treetops. One of Farley's hunts? Their cries make my skin crawl. "Sorry," I say, wiping at my shirt. "I forgot I have a paper to do."

Mom nods. She's not surprised, and she doesn't believe me. This is normal, too.

I think I might hate this Grace.

I pour the coffee down the sink, refusing to look at the tiny, tidy kitchen desk and its folder full of cash. I check my school email before going back upstairs. There's nothing from Ander.

And still nothing by lunchtime.

Nothing at dinner.

Nothing when I finally fall asleep. This has never happened before.

Something's wrong.

*then...*

We were in the third week of triple-digit temps when Calvin Bishop killed his wife. Everyone was shocked, which was shocking to me because everyone knew Calvin Bishop had been threatening to kill her for years. I knew this the same way everyone else knew this: Boone was a small town.

People worried it would scare away the tourists. It was one thing to be known for a bed-and-breakfast that was haunted by a murdered Confederate soldier. It was another to have an actual murder.

Our parents thought everyone was being stupid, but I heard Mom whisper about how her tips were down at the diner and Dad start to say something about how it was because of hour cuts at the mill. Then I came into the kitchen, and suddenly he only wanted to know what I thought about the new-to-us Stephen King book I'd been reading.

Ander disappeared for almost a week. Jem said it was because his mom knew Mrs. Bishop so well. They cut hair at the same place, and sometimes Mrs. Bishop stayed over.

Ander's mom took it hard.

I thought about calling and didn't. He was my friend and yet now he was also…I had no idea. Was there a word for wanting to kiss your best friend? Because the only one I could think of was "stupid."

We were seventeen, and I felt like a little kid again. He was Ander, and somehow that was familiar and weird and something I craved.

Which was even weirder.

So for a week, I sat at the house and read while Jem went off with Callie. Then, quite suddenly, Ander reappeared. He stood in the kitchen doorway like he'd never left, his shoulders blocking the sun behind him.

"Are you reading *Hitchhiker's Guide* again?" his shadow asked.

"I'm looking for the answer to the question of life."

"It's forty-two."

"You *do* listen!"

His laugh was the softest huff. "You could have real friends, you know."

"They *are* real. Haven't you ever met a character who's more real than someone standing next to you?"

"No."

"Fine." I closed *Hitchhiker's,* but I could still smell the pages on my fingers like the words had bled through my skin. "I just like book characters more."

Another huff, and the way my gut twisted told me he smiled. "Want to take the boat out?"

I answered by following him.

Outside, the heat had weight. It wasn't even noon yet, and I already felt like there was a three-hundred-pound man sitting on my chest. I wheezed and Ander paused.

"You okay to be out here?"

"God, yes."

He grinned. We thumped across the small dock, and Ander unlooped the frayed yellow tie and swung into the boat in a smooth arc. I hopped in after him, bracing my hand on the metal edge for support and burning my palm in the process.

Ander laughed. "*Grace*ful," he said, making it sound less like a joke and more like a version of me that belonged to him. My dad did the same thing. He'd named me. Sometimes I was Grace because of writers he enjoyed (Atkinson, Jordan, Bauer). The rest of the time I was Grace because of mathematicians he admired (Alele-Williams, Wahba, Young).

"Don't you have work?" I asked.

"Finn said he could handle it—did you know he's some sort of super genius?"

"No."

"Amanda said he's going to give you a run for that valedictorian spot."

I stiffened. "Oh. What did you say back?"

"I said it was highly doubtful." Ander's smile split me open. "You ready?"

He pushed us off the dock before I could answer, and we powered south. Ander popped open a beer and took his usual time weaving us past the sunken logs that lay just under the surface. Once we passed the last bend, he accelerated, steering us for the left-hand river fork.

"Are we heading for town?" I yelled, my hair blowing loose around my face.

"Does it matter?"

I shrugged. The sky was a burned-out blue between the drooping leaves, and the faster we went, the better I could breathe. Hot wind pushed underneath my hair, my clothes. I think I would've been happy going like that for hours, but he cut the motor after another ten minutes or so. We drifted along, caught up in the river's current until it pushed us toward the shore, weeds brushing the sides of the boat.

I sat up. "What are we doing?"

Ander didn't answer. His eyes were pinned to something farther up the bank. I turned…and saw a lone police cruiser parked in the sun. We were below the Bishops' place: a small, peeling trailer tucked just off the river. Yellow caution tape snapped in the breeze.

"Ander?"

His attention still was fixed on the trailer. There was the slap of a screen door, and I turned back in time to see an officer—with that red hair, it had to be Gary Westin—lift his hand in a small wave. Ander returned it.

"How could you kill someone you love?" he asked without looking at me.

"I don't know." We watched Officer Westin turn his cruiser around in the Bishops' drive, rumbling away in a cloud of red clay dust. Everything was dusty that summer. Between the drought and the soaring temperature, it felt like the world wanted to explode. "Why are we here?"

Ander slid his gaze to me. "She was friends with my mom. Nice lady. She really loved him."

"I don't know what anyone could love about Calvin Bishop." Deep in the swamp behind us, a loon screamed. I shifted on the hard, wooden seat. My legs were going numb, and it felt like the sun was burning a hole through the top of my head. "I don't know why she stayed."

"Nowhere else to go." Ander stood and the boat tilted. His eyes were pinned to the trailer again. It was like he saw something I couldn't, and cold curled inside of me.

*All the time Ander spends at our home…all the time he spends avoiding his…*

Without the hum of our outboard, the cicadas were the

only sound. A week before—when Mrs. Bishop was shot—the cicadas had been almost deafening. I'd had to close my window. Chills rippled up my arms. Was that the last thing she heard? The insects' chatter and whine?

"Ander…" I rubbed my goose bumps with both hands, but they wouldn't go away. "Do you think people know when something bad is about to happen?"

"What?" One corner of his mouth turned up, exposing a single dimple. It looked like a tiny crack, and I had a sudden urge to press my fingertip into it.

I pushed my hands under my thighs. "Do you think people know when something bad is about to happen?" I repeated. "Do you think people get premonitions?"

Hot wind lifted sticky hair from my neck, and I leaned into it, closing my eyes. When I opened them, Ander was watching me. "I don't think we get that lucky," he said.

"Lucky?" The current pushed us closer to shore, and the weeds reached into the boat. I pulled the head off a cattail and flung it into the mud. "Why would you call it lucky?"

"Because you could do something about it." Ander sat down—heavy enough to rock us—and I held on with both hands.

"Like stop it?" I asked. "What if it's your destiny, or whatever?"

A gross thought. I tried to ignore it, but it still left an image I had cooked up just this second: of a woman running barefoot down those warped wooden steps, her husband right behind her. What if the neighbors had heard? What if the neighbors had done something?

I pulled my arms tight around me. "What if you *can't* stop it?"

Ander looked away. "If I knew something was going to happen to you," he said slowly, so slowly I suddenly realized how close we were, how we had never been this close before even in the darkness of movie nights. "If I knew something was going to happen to you," he repeated, "I would do everything I could to stop it. Do *you* believe in destiny? Do you think we get a choice in what happens to us?"

I nodded, because in that moment I wanted to choose him.

And I wanted to be chosen.

He leaned closer, and I couldn't name what was in his eyes, but it heated me anyway.

"I only have to look at my old man to know my future, Grace."

"Then don't look at him." I licked my lips, and his eyes dipped to my mouth. "Look at me instead."

He did.

"That's not your destiny," I whispered. "You will never be like him."

I believed it with everything I was, and after my very own personal forever, Ander nodded like he believed it, too.

And then he kissed me.

*now...*

Monday is different. Everyone is quiet during breakfast, and it kinda drives me nuts. How can they *not* talk? Jem and I will be at school all day and they'll be working all day and no one will be home until late and then we'll be tired and then who will want to talk?

Nobody, that's who.

In my original life, my family ate together whenever we could. And even though there were only five of us at the table—Mom, Dad, Ander, Jem, and me—we sounded like fifty. We were *loud*. My dad always had work stories. Jem and Ander were funny. My mom didn't laugh often, but when she did, she laughed with her whole body, like she was going to shake apart.

This family? It's just…silence. They could have so much more. I know they could. I *lived* it, and yet this is what we have instead.

I bounce my leg and pick at my toast and remind myself this is normal to them. This is how their family operates, and I shouldn't interfere. I should go along with it. After all, I'm one foot out the door already. More than one foot. I have clean clothes packed in my backpack, a hundred bucks of their cash rolled into the clothes. I'm ready to *run*. It's the third day, which means we're already behind. Ander and I should be long gone—and we will be once I find him.

*If* I find him. Ander never responded to my email. Because he can't get into the account? Or because something happened?

*Don't think about* that. *Think about running*.

Only every time I hear Mom's soft sigh or watch Jem roll his eyes at whatever article he's reading, I'm not sure I can run. What if I never have a family this close to *my* family? What if I never see Jem again?

*This is not your real family. This is not your real family*.

Except it *feels* like my real family, or awfully close to it. Jem looks up at me, and I can't stop my smile.

"What is *wrong* with you?" he asks.

My stomach knots, and I stop bouncing.

Our parents glare at Jem. "Don't talk to your sister like that," Mom snaps. It should probably make me feel better, only it doesn't. My Jem never talked to me like that.

*This is not your real family*.

My stomach settles, and everything under my surface smooths. There. That worked. I study my toast and feel normal again. Normal's good, though. Normal is in control. I throw away my breakfast, put my dish in the dishwasher, and check the time. Seven twenty. I have no idea if I need to leave for school.

"Grace is right, Jem," our dad says around his newspaper. "You're going to be late."

Jem rolls his eyes at me or maybe at both of us. "Five more minutes."

No one says anything. I guess everyone agrees to give him

more time. Or maybe no one cares. You can say a lot with silence; I've just never been good with it.

I'm not sure if Jem and I ride to school together or if someone else picks me up, so I sit on the bench by the side door, watching the window and watching the kitchen. Five minutes stretches into ten. I want to check my email again. I occupy myself by going through my backpack instead.

"Get oriented," I mutter to myself, and honestly it's not that hard. This Grace is remarkably easy to step into. I'd found her backpack on the closet floor. It had been tightly zipped, all the folders coordinated by subject and class period. It would be easy to say she's super organized, but it felt…anxious. Like something I would've done to combat my nerves, and the similarity threatened to pull me under.

I take my class schedule out of the book bag, carefully arranging my folders so they hide the clothing I took, and skim one finger along the list: bio is first, then English, then…

I grin. Art. I have art class this time. I haven't had art since my real life.

"Let's go," Jem says, brushing past me. He takes his own bag from the hook by the door and trots down the porch steps, heading for the truck. I rush after him, cramming all the folders into my backpack. So much for being organized.

The whole way to school, Jem ignores me. I almost don't mind. I watch our route, making mental notes about turns and landmarks. When we finally pull into the high school parking lot, I recognize the squat, two-story building—same flat black roof, same dark brick. This time, the school colors are gold and blue.

I lean forward, peering through the windshield at the stream of students walking toward the entrance. I spot Becca right off, and my stomach twists hard, then settles on its side. No Finn, though—a small mercy, but one that I cling to. Based on the past timelines, I should see him tomorrow.

It'll be another two days before he makes his move, though. I still don't understand, and he never explains why. Maybe it's an inexorable pull. We are the boats, and Finn is the tide.

*Not if I run fast enough.* I roll my hands into fists. Fall 29, we almost made it out of Boone—would've made it, but the truck Ander stole died, and Finn was waiting for us on the side of the road. Fall 30, we got lost in a tangle of unfamiliar streets. Fall 41, we ran, just took off, and Finn followed, chasing us deep into the swamp.

Ironic, how desperate I'd been to escape Boone in my original life, and I still can't get away.

Wait. I rub my stinging eyes until colors starburst behind the lids. Is that irony? Because mostly it just feels tragic right now.

Jem grabs his bag and wrenches open his door. "Try setting your broomstick to fly at a lower altitude today, okay?"

*What? Oh.* We stare at each other, and ever so briefly I think he's about to say something. He searches my face, then shakes himself and slides off the bench seat. I hop out after him, ears burning.

I'm not the kind of person who has a broom—except, of course, I am in this life. I trail along behind him, kinda sorta hoping Becca won't notice me.

"Grace!"

I plaster on a smile, reminding myself that Becca is this Grace's best friend. I can't ruin that for her. For either of them.

"C'mon!" Becca grabs my hand, and if she notices it's sweaty, she doesn't say anything. If she notices I'm still looking from face to face for Ander and Finn, she ignores it. She drags me along, and for the first time today, I feel safer.

...

Inside, the hallway is cool and overlit and smells faintly of cleanser. It's so crowded I lose sight of Jem immediately. Becca sticks close, though. Her shoulder presses against mine as she tells me about her Sunday.

"You should have answered your phone," Becca says, sidestepping two skinny guys chasing each other. "You could've come swimming."

"Sorry." I should say more, and I can't. I'm looking everywhere and nowhere and I can't spot Ander.

Becca's mouth flattens. "Would you hurry up?"

*She doesn't like to be alone.* The thought drops into my head so fully formed it feels like it belongs to someone else. Becca hates being alone—it's almost hilarious considering we're surrounded by so many people who would love to be her friend. They watch us like we're something that needs to be memorized.

Funny. I belong more now than I ever did in my real life. For as long as I could remember, fitting in had been going through the motions, touching the world through plastic wrap.

"Just keep faking it 'til you make it," Mom had said. "Sooner or later, it'll become real."

It never did. To everyone else, I looked fine. I knew I was just pretending, though. It actually prepared me pretty well for Falling. Maybe this was always supposed to be my destiny.

We turn a corner, and a dark-haired boy meets my eyes. I flinch. It's not Finn, but for a heartbeat I thought it was.

My chest winds tighter. Why didn't Ander respond to my email? Is he sick? Is he hurt?

Is he drunk again?

Unfair of me. Stupid, too. Ander hasn't touched a drop since the last night of our lives, the first night we Fell. Yeah, he'd had a problem for a while, but when he'd called me back—and I'd gone to him—it all turned around.

We're okay now. I mean, *yeah*, we're both unraveling, but we don't let go of each other. It's the only good thing to come out of this.

Becca stops. I stop. She arches a single delicate brow and cuts her eyes toward the lockers on our left. "Don't you need anything?"

"Oh." I grab the closest locker and spin the combination lock.

Becca covers my hand with hers and moves me one locker down. "Are you okay?"

*No. Not at all.* And I suddenly miss Ander so much it threatens to suck me through the floor. Dirty White Visor Boy joins us, leaning one shoulder against the locker next to mine. "Missed you yesterday, Grace. Why didn't you come?"

"Sick."

"Oh. Sucks for you." He turns his attention to Becca, whose smile is werewolf white under the overhead lights. "Hey, girl."

"Hey yourself, Sam." Becca looks at me, rolls her eyes, and retreats to a locker farther down from mine. DWVB—Sam—follows her. I check the locker combination printed at the top of Grace's binder and swap my books around. I have biology first, then English—someone laughs, and my heart thumps behind my teeth.

I know that sound. I would recognize it anywhere. I turn, searching...searching...

Ander steps around two kids carrying instrument cases, smiling a smile that nearly drags me to my knees.

Our eyes meet and I rush him. I wrap both arms around

his waist and try not to cry. He feels so good, so right, so *normal*.

Until he stiffens.

"Hey…uh…what's up?"

I tilt my head so he can really look at me. We always recognize each other. Always. In every lifetime, Ander's eyes have been so light, they're almost colorless. In every lifetime, his cheekbones have stayed sharp, like every version of him doesn't eat much. He looks exactly the same, and the relief makes my bones mushy.

"What's *up*?" I ask. "Did you not get my email? Jem's *back* and Finn's my *friend* and—"

And he's not listening. Ander's attention is pinned to my neck, and the tiniest fissure of unease curls in my gut. I don't like his expression. It's worried.

"I'm already packed," I say. "I'm ready to go. I'm…" I'm *pleading*, because there's something cold and hard growing in my stomach.

"Grace…what are you talking about?"

My feet…my hands…my face…everything goes numb. "What?"

"Where did you get that tattoo?" he asks.

*From you*. I press one hand to my neck…dip to the curve of my shoulder…slide across my collarbone until I feel the faint bump of my scar tissue.

"Did you *seriously* get my drawing tattooed on you?" Ander carefully untangles himself and sets me aside. He keeps one hand on my upper arm. Can he feel my shaking? It's not supposed to work like this. It's *never* worked like this.

"Why'd you email me?" he asks. "We haven't talked in months."

"I…I…"

"Are you okay?" He's studying me so closely I get the

briefest surge of relief, because surely Ander will recognize me. Surely. He *always* recognizes me. It's one of the few things I can count on.

"Grace?" He gives me the tiniest squeeze. "Should I call a teacher or something? Are you okay?"

"No," I manage at last. "I'm fine."

"You're not fine if you're talking to me again." His smile is still crooked. It hits me like a sucker punch. Ander's eyes flick behind me and hold. "I believe that's your flying monkey headed this way."

I turn. Becca is power walking toward us, her white skirt frothing around her knees. "It's not like that," I say, pivoting to Ander. He's already backing away, though, hands raised like he's surrendering.

That half-assembled smile widens. "It's exactly like that, Freeman."

I step toward him—I can't help it—and Ander cocks his head like he can't believe what he's seeing.

"Grace!" Becca's fingers dig into my arm. She pulls me around. "What are you doing? You just took off like a freak. What's the matter?"

I stare at her and can't come up with a single answer, because Ander doesn't remember. No, that's not right. He doesn't *know*.

My stomach clenches. That means I'm going to have to tell him. How's that supposed to work?

*Oh, hey, Ander, I'm your girlfriend from another universe. Or better yet, Ander, I'm your girlfriend from another universe and I'm here to warn you. Warn you about what? Oh, you're about to be murdered.*

"I wanted to say hi to Ander," I say at last.

"Why?" Becca's tone is so incredulous, so dumbfounded it should be funny. It's not. "You aren't thinking about getting back together, are you?"

Back *together*? I wheeze. Hard. "It just…seemed like a nice thing to do."

Something watchful enters her expression. I look away and concentrate on Ander's laugh—disappearing—and realize the only thing I can possibly think of is: he forgot me.

# chapter
# eleven

*then...*

Ander throttled back the motor as we drifted closer to the dock. "Looks like your dad's home," he said, nudging his chin toward our house. I turned in my seat and shielded my eyes with both hands. A blue pickup was parked next to the back steps, a small green sedan beside it. Not only was my dad home, but we had company.

"Maybe he knows you've been kissing me."

Ander went pale. "That's not a conversation I'm ready to have."

"I was kidding. He's not psychic."

Ander worried his lower lip.

"Is this even worth having a conversation?" I asked.

His eyes bored into mine. "You know what you mean to me."

Of course I did. We had over ten years between us. That had to count for something. More than something.

So why did I want *him* to say it?

Because I'm an idiot.

I stood and the boat rocked. "It's okay. Whatever this is,

I'm not ready for everyone to know about it, either."

*This*. Like kissing and boys and best friends were things I could pick up and set down and walk around as I analyzed them.

Ander nodded. "Fair enough."

Then he leaned closer like he might kiss me and it took everything in me to lean away. "My parents could see us."

Another nod.

"See you tomorrow?" I asked.

His smile went slippery. "That's kind of the way things work with us."

Now I was smiling. In fact, I was still smiling when I pushed through the screen door, still smiling when I stepped inside. It took my eyes a beat to adjust and then I saw them: my parents were standing at the kitchen counter, and the high school counselor, Mrs. Holland, sat at the table.

I hesitated. "Is everything okay?"

Mom nodded, her mouth wound tight. "Could you sit down with us for a few minutes? Mrs. Holland wants to talk to you."

That couldn't mean anything good. I slunk across the floor and took the closest chair. Had Jem done something? Had Ander? Mrs. Holland was new to Boone, and I knew her the same way everyone at school knew her: she was our guidance counselor and her office was filled with *New Yorker* magazine covers in Walmart frames. She talked to everyone, but I don't think she liked anyone, and I was pretty sure she'd never been sixteen.

"I have some very good news, Grace," Mrs. Holland began. "You remember at the end of last year when we got your test scores back?"

I nodded. We'd all been excited. College finally started to feel real rather than this thing my dad talked about.

"Honestly," Mrs. Holland continued, "I just couldn't stop thinking about how well you did, so I started doing some research into schools that might better accommodate your potential, and I kept coming across Alton Preparatory."

"The fancy private school?"

She straightened in her seat, eyes terrier-bright and focused. "You know it?"

I shrugged. "They come to town every year for that project they do about the mill and the cemetery and the local history."

Alton students returned to Boone every May, "just like herpes," Jem always said. He didn't like the prep kids—although honestly no one really did. They always stayed for about three days, renting out both floors of the Nine Bells Bed-and-Breakfast, and everyone said they were worse than the regular tourists.

They didn't tip.

They never said please.

"They watch us like we're lab specimens," Ander had said.

"I think they look at everyone like that," I had returned. Even during heat waves, the students walked around in clusters of hunter green and gold, wool slacks, and wool knee socks. They didn't look like they ever sweated.

Mrs. Holland leaned a little closer, and her fingers dug into her bag a little more. "Alton Prep has a few select openings every year for deserving students, and I think you should apply."

"To *go there*?" It was stupid question. I realized it as soon as I said it, but still. It was Alton Prep and I was…me.

"Yes." Mrs. Holland's eyes flicked from me to my mother. "I think you have a very good shot at acceptance, too. You see, Grace…"

It was the weirdest thing. Here was Mrs. Holland talking about Alton Prep, going on and on about scholarships and how I was an excellent fit for their program…and I couldn't stop staring at how she clutched her bag to her chest.

Was she worried my parents were going to yell at her? Steal it? It was like she was trying to hide.

Or make herself smaller.

I didn't understand—but then I noticed how her gaze kept straying from my parents to the kitchen around us, how her attention snagged on the breakfast-stained dishes on the scabby counters, how she kept looking at us. Only she wasn't seeing *us*, she was seeing the turned-up linoleum in the corners and how my dad's hands were still oily from the mill.

She wasn't trying to make herself small because we made her feel small. She was trying very hard not to touch anything, like my family was something that could rub off on her.

And judging from how my parents' eyes kept bouncing to the floor, they knew it, too.

"It would be a full ride," Mrs. Holland said to my parents, fingers flexing and releasing the edge of her bag. "Considering her…circumstances, the school would subsidize everything."

"It's all the way in Atlanta, though," Mom said. She kept fisting her cardigan tighter and tighter around her frame. "The commute—"

Dad shook his head. "She would have to live there, Layla."

"But she would hate that. Her friends are *here*. Jem is *here*. We're *here*."

"Alton is an excellent school," Mrs. Holland added. "Grace would have academic opportunities she would never receive here. The math programs alone—"

"She would rather paint," Mom said. "Grace loves painting. Do they even have an art program?"

"They do." Mrs. Holland's tone somehow managed to pull the two words into a verbal eye roll. Of *course* Alton would have an art program. They had everything.

"She doesn't need art, Layla," Dad said. "She needs to focus on math. That's where her future is going to be."

Mom stuck a finger in my direction. "She doesn't even know what she wants to do with herself."

Mrs. Holland's lips wadded together. "You haven't chosen a course of study, Grace?"

I shook my head, studying my hands. It seemed like everyone already knew what career they wanted, and I still had no idea. I took a deep breath and kind of regretted it. There was the faintest scent of mold in the air. The disposal again, probably.

I wondered if Mrs. Holland had noticed, too.

"Why drag her off to some school that might prepare her for a career she won't ever want?" Mom demanded.

"Because Alton Prep could prepare her for almost *any* career she might want." Mrs. Holland pushed to her feet, and my father was right behind her. I'd never seen him smile so wide.

"Well, clearly it's a great deal to think about," Mrs. Holland continued. "I do hope, however, you'll give it careful consideration."

My mom's chin lifted. "Of course we will. She's our daughter."

"And I know you want what's best for her." Mrs. Holland's smile was stapled on. She hoisted her bag to her shoulder and left a fan of brochures on our tabletop. "Please let me know if you have any questions."

Our front door was less than ten strides from our kitchen, but Mom walked Mrs. Holland out anyway, and when she returned to us, her gaze went straight to the dishes. "You know," Mom said, "*considerate* people *call* before they show up."

Dad's eyes were only for me. "I want you to do this. This is your chance to get out."

"Dad—"

"Why does she need to get out?" Mom slammed plates together as she filled the sink. She dumped a handful of lemon soap into the water and then dumped a bit more. "You're acting like she can't have a perfectly good life here."

"I'm not saying she can't have a good life," Dad continued, his voice climbing. "I'm saying she could have a *better* life. Opportunities like these don't happen in Boone."

"I didn't realize we had it so bad!"

Dad winced, I winced, and when he finally looked at me again, his expression promised that whatever was coming, he didn't want to say.

And I was sure I didn't want to hear it.

"I regret not going on, Grace."

My mother slowed. She groped the counter edge like her feet had slipped.

"I regret not getting out," Dad continued. "I regret not trying to see what I could do beyond Boone." A pause, just long enough for me to hear the rushing in my ears. "I regret staying."

The rushing turned into a roar. He regretted the life he had? He regretted marrying my mom? Having *us*? My chest funneled shut. It hurt.

But it didn't hurt enough to keep me from admitting part of me understood.

*I'm afraid of the same thing.*

Mom braced her spine against the sink edge, no surprise in her face. She'd *known*.

"Well," she said finally. "I guess it was different for me. All I ever wanted was love, family. It filled the cracks in me."

Like it hadn't filled my dad. I swallowed, mouth suddenly sticky.

"I don't want you to have the same regrets," Dad whispered.

"I'll think about it," I said, which made my father smile and my mother wince.

They argued for hours that night, hushed hisses that sounded like snakes. In the end, my dad slept on the couch, and my mother cried.

No matter what I chose, I was going to disappoint one of my parents.

# chapter twelve

*now...*

*A*nder doesn't remember.

Becca squeezes my upper arm. "Grace, breathe! You sound like a damn train!"

I blink. I *do* sound like a train. I'm wheezing hard, fighting to suck oxygen around my loss. Ander and I were all we had. We lost our original lives. We lost Jem, our real parents. Forty-two lives, and Ander and Finn have been the only constants.

*My* only constants.

"Where's your inhaler?" Becca grabs my book bag, and I have just enough left in me to pull away. She'll see the clothes. I won't be able to explain.

*I need to run. How can I run without him?*

"I'm okay. Just…allergies," I say, sounding perfectly reasonable even though all I can think is: Was I always destined to lose Ander, too?

Then, almost on top of it: Will Finn have forgotten as well?

I inhale so hard, the edges of my vision go gray and Becca's fingers dig deeper. "Grace?"

"I'm okay." I shake her off. "I'm okay."

Becca makes a disgusted noise. "You're not okay if you're talking to *him* again. You've been broken up for months."

Another wheeze. *We were together. Now we're…not.*

"Don't start up again," Becca says.

"I'm not. Just forget it, okay?"

Two other guys join Sam at Becca's locker, waiting for her to retrieve me. I focus on their flip-flops, their candy-colored polos, their seriously unfortunate madras plaid shorts—anything to keep the thoughts in my head from escaping through my mouth.

*Ander doesn't remember. He doesn't* remember. The words deafen me, looping and looping until: *I will have to face Finn alone in two days.*

"How am I supposed to forget my best friend acting like a lunatic?" Becca asks, putting her face almost against mine.

"Sorry. I'm just…sorry."

She studies me with narrowed eyes. "C'mon."

I do. At the lockers, the boys watch Becca and me like we are everything shiny. Or maybe like she's everything shiny. Becca's laugh has a bounce to it, hard and round and high enough to reach the sun.

She links her arm through mine and leans into me. "You'll come, right?"

I nod and then wonder why I did. I have no idea what Becca's talking about, but it's like her superpower to get me to agree. Is that a this-timeline thing or a me thing? I glance away, spotting Ander a few yards off. He smiles at some pink-haired girl and his eyes lift, catching mine.

Then someone moves behind me, sliding to my side. I jerk around, and suddenly we're face-to-face, breathing the same air.

Finn.

I know not to scream (Falls 2 and 4 and 5) and I know not

to beg for help (Falls 3 through 9). Finn looks like a come-to-life Prince Charming. He's all dark hair and amber eyes and a smile that promises you are his only. No one ever believes he's capable of murder. "Get away from me," I whisper at last.

He edges the tiniest bit closer. "Hey, Grace."

*Finn's never found us this fast before.* Never. *Is this how it's going to end?*

I pull up my chin. No way.

"Touch me," I say, "and everyone will see. You won't get away with it."

He's so close all I can see is him. The thin skin of his throat slides as he swallows.

"I know," he says.

"Get away from me," I repeat, and Finn shifts, stops, and watches me for so long I start to wonder what he's searching for.

He looks exhausted. So am I.

His eyes switch to his left, lingering on Ander. "Does he remember?"

"Of course he does."

Because I'm not alone in this nightmare. I'm *not*.

"Finn!" Becca shimmies to my side with a smile that overstretches her face. "You're not usually on time for class."

"First time for everything, right?"

Pink tinges Becca's ears. She likes him. I get that. Finn has the kind of lazy smile that makes you want to know—beg to know—what he's thinking.

"God, Grace, do you treat all your boyfriends like that?" The leggy brunette from the party pushes in next to us. She slings one arm around Finn's shoulders, and he stiffens.

*Boyfriend? Nonononononononono—*

"Stop looking at him like you hate him," the other girl continues. "Unless you *do* hate him, in which case tell me so I can have him."

Dusky red crawls up Finn's throat, and he looks at the floor. I can't look away from the brunette. She's pinned me to the spot.

"Stop being such a cow, Morgan," Becca says, but she sounds amused, and I suddenly feel sorry for Grace. These are her *friends*? The crowd around us is growing thicker, and it presses us tighter and tighter together. I'm almost touching Finn, and I'm convinced I can smell water, *swamp*. For a single second, I think I'm going to be sick.

"Seriously, though, Grace." Becca turns to me, and there's something watchful in her expression. Mean. "You should probably make it up to him after flinging yourself at Ander."

Finn flinches.

"Make it up to him?" My voice is Minnie Mouse high.

"Yeah, make it up to him," Becca says with a smirk. "You gonna hold on to that V-card forever?"

"Probably," Morgan adds.

I open my mouth and close it. I don't know what to say. I don't know what to *do*. Usually, I'm so careful not to disrupt all the Graces' lives. I don't know what happens to them after I Fall. If they come back and I've created a mess, they have to fix it. It's not fair to them.

What if the real Grace returns to her life and I've ruined it? These are her friends, and I'm making her look like an idiot in front of them. Somehow, I don't think they'll forgive her for that. What if I ruin something she can't get back?

"Are you two actually going out?" Morgan tilts her head so her chocolate-colored braid drapes over Finn's shoulder. "I've never even seen you kiss him. Finn? Have you kissed her?"

"Yes," he says.

Heat fills me like floodwater. *Liar*. Only as soon as I think it, I feel Finn's fingers in my hair, feel his breath coast against my skin.

I jerk back, definitely smelling water and mud now. I'm not remembering kissing. I'm remembering our last Fall.

"Kiss her now." Morgan slaps Finn on the shoulder, shoving him toward me. Suddenly, we are toe to toe, and my stomach is in endless free fall. "I want to see it."

"Yeah," Becca says to me. "Kiss him."

I shake my head. "No."

"*Yes*." Becca's tone is so sharp I suddenly realize she's not used to Grace saying no. I'm changing their dynamic, and I have a very bad feeling Grace wouldn't want that.

"C'mon," Becca continues, that watchful look still in her eyes. She's making note of every misstep, and it makes my insides topple. "It's just a kiss."

*Think of this Grace. Think of Ander. You can't slip away if you're causing attention.*

And Finn can't hurt me with all these witnesses. As this Grace's boyfriend, he might be able to *touch* me, but he can't *hurt* me.

I wrench myself forward and Finn shakes his head, focuses on Morgan and Becca. "Leave her alone."

Becca laughs. "It was a joke. Lighten up."

"I mean it. Leave her alone."

I wheeze and catch myself. What. Is. Going. *On*? Becca and Morgan turn their attention to Ben and the others, and Finn's eyes meet mine. A single muscle ticks in his jaw.

"What are you playing at?" I whisper.

He eases into me like we really are boyfriend and girlfriend, and my shoulders hit the lockers behind me. "I'm not playing at anything. I'm keeping up appearances."

He says it like it's funny, and it's not. It's *so* not. I'm close enough to strike, but Finn doesn't move. I'm close enough to grab, but his hands roll into fists. Is he holding himself back? He tilts toward me and I hold my breath and for two whole heartbeats, the world stands still.

Then someone shouts, and we both flinch, turning to see Ander weave past. He doesn't glance even once in my direction.

"Ander doesn't remember," Finn whispers.

I shudder and force myself to turn around. "He remembers."

Finn's eyes are so sad it makes that slow smile look accidental—a rainbow in spilled gasoline. "When it comes to him, you've always been such a liar."

*then...*

I stayed up that night, listening to my window AC unit drip water into its plastic bucket and going through all the brochures Mrs. Holland left behind. It was fluff stuff. I *knew* it was fluff stuff.

And yet I couldn't look away. I studied the pictures, tried to pick out kids who looked like me and couldn't. Everyone was the same—jackets pressed into knife-sharp pleats, faces round and pale as the moon.

Although I was pretty sure they used the same Hispanic guy twice.

I closed my eyes, took a breath so deep it felt like I'd overfilled my lungs with the smell of damp carpet, and tried to imagine myself at Alton: navy blazer, green skirt, "endless opportunities to become the adult your child is meant to be."

It wasn't me and yet it felt like it…might be. It felt almost like meeting another almost-could-be-maybe version of myself. I could do this. I could—and yet at the same time, I knew part of me was still lingering over how if everyone looks the same, then no one stands out.

I could disappear.

I could *disappear*.

I swallowed, and when I heard the coffeemaker hiss and spit a few hours later, I walked into the kitchen and told my hollow-eyed parents I wanted to apply.

The look in my mom's eyes when I told her scared me. The look in my dad's eyes when he talked about regret scared me more. Dad was so excited, and I smiled like I was, too, like dread hadn't wrapped around my bones.

I wrote the personal essay that morning and turned it in to Mrs. Holland. She attached it to my transcripts and letters of recommendation, and sent everything off. I never expected to hear a word.

Which helped when dealing with Jem, who couldn't believe I would willingly miss senior year.

"I'm not getting in," I told him after Dad and I got home. Jem was lying in wait by the door already dressed for work and already late and in no hurry to leave. He followed me from the living room to my room to the kitchen.

"But what if you *do* get in?" he asked.

"I won't."

His face screwed up. "But what if you *do*?"

I sighed. "I'll introduce you to all my roommates."

"A promise is a promise." Jem's grin faltered, tugged down at the edges. "Have you told Ander?"

"No." I paused. "Don't say anything, okay? It's not a big deal, and I don't want to go into it."

"Whatever. I can't believe you would even think about leaving. These are the best years of our lives."

He was only half joking. I rolled my eyes. "Oh my God, my brother is Peter Pan."

He pointed two finger guns at me. "I could totally pull those tights off. I'd make Peter look manly."

"You're missing the whole point. Peter doesn't want to be manly."

"Peter doesn't know what he wants." Jem grinned, and suddenly I was grinning, too. He could always make me laugh. If I went away, I wouldn't have that anymore.

And when his eyes darkened, I knew he was thinking the same thing.

"I'm *not* getting in." I repeated it like a mantra, like a prayer. I believed it, and that's why I never told Ander I applied. What was the point, right?

But he was there when Dad came home with the first-round acceptance letter. Jem, Ander, and Finn were working on Jem's truck. I was reading in the shade, and when Dad drove up, I knew. His grin was so wide I could see the gleam through the cracked truck windshield. I'd never seen him so happy.

It almost was enough to ignore how my stomach had curled into a knot.

"You're on to the next round! You made it!" Dad grabbed me in a bear hug and twirled me around. His yelling should've buried Jem's hushed and hurried explanation to Ander and Finn about what was going on, about what it meant. Only it didn't.

I felt every word dig under my skin to simmer.

"I'm so proud of you," Dad breathed into my hair.

I hugged him harder. "I haven't done it yet."

"You will." Dad set me down and waved Ander over. "I bought Layla some new plants for out back. Help me bring them in?"

Ander nodded and Jem joined us, wiping his hands on

the front of his jeans. Dad's truck bed was filled with lacy pink and white azaleas. They were my mom's favorites and at first, I thought it might be an apology. Dad was sorry he said he regretted staying. But he's done things like this for her before—many times, for as long as I can remember—and I don't know how to reconcile what he says he regrets and the love he shows. Which one's the truth? Or are they both?

Ander and Jem grabbed the closest plants and followed Dad around the back of the house.

"Why don't you want to go to Alton?"

Finn. He so rarely ever spoke, I almost didn't recognize his voice.

"I didn't say I didn't want to go. I said I wouldn't get in." I tried to summon a smile and failed. He made me anxious. Jem would say it was because everything made me anxious.

"Are you looking forward to the new school year?" I asked at last.

No response.

Part of me knew I should just shut up, and yet I couldn't seem to. "I know it's hard to start at a new school," I continued, picking up speed. "It'll get better, though."

"What?" Finn stared like he couldn't understand a single thing I was saying, and slowly, my cheeks began to flame.

"I mean," I added. The words were now running into themselves. It was like I'd lost control of my mouth. "It's hard to be shy, but the school year eventually ends, right? And we always survive."

"You think I'm shy?" His face had gone pale underneath his tan, but his tone was amused.

"Well…yeah. You're always so quiet. I figured you were having a hard time fitting in."

"You think I'd *want* to?"

I froze. He was angry, and I didn't understand what I'd said.

"This"—Finn waved to himself and then to the driveway and the house and the swamp in the distance—"isn't me, okay? It's not who I am."

I straightened. "Oh yeah?"

His mouth thinned, and there was something in his eyes I recognized. It was the same look Mrs. Holland had. Like we were dirty. Like we were *less*.

I drew back. "But acting like a pompous ass is?"

"Hey, Finn!" It was Jem. He had curling white petals stuck to the front of his T-shirt. "Could you grab the shovel from my truck?"

"Sure," Finn said, still staring me down. "No problem."

And after another beat of us glaring at each other, he did. Finn left maybe ten minutes later, and I was relieved to see him go. One less person to have to negotiate. Except Dad went inside to fix dinner and Jem went back to the truck and I couldn't avoid Ander's eyes any longer.

"Why didn't you tell me?" he asked.

"I didn't think it mattered."

"You didn't think I'd *care*?"

"No, no, I just…I only applied because I felt like I should." I took a deep breath, felt the humid air reach all the way to the bottom of my lungs. The atmosphere had a weight to it, and in the distance, the cicadas whined. "I truly didn't think I would get in—I still might not. This is just the first round…" I trailed off, because Ander was supposed to nod or say something or do something so I would know we were okay.

He didn't.

He looked at me like I'd lied to him.

"I didn't think it mattered," I repeated. "I'm glad you know now."

He studied the envelope. "Yeah, I am, too."

# chapter fourteen

*now...*

Becca thinks my asthma is making me woozy, and I don't argue. It's easier to let her lead me to homeroom than find it myself. She drops me off, and briefly, I worry about screwing up even more, but there are perks to being popular. I don't have to raise my hand during roll call—the teacher knows me. I don't have to figure out my seat—the other kids melt back. I smile at one girl, and she flinches.

Two seats from mine, Finn finally finds a desk. We don't look at each other, but it doesn't seem to matter. He didn't touch me and yet I still feel him *everywhere*. Is it an effect of this Grace's body? If they were dating, maybe her body recognized his on some biological level, some cellular level. Love changes you—maybe I just didn't realize how *much* it changes you. Every time I smell the river, I think of Ander. Maybe every time Finn gets close, this Grace recognizes him.

The bell rings, and I launch myself into the hallway, nearly colliding with Sam as he leaves his homeroom.

"Whoa there," he says, putting one hand on my elbow. "You okay?"

"Totally." I force a grin, and he studies my face. I grin wider, and he shrugs.

"Bio?"

I nod, and together, we press through the crowd. Sam tells me about his soccer practice and how he didn't do his history homework. I don't think I'm expected to respond. I smile and nod at the right places, and he seems happy enough with that.

We walk down a flight of steps and meet Becca at the bottom. She wriggles between us. "I need more coffee to get through this. He's going to put me to sleep again, you watch."

Thanks to Grace's organization, I'm pretty sure "he" means Mr. Manson, our bio teacher. We turn right at another set of lockers, and I follow Sam through the closest door.

Bio is basically one big room with row after row of lab tables. I have a momentary panic attack because people seem to have assigned seats and then I see an empty chair sitting next to a petite blonde. The blonde looks at Becca, at me, and swallows hard.

Guess this is where I sit. Sam and Becca take the lab table behind her and I slide into the empty chair, careful not to let my bag spill onto her side of the table. Her hands go to her lap, the tabletop, under her thighs.

At the end of the late bell, Ander flies in and takes a seat across the room. Mr. Manson wanders in after him, telling everyone to get out their notes.

The teacher then turns to the whiteboard, giving us a great shot of his bald head, and starts outlining free energy change and entropy. Ugh. *Again?* I've had this stuff at least five times now, but I still take out my bio notebook, flipping it open to the next empty page. At least I can leave this Grace with something she can use.

Or I could, if I could concentrate. Finn's face crowds my thoughts. The timeline's speeding up. He's never found us this fast before. He's also never gotten so close without trying to hurt me.

Chills creep up my arms as I remember Finn's heat, the weight of him. He held himself back; why? Too many witnesses?

I sneak a glance at the girl next to me. She's written "Abbie" at the top of her paper and is scribbling furiously.

I fumble for my pencil. *I should be doing the same thing. I should be—*

A small square wings through the air and hits the table. I look down. There's a condom wrapper sitting between Abbie and me. For about a nanosecond, I'm confused, but then another arcs past Abbie's shoulder and joins the first.

My stomach rolls.

Becca and Sam are throwing condom wrappers at this poor girl.

Abbie grips her pencil harder.

I glance over my shoulder and Becca grins at me. This is my best friend. I glance ahead, and the teacher's still droning away. This is their normal. My normal.

*It's not your problem. You know what is your problem? It's the third day.* Ander's voice is so clear in my head I sit up straighter. He's right. This isn't my problem—and moreover, I can't risk calling more attention to myself.

We don't know the fallout we're leaving behind. We know Ander dies, but does Grace survive? Am I just borrowing her body, giving it back after I've used it? If so, I can't hijack her life.

I can't just sit here, either.

Behind us, Becca giggles as Sam throws another condom wrapper. It bounces off Abbie's ear and lands on the back of her hand. She studies it for a beat, then flicks it to the floor to join the others.

*Say something. Tell the teacher. Call them out.*

She doesn't. She just hunches into herself like she wants to disappear entirely.

Is this what she lives like? Day after day, week after week? Is this the hell they put her through?

"Say something," I breathe. Abbie cuts her gaze to me, white showing all around her eyes.

"Say something," I whisper again. "Tell Manson."

She cringes, and I want to grab her hand. *I'm not who you think I am.* Except I am, or rather, I'm supposed to be.

Another wrapper hits the table, and I bounce to my feet, overturning my chair. "Knock it off!"

Becca gasps. The room gasps. Everyone stares at me as heat crawls up my neck. No one ever tells Becca to knock it off. Ever. I don't need a diary or color-coded folders to tell me that. No matter the universe, some things stay constant.

"Miss Freeman." Mr. Manson glares at us, breathing so hard his nose hairs quiver. "What is that about?"

I look at Abbie. *Here*, I want to say. *I got you halfway. Tell him the truth. It's sitting all around our feet.* But Abbie won't meet my eyes. She's staring straight ahead, barely breathing.

"Miss Freeman! What is going on?"

"It's—" I bend down for the condom wrappers and go cold. They're *gone.* How can they be gone? I saw them. They were all over the floor, all over our lab table.

"Miss Freeman!"

I pop back up, face nuclear. Our desk is clear, too. That's not possible. I *saw* them. I swallow and look at Mr. Manson again. His eyes are half bugged out of his head, and his face is flushing pale purple. "Sorry. I—sorry."

"What were you thinking?"

I look at our teacher, at Abbie, at the class. Becca's drawing curlicue doodles in her notebook, and Ander has tilted back in his chair, watching me. My face goes hotter. He's watching me because I look like a lunatic. I *am* a lunatic.

I'm freaking seeing things, and even if I weren't, I know better than to behave like this. You can fight against the Falls all you want, but you won't win; you'll never win.

"Sorry." I slam my chair upright, flop down, and focus on the board. "Sorry."

It's all I say these days. We take notes in silence for the rest of class, and when the bell finally rings, Abbie bolts. Did I make things worse for her?

I stand, stuffing my notebook inside my bag as Becca passes me.

"What is your *damage*?" she hisses, ramming her shoulder into mine. I stumble as Ander slips past. Everyone else files out. In their wake, there's a charged silence, the kind of quiet that promises storms.

"Miss Freeman?" Mr. Manson plants both fists on his desk and leans forward. "I'd like a word, please."

I haul myself to the front of the room and study the toes of my shoes while he lectures me on interruptions.

"Do I make myself clear?" he asks at last. "Look at me."

I do. I look at him and think about the wrappers that were lying on our table. Then I think about how Abbie hadn't asked me to play hero. Maybe the shame of confronting Sam's behavior was worse than actually enduring Sam's behavior. If she doesn't want the truth to come out, who am I to force her?

"Yes, sir," I say. "Sorry."

"Good. Don't do it again."

I nod, a bile-tinged laugh creeping up my throat. I don't want to be this girl, this Grace. And for the most horrible second, for the first time *ever*, I think I will be glad to die.

*then...*

Boone was all about traditions. We had parades every Fourth of July, strawberry picking every June, an apple cider festival in the fall, and the Boone High School Senior Pick Up Day every August.

"Free labor disguised as tradition," Jem explained to Finn the night before. As usual, Finn seemed unimpressed. He might've even looked at me to underscore his unimpressed point, but I stared straight ahead like I never noticed.

We were late—so very late—and my skin felt too small for my body. As Jem had made sure to point out, it wasn't like I *had* to be there. I probably wouldn't be at Boone High in the fall, I'd be at Alton Prep. But since I'd stuck with my "I'm not getting in" for the past two weeks, I signed up anyway.

I didn't want to go, and I definitely didn't want to show up late. Late was worse. Late made me want to vomit.

"It's just school stuff," Jem said, not taking his eyes from the barn. We were waiting for Ander and Finn to finish their early-morning prep work at Farley's. We'd parked almost ten minutes ago, and there was still no sign of them.

"It doesn't matter if we're late," Jem continued. "People know me. They know what to expect."

"Which is?"

"Very little." Jem leaned toward me, grinning like he had the greatest secret ever. "Stop worrying. Everyone knows us."

He really didn't care—correction, Jem actually enjoyed their eyes on him. Why couldn't I be a little more like him? I gritted my teeth. "Yeah, and everyone will stare as we come in."

Jem shook his head, drumming his thumbs harder against the steering wheel. We both knew what came next in the argument. He would ask, "Why would you care?" And I would try to explain and fail to explain and finally give up because you can't make someone understand you, no matter how much you might want to.

"It makes my skin crawl," I said at last.

"Why would you care what they think?"

"Forget it." There were gunshots in the distance, and birds burst above the tree line. I leaned out the open window, watching them arc above us. Farley must've had another hunt going or maybe a group doing target practice.

"I'm worried you're going to end up a hermit. People shouldn't make you anxious. They're just people."

"Maybe it's a genetic thing. Maybe one of our great-great-great-whatevers was agoraphobic or something."

"No way. You're closer to me than you are to anyone else." Jem leaned forward, draping tanned forearms against the dashboard. Ander and Finn had appeared, walking out of the barn with their book bags slung over their shoulders.

I frowned. Farley—shorter than both boys, his soft belly pushing hard enough through his T-shirt to see the indentation of his belly button—walked between Ander and Finn, gesturing his hands in short, hard jerks.

I slumped into the truck seat. "I think Farley's mad."

"Hope Ander didn't start in about those stupid birds again."

Ander nodded along with whatever Farley was saying, his dark blond hair falling in his eyes. Finn ignored both of them completely. He stared off into the fields like Farley didn't even exist.

Considering this was Finn, Farley probably didn't.

Jem suddenly turned to me. "I saw some brochures for Vanderbilt in your room. What's up with that?"

My stomach flipped. "It's called *boundaries*, Jem. You should look them up."

"I know. I know, but…just tell me, okay? First Alton Prep and now you're considering Vanderbilt?"

"No." *Yes*. I focused on Farley. "I just wanted to look."

"Why?"

"Maybe I want to go there. I don't know. When we drove past last summer, it felt…I haven't been able to stop thinking about it." I glared at him. "Don't make me feel bad about wanting to go away for college."

Which was stupid, because I already did.

Jem picked at his steering wheel and wouldn't meet my eyes. "I don't understand. Why would you want to go to school with a bunch of strangers?"

*Because* they're strangers. Because I can hide in plain sight. Because no one knows who I'm supposed to be.

"Have you told Ander you're thinking about going away for college, too?"

"No." We had barely seen each other since my acceptance letter came. I had stuff at home and he'd had work and… "Why would he care?"

"You've noticed the way he looks at you. I *know* you have. It's not just that, either—it's how he always waits for you, how he always seems to find you."

Or he used to. Since the acceptance letter stuff… I tucked

my hands beneath my knees. Jem said the things about Ander the same way he said, "You're closer to me than you are to anyone else," like it was the truth. No, more like it was logical, predictable, like two plus two will always equal four.

Was it?

"Always finds me?" I echoed. "Are you talking about when we take the boat out? Maybe he's trying to make sure I don't fall in—which is more than you do, by the way."

"Whatever. I know you can swim your way out." Jem paused, digging his thumbnail into the steering wheel. "Maybe you're meant to be together. I mean, it would make sense, right? It's always been the three of us. Maybe it's inevitable."

Jem was fishing, and I refused to respond. He grinned like he knew it. "Look, as much as the thought of you being with a guy makes me want to barf, if you were with Ander…it might not be the worst thing. I'm not exactly thrilled, but you're really good for him. If anyone can save him from himself"— Jem waved one hand in the boys' direction—"it's you."

"What a glowing recommendation."

"All I'm going to say."

"Good."

"Hey." Ander leaned through the open window, and just as Jem said, his gaze never left me. It made my mouth go hot and dry. "Sorry about that," he said, rubbing one hand through his sun-streaked hair.

Jem sighed. "Get in before she explodes. You need a ride, too, Finn?"

Finn stood a few strides behind Ander. His fingers—long and tapered—were playing with the ends of his backpack straps.

"If you don't mind," Finn said, lifting one shoulder. It made his faded button-up stretch tight across his chest and for a moment, I couldn't reconcile the preppy kid with the pretty face and the deep Southern accent. Who was he fooling? He could dress however he liked and yet the minute he opened his mouth, everyone would know he was country.

"You'll have to ride in the back," Jem said. "No room up front."

Finn nodded and tossed his bag into the pickup bed. He jumped in after it, settling with his shoulders to the cab as Ander climbed in next to me. Jem shifted into first and his leg brushed mine. We turned onto the main road and our knees bumped. My brother pushed the truck faster and faster, but he couldn't outrun the heat. Hot wind whipped through the cab, making it impossible to talk.

Which was just as well.

*Maybe it's inevitable*, Jem had said. Was it? I didn't have memories where Ander wasn't at the edge. I didn't have birthdays where he wasn't there, rides to school where he wasn't next to me... I didn't have me without him.

Without either of them.

Jem and Ander had been my only real friends for years, for *always*, and the thought erupted in a cold rush: *Am I in love with my best friend?*

I looked at Ander, and he shifted like he knew.

Another chill swept over me. *I don't think "love" is a big enough word.*

Thanks to Jem's driving, we were only fifteen minutes late—although he was going so fast, he almost clipped the curb *and* the gym teacher as we came in.

"Sorry, Mr. Daley!" Jem yelled, waving furiously.

Mr. Daley actually waved back. No one would be running sprints today, but he was prepared anyway. The teacher's shorts were short, and his white tank top was tight. The only thing he was missing was his perpetually gleaming whistle.

"Someone's excited about the upcoming year," I said, already tugging off my seat belt.

"He really needs a bra," Ander added. He leaned back and knocked on the half-open window that divided the front cab from the truck's bed. "Did you see that?" he asked Finn.

"I tried not to."

I nudged Jem. "Anyone else would get detention for nearly running over a teacher."

My twin made a scoffing noise. "Please. I'll just tell him I had to get Boone High School's favorite student to class on time." He screeched us into the last parking spot in the shade and turned off the truck. "See? We made it."

"Barely."

"And yet somehow I think you'll survive." Jem caught my arm, already laughing at whatever was about to come out of his mouth. "First day of school, I'm going to make you wait until the late bell rings, see if your head really can twist off from anxiety."

He tilted toward Finn, who was getting his own stuff from the back, glancing at us through the rear window. "She has to be early to every class because she likes to be dead center," Jem explained to him. "Exactly two rows back. Wait until you see. It's hilarious."

I glared at him.

"I thought you weren't going to be here for senior year," Finn said.

It was the first time we'd spoken since the acceptance letter, and I couldn't help how my shoulders went stiff. "I might be. I mean, I haven't been accepted by Alton. Nothing's set in stone or whatever."

"Of course you'll be accepted," Jem told me. He turned to Finn again. "She only applied to make our dad happy. She'll turn it down."

Finn's expression was carefully blank, but I spoke Jerk well enough to see the "You're going to turn down an offer from Alton Prep to go...*here*?" written in how his mouth went thin.

"Move it, ladies." I shook Jem off and followed Ander, sliding across the bench seat and hopping to the asphalt. "Some of us have things to do."

Boone High School was a squat cinder-block building punctuated with long, slender windows. It sat just on a rise outside the swamp and was probably the newest thing in the whole town. A tornado flattened the old school when Jem and I were in third grade, and the town council built the new high school in the same place. When it rained, the hallways smelled like old milk. When it didn't rain, the hallways smelled like people.

Ander bumped open the metal door, and I followed him through. Even though we were late, Mrs. Holland and Mr. Daley were nowhere to be seen, and everyone was milling around. Boone was pretty small, only about a hundred kids in our graduating class. Pressed this tightly together, though, it felt way bigger. Everybody knew everybody, and everyone wanted to give everyone else a hug.

Finn's eyes went wide, and I had to smother my laugh.

Above our heads, there was a limp banner draped across the main hallway's entrance saying: Welcome Seniors!

Jem grinned. "This is going to be our best year *ever*." He was talking to me, but watching two blondes standing by the lockers. One of them looked up and noticed my brother. She grinned like she couldn't help it.

"Grace?" Coach Daley squeezed closer, holding a pile of binders in his arms. Papers were escaping at odd angles, and I knew what was coming before he even asked. "I can't seem to get the receipts and the ledger to line up. We have to do a new order for basketballs and mats, and I don't think the receipts match and…could you look at it?"

"Sure."

"Thanks." Coach Daley heaved everything into my arms, and I wobbled.

Ander quirked a brow. "I guess they were right when they said we'd use word problems in real life."

"Lucky," Jem added, frowning. "You're going to get air-conditioning."

In the end, I didn't. I sat on the bleachers by the football field that was also our soccer field and sometimes baseball field and sifted through order forms while everyone else repainted stairs or swept up or goofed off behind the concession booth. Jem and the blonde were nowhere to be seen, and Ander was helping Coach Daley, which was especially nice of him because they hadn't gotten along since Ander quit soccer two years ago.

Maybe that was why I wasn't surprised when Finn's shadow crossed Coach's paperwork; Jem and Ander were busy and we were waiting for them. It was what the two of us did.

"I'm sorry I acted like an ass."

I didn't look up. "You were an ass?"

A pause. "Yeah, when I gave you shit about Alton…and Boone."

*And for being nice to you.* I wasn't done with the receipt reconciliation, but I turned the top page anyway. I wanted to make a point. "Whatever."

Silence…more silence. Finn still wasn't moving, and he still wasn't saying anything.

*And I'm still not looking* up. I turned another page and made a notation in the margin for two payments. *Keep walking, jerk.*

"You must read superfast," Finn said, and I didn't have to

see his face to know he was smirking.

"Yeah, it's a talent."

"I really am sorry, Grace."

My pen wavered a bit. He actually sounded sorry. I squinted up at him. "I was just trying to be nice."

Finn nodded slowly, chewing hard on his lower lip. "Yeah, I know," he said at last. "Everyone around here is just so damn *nice*."

Sarcasm? Hate? I couldn't tell, so I ignored it. "Yeah, well, good manners don't cost anything."

He scoffed. "Clearly. That must be why people around here have them."

I slammed the receipt book closed and grabbed my backpack strap.

"Shit." Finn caught my wrist. "Sorry—*sorry*."

I eyeballed his hand, and he dropped my wrist. "I'm sorry," he repeated.

"You're also an ass."

"Agreed." Finn scowled, studying the tops of his shoes… the palms of his hands…then his eyes swung up. They speared mine. "Can we try again?"

For a second, it made my heartbeat stutter. In the next second, I kind of hated him. Why did he affect me like this?

"Why should we try again?" I asked, opening the receipt book and smoothing the pages. "How could someone like me possibly keep up with someone like *you*?"

At least he had the good grace to grimace. Finn pushed one hand through his hair, leaving it in messy dark spikes. "Would it help if I apologized again?"

"I'm not sure. Try and we'll see."

Something flickered in Finn's eyes. Amusement? Interest? *I don't care. I don't care. I don't care.*

"I'm really sorry," Finn said softly. "I hate it here. I didn't want to come, and I know that's not your fault. I shouldn't take it out on you."

He sat down next to me, and I forced myself to turn, to really look at him. He held my gaze and didn't waver. Maybe he was being honest? Then again, Jem had quite a few pretty speeches about making mistakes and wanting to be a better person. They were really touching, too.

Until you realized he'd just memorized a bunch of Hallmark cards.

Why did Finn feel different? Because he was being truthful? Or because he wanted me to believe?

"Wow," I managed. "That's…really evolved of you."

"I've had a lot of therapy." I kept staring at Finn, and he raised one brow, panned his hands in a *what* gesture. "It's true. You're telling me Jem doesn't know how to own his actions?"

"Jem doesn't even know the words 'own his actions.'"

He grinned, and my heart stuttered. That shouldn't happen. I shouldn't feel like this when he looks at me.

"So how'd you end up in Boone?" I asked.

Finn's grin drained from his face. "My dad was called up for another tour. I had to crash somewhere."

"I'm sorry. Is he…?" I had no idea what to say.

"He's okay." Finn leaned back, resting his elbows on the bleacher seats behind us. "I mean, since we last talked, he's okay. But the situation is kind of day-to-day, you know? Minute-to-minute sometimes."

"You living with family then?"

A scowl ghosted across his mouth. "Yeah, my dad's parents. They're okay, I guess. Life didn't really work out the way they expected—my dad marrying my mom, I mean."

"That's got to be hard on her."

Finn shrugged. "She died when I was ten. Cancer."

"I'm sorry."

"Don't be. And don't tell me 'everything happens for a reason.' She didn't die in agony because there's a big huge point." His smile is fake as hell but lightning-bright. "Anyway. My grandparents aren't horrible. We just don't have a lot in common. Happens in families."

Yeah, it did. Finn waited for me to agree, and I kept my face blank like I had no idea what he was talking about. It felt like a betrayal to agree to anything with him.

"This place is like a time warp," Finn continued. "You know I actually met my dad's high school girlfriend, the one his parents wanted him to marry? She's still here. Boone is like a black hole. No one escapes."

"Most of them don't want to."

He smiled, tilted toward me, and suddenly I could smell sunshine and soap and *boy*. "So you were nice to me because you thought I was nervous?"

"Yeah." I frowned. The whole thing felt super stupid now, and even though I had done it for Finn, I felt like I'd just revealed way more about myself. "I thought were you quiet because you were shy."

"And that meant what? You were going to save me from myself?"

The question was designed to make fun of me, but Finn's tone was so quiet, so serious, it didn't seem like a dig. I looked at him—a mistake because now I could see how those yellow eyes of his were really closer to dark gold.

We weren't touching. Why did I feel like I was being pulled apart?

"I wasn't trying to 'save' you," I said at last. "I just know what it's like to be on the outside."

Finn's eyes went wide. "With a twin like Jem? He's practically king of Boone."

"Doesn't mean *I* belong."

"I get that." Finn paused and then chuckled. "You know, for someone who's so shy and quiet, you don't hold back when you're mad."

"Jem is my twin, and Ander has been my best friend since we were little." I stopped, realizing that didn't exactly explain anything, and yet for me, it explained everything.

Another smile. "So you have no issues about standing up for yourself, just issues about standing in front of other people?"

I thought about it. "Yes."

"Sounds reasonable to me."

I searched his face for the joke, and there wasn't one. He wasn't laughing.

Finn shrugged. "It *does*."

"Glad it meets with your approval."

"Grace!" Ander stood with Jem by the staircase that wound down to the parking lot. They must have finished already. "C'mon!"

"I've got to drop this off!" I tugged my backpack over one shoulder and lifted the paperwork into my arms.

"You're not done?" Ander made a face. "You're killing me, Smalls. Let's go."

"I'll meet you at the truck."

He groaned but turned around, heading for the parking lot with Jem close behind him. I glanced at Finn. "You coming?"

"No. I'm meeting a friend."

The way he said "friend" sounded more like "girl." I hoisted the binders a little higher. "Okay, see you around."

"No doubt."

I made it almost down the whole hallway before I dared a glance backward. Finn was watching me.

And he was still smirking.

*now...*

Becca doesn't speak to me for the rest of the day. I tell myself I'll fix it. I tell myself even if I can't fix it, it doesn't matter. It's the third day. I have way bigger problems. Screw this Grace. Screw this life.

Except it doesn't help, because it feels like something's growing. People slide me glances as I struggle to find my classes. No one says anything, and I can't tell if that's because I'm Grace, or if it's because I've pissed off Becca.

I spend lunch hiding in the library, at a table in the back under an overhead light that has a beehive hum. I don't realize my tactical mistake until I hear his footsteps behind me.

Finn.

I wrap my fist around my pencil and pin it to my side as his shadow slides over me. I kick to my feet, but Finn doesn't move. He keeps the table between us.

"Heard what you did." His gaze drags up and down me, lingers on my fist and the upturned pencil. "It was nice of you. Even after all of this, you're still you."

He leans forward like he might reach for me, and I lean

back. "I will stab you," I whisper. "You know that."

Finn nods, dropping into the closest chair. "I would let you...do you think it would help?"

"Is that supposed to be funny?"

A younger girl emerges from between the bookshelves, looking for a place to sit. Her gaze flicks from Finn to me to the empty table on my left, and I go light-headed with relief when she sits down.

*Safety in numbers, sucker.* I glare at him. "What do you want?"

"I want to know what changed."

"I have no idea what you're talking about."

"What changed?" He leans forward and I lean backward and surprise tinges his expression. "This is the closest you've let me get to you in forever."

"It's not by choice."

"Isn't it?" He pauses, his mouth working around something he cannot or will not say. "Grace...what happened?"

Nausea sweeps through me in a wave. "You tell me. I don't know why we're stuck on this loop."

Finn tilts closer. "Yes, you do."

I cannot stop myself. I lean forward, heart thumping in my teeth and toes. From rage? Fear? I can't tell. Everything is tangled. "No, I *don't.* Get away from me."

The poor younger girl glances at us, shifting in her seat. She's worried. That makes two of us. Finn doesn't notice, though. He doesn't move.

But his eyes are all over me: searching my face, lingering on my mouth. Is he remembering how I begged? Because I am.

I start to tell him to get lost, and the librarian appears between the shelves. She pushes her book cart past us, glaring. Finn's eyes drop. It should be a relief, and it isn't. I still feel the heat of his gaze everywhere.

"Why do you always do this?" I whisper.

"You don't give me a choice."

"You're a monster."

He pushes to his feet. "You would know."

*I* have art last, and I'm nearly late because I took the wrong hallway and wandered almost back to the science wing before realizing my mistake. I skid into the art room just before the late bell.

"Sorry!" I gasp to the teacher—Mrs. Johnson according to Grace's folders—and her mouth goes paper-cut thin. The other teachers might let Grace slide, but this one doesn't. Her eyes narrow and I realize she might not even *like* Grace, and for some reason, that makes me even sadder. We love art…don't we?

Mrs. Johnson faces the other students and flicks one hand in their direction. "You may begin."

I hesitate. Where do I sit? All the easels are taken. There are no empty chairs.

Wait a minute.

My stomach free falls. No empty chairs except for one, and it's next to Ander.

"Of course it is," I breathe and stalk across the room. He doesn't acknowledge me as I sit down, and I'm kind of grateful. I don't want to talk about what I did, and I definitely don't want to talk about what I'm about to do.

The canvas is covered with a paint-splattered drop cloth, and I don't move to take it down. There could be anything under there. This Grace could be great or mediocre or have an excellent grasp of stick figures and I'm not sure I'm ready to find out.

"Miss Freeman, you don't have all day," Mrs. Johnson says, watching me from above her pale-yellow glasses.

Isn't that the truth? I tug the drop cloth's corner and it slides to the floor with a whisper, revealing a canvas stained with vibrant blues and impossible greens. It's…an ocean? A scene underneath the ocean? A Rothko imitation?

Whatever it is, it's beautiful, and my held breath rushes from me. This Grace is far and away better than I was—am— whatever. Her bands of color have been built and blended until you can't separate them. It feels like a crescendo. I've never done an abstract this well.

It happens sometimes. I was a theater kid in Falls 10 and 16. It was okay. I liked the idea of being someone else, but I didn't like the audience part. It felt too exposed, too public. I invented flu symptoms to get out of practice. Which was best for everyone, because it wasn't like I knew the lines.

I was a musician once, Fall 11, and somehow that idea felt closer to being the real me even though I couldn't play a note. Losing myself in the music was easy (even if finding excuses about why I couldn't play wasn't).

Only I hated how there was nothing to show in the end. Once the playing stopped, the music disappeared.

"It's not like math," I had told Ander at the time. "When you finish a problem, you can see your work. It's there. You can almost touch it."

Ander laughed and laughed. "It drives you crazy because you like to acquire things. It's the effects of Falling. You're holding on. You're grabbing at anything."

I glared at him. "And you aren't?"

"*You're* my everything."

And then he'd kissed me.

One day later, Ander died and I watched and we Fell and

I haven't painted since. None of the other Graces were into it. Giving me back my painting now? It feels like coming home. I shouldn't be blinking away tears, but I am.

"Why did you do it?"

Ander. *This* Ander. He leans closer and I flinch. "Did you finally get tired of your game?"

"It wasn't my game."

"Oh, come on. Don't be modest now."

"It wasn't my *game*."

"*You* came up with it."

My whole body hot and then cold and then hot again. I would never start something so horrible. I would never—I tug my chin up. This actually isn't even about me, even though Ander's glaring at me like it is. It's about the other Grace, the one I'm inhabiting. And I get it, I really do. This Grace is awful, but she's also broken.

I want to tell him about her friends who aren't really friends, about how she lost her Jem, and I can't tell if I want to tell Ander because I need to share everything or because I've always shared everything with him.

Or the Ander that he used to be.

I face my canvas. "I didn't see you doing anything to stop it. If you want to play hero, talk to someone who doesn't know how you sat there and said *nothing*."

He exhales hard.

*Good. I hope he hurts as bad as I do.* I rub one palm across my face, feeling the beginning of an oncoming headache, like my edges are unraveling. From the Falls? Or something else?

Ander doesn't know. Will that save him?

I doubt it. Ignorance isn't bliss, much less a shield. Ander may be innocent, but Finn will come for him anyway...right?

Because for a single second, I'm actually not sure. When Finn looked at Ander this morning, there wasn't bloodlust or whatever in his eyes. He seemed tired. Resigned. He seemed like the boy I knew before.

Hope and doubt twist my chest tight. I think about how Finn looked at me, how close he'd been, how insistent he was that I knew what was happening.

And I don't.

We had been friends, but Finn came into my life when things were kind of, sort of, possibly changing. There was Alton, but there was also something else, something swimming just beneath our friendship's surface.

Our last night and first Fall, we'd all been at Amanda's for a party. I hadn't wanted to go. Jem and I had been fighting and Ander and I were a mess and I was pretty sure everything was ruined. Ander had asked me to play along for Jem's sake, to be normal, and I'd agreed because…because it was Jem.

And because Ander and I both knew we'd hurt him.

Only as soon as we were there, I realized (again) how pointless it was. For me, parties were always the same thing: me on the edge, praying no one would notice me.

And no one did until they needed me to take care of Ander.

I'm not cold, but I still shiver as I remember how I found him in Amanda's bathroom. His hand had been so warm. His fingers had twitched, and I knew he was going to reach for me.

And then he did.

Ander lifted one hand, palm upturned, and said my name. We could have been finished, but I took his hand…and we Fell.

After that, it was always the same: we ran and Finn chased and we Fell until all that's left is me—a girl who keeps crawling back from the dead.

*We all have to pay for what we did.*

I grit my teeth. We didn't *do* anything.

Next to me, Ander shifts, stretching the space between us.

He can't stand this Grace. He can't stand *me*.

*Don't think about it. Don't. Now is not the time to cry.*

Maybe that's because now's the time to give up?

I blink, blink again. Jem is back, Visa is back, my art is back, and now I want a Fall to happen. First time for everything, I guess. Maybe in the next universe, Ander will be back.

Or maybe he's gone for good.

Panic shrinks my lungs two sizes. What if Ander's death finally took? What if this Ander doesn't remember because he isn't my Ander, because my Ander—for whatever reason—didn't survive the Fall?

Which means if Finn comes for him, this Ander has no idea what's happening.

Would he die? Or would he Fall?

Pity chews through my horror. Falling would be worse than dying. I remember my first Falls—how I couldn't stop crying when I realized I would never see my parents, my Jem, ever again. How every passing moment started to fill lead-laced, so heavy because Ander and I both knew it was taking us closer and closer to the fifth day.

How terror was always my last breath.

I wouldn't wish it on anyone. At least I'd had Ander from the beginning. We figured it out together, patched the holes in what we were and what we knew.

I don't know what to do for this Ander.

Or for me.

I could walk away—run, just like we planned. This version of Ander is not my responsibility…and yet I know I can't do it. I cannot abandon him. This Ander is innocent, and if Finn won't stop and Ander doesn't know, I'll have to save us both.

But how?

# chapter seventeen

*then...*

It was Ander's idea to start bringing Finn everywhere, and it made hanging out feel like a bad sitcom. Jem was the heartbreaker, Ander was the boy next door, Finn was the snob, which made me the bookworm? The shy girl?

The social moron?

That sounded about right.

"We're taking Finn to the river tonight," Jem told me. "You're coming."

"I have plans."

"No, you don't." Jem stood between the window and me, glaring at me in a way that probably worked on every single girlfriend. I glared right back.

Did he know I was waiting for the mail delivery? Probably.

"You're coming," he repeated. "It'll be good for you."

Like my shyness was something he could cure, *fix*.

We took Ander's boat from our dock just as the sun dipped behind the trees. Jem's yellow spotlight turned the bugs bright white and caught all the ways the water rippled ahead of us.

Snakes.

"Why are we going at night again?" Finn asked. He sounded ever so slightly worried, and it made me ever so slightly glad. Maybe more than ever so slightly.

"We want you to have the full Boone experience," I told him, making sure my tone slid extra sweet. "I know how important that is to you."

Finn scowled at me like he wanted to set me on fire.

I smiled like I was going to bite his head off.

Jem never noticed. He kept complaining about Callie (they had broken up) and Bailey-Ann (they were fooling around). She'd wanted to come and had been mad when he said no. "It's like she doesn't understand we're not attached at the hip," he finished.

"It's because Grace came," Ander said, throwing the spotlight a little left so he could negotiate us around another fallen log. Between the shadows and the paint stains, his fingers were almost black. "She doesn't realize Grace isn't a girl."

"Hello? I *am* actually."

"I meant you're Grace," Ander added. "It's different."

It felt even *less* when he said it like that. Something plopped deep into the water by my hand, and I drew farther into the boat.

"Considering you dumped Callie," I said to Jem, "you still talk about her a ton. You in love with her?"

"*Callie?*" Jem's eyes went huge.

"Yeah. You love her?"

"He loves her so much it hurts," Ander said.

"But only when he pees," Finn said. Now they were both laughing, and the shadows turned Jem's scowl into a slash.

"You know," he said, "household cleansers come with warning signs. Girlfriends don't. It's a serious problem."

"Or it's natural selection," I said, adjusting my ponytail. It was glued to the back of my neck. This deep up the river, the trees were close, and without the breeze, we were breathing in a sauna. "Eventually, one of your hookups is going to shoot you in the ass, Jem."

Ander laughed. "I want to be there when it happens."

"Whatever," Jem said. "It's not like you two know anything about girls."

"Oh, I know a few things." There was a smile in Ander's voice that made my stomach flip-flop, and when I glanced up, that smile was focused on me.

"Oh God." Jem again. His face is bone-bright under the moon. "Are you two having…a moment?"

Ander's smile slid into a grin.

Were we past the Alton thing? We hadn't talked about it. Because maybe it didn't matter?

The low-hanging tree limbs parted, and as Ander picked up speed again, Finn leaned close. "I would've thought he's like your brother—is that the appeal? I heard that's a thing around here."

I tapped one finger to my chin. "Cute. Especially coming from someone who's proof evolution really can go in reverse."

Finn resumed his scowl and settled back against the seat, oozing into my space. Annoyed, I scooted over and in a desperate (and possibly successful) attempt to annoy me further, Finn nudged his Converse into my tennis shoe.

"I've been single for a while." Finn was talking to Ander and Jem, but he was staring at me. "It's working out really great for me, too. I think I'm The One."

*Do not laugh. Do not laugh. Do not—*too late. I laughed, and Finn smirked like he'd won.

"You won't be single for much longer," Jem said to Finn, scratching the side of his neck. "Callie's sister can't shut up about you."

Ander cut the engine and we drifted, catching the sluggish

current. It twirled us in a lazy circle. The trees opened up, revealing acres and acres of the Morton family's cow pastures, and in the distance, you could see the lights from the mill, a pink haze along the horizon, always there.

Then Ander spun us too hard and the boat bumped against the shore, sliding against mud that was soft and sticky as melted toffee. The cows startled backward, slamming into one another, and Ander and Jem laughed. We smacked against the shore again, and somewhere farther up the bank, a cow lowed. Their hooves made shushing noises against the grass.

Finn stiffened. "Please tell me we aren't going cow tipping."

"Nah." Jem was already climbing out of the boat and onto the bank, sticking low to the ground. "Just give me a few minutes and be *quiet*, okay?"

Ander flashed me a grin and followed him. This couldn't be good. I dabbed at the bead of sweat running along my collarbone. They were up to something.

Both boys disappeared over the top of the embankment and even when I stood, I couldn't see a thing. I sat back down and regretted it at once. Now I was sitting with Finn.

And was he closer? Because he felt closer.

"So what's your deal, anyway?" Finn asked.

"'Deal'?"

"Are you going to Alton or not? Because you should."

"Like you know so much."

"About this, I do."

I blew out a long, *long* sigh. "Are you seriously trying to tell me what's best for me?"

"Well, no one else in your life is. They're too busy trying to get you to stay put. You leaving is all Ander talks about. He doesn't want you to go."

I stiffened. "Huh. You're Ander's friend and you're trying

to talk his girlfriend into going to school hundreds of miles away? Interesting."

"I am."

"And humble."

Finn nodded. "Only when necessary." He paused. "Why aren't you like this all the time?"

"What do you mean?" I knew exactly what he meant, though, and Finn did his stupid smirk again because he knew I knew.

"When you want to be, you're funny. I bet you could have a ton of friends."

"No."

"Yes."

I scowled. "So could you."

"I'm an ass, remember?" Another pause, and this one stretched long and thin as melted caramel. "Why are you so shy?" he finally asked.

Later, I realized it was the way Finn said "shy," not like it was something cute that I would outgrow, but like it was something that turned my head to static.

Like it was something he understood.

Or wanted to understand.

There was thumping above us, coming fast. *Hooves? Is one of the cows running?* Finn and I both popped to our feet, and the force shook the boat, bumping us into each other.

I spread my arms for balance, and Finn's hand found my upper arm, my waist. He pressed against me and it felt…good. Like all the parts of him fit all the parts of me.

And they shouldn't.

Finn exhaled hard. "Grace—"

Ander leaped into view. He skidded down the embankment with Jem hot behind him.

"What did you *do*?" I demanded, because I knew they'd

done something. I could hear it in their giggles.

"Keep your voice down," Jem whispered, holding up something shapeless. It was…pants. He had someone's pants. "Callie's making out with Beau Landers to get back at me. I had to do something."

"Because taking Beau's pants is making a statement?"

"It will be once I call the cops about someone disturbing Morton's cows," Jem said. He flopped down next to Ander and stabbed one hand against the bank to push us back. I sat down before I fell down and we were almost to the first bend when someone far behind us started yelling.

Ander and Jem cracked up.

"Welcome to Boone," I said under my breath, and Finn smiled like we had a secret.

# chapter eighteen

*now...*

I wait for Jem by the truck. The sky is a faded blue, not even a single cloud, and the relentless sun gives everything a hard edge except in the distance where the heat makes the horizon wavy. I'm baking on the parking lot asphalt, but I'm too afraid to move. I don't want to give him an excuse to leave without me. I'm not sure I remember the way home.

I pick at my book bag straps and try to ignore how standing in the open like this freaks me out. I should get out now. Leave. Run.

And I can't. No matter how many times I tell myself I'm being stupid, that this Ander isn't *my* Ander, that he isn't my responsibility…I can't leave him. I couldn't live with myself if I knew I had abandoned him to Finn.

Of course, that doesn't mean I'm ready to be a hero, either. Deep in my purse, my cell beeps. I fish it out and the screen is blank. Great, now I'm hearing things. I toss it back in, catching a glimpse of myself in the truck window. This Grace is starting to feel so familiar. I touch my fingertips to the tattoo and frown. It feels tender, almost sore. Even the edge of my shirt irritates it.

I keep the tattoo covered, always. It's not that I'm embarrassed. Ander—my Ander—had wanted me to have it in our fourth Fall and I'd wanted to wear it, but it was something that belonged to us. It was private.

Now? Now it feels raw, *wrong*, like I stole it.

And I didn't. The tattoo had been a promise. We were going to stay together. Ander had sketched it on my skin thirty times before we'd sneaked off to the truck stop by the interstate.

I should've felt lucky I didn't get hepatitis. Instead, I felt lucky I was his.

I pick at the white ink. It was supposed to be subtle. It ended up looking like a scar.

*A* little after four, Jem appears in the distance. Even if I didn't recognize the red band T-shirt he put on this morning, I'd know the walk anywhere: loose, confident, like he's slinging his body around inside his clothes.

I dip my gaze, focusing on my too-white tennis shoes, and I don't look away until Jem's next to me. The tips of his boots almost touch my toes.

"I heard what you did," he says.

It's a small school. I'm not surprised he heard, but I'm not sure if he means the screaming at Becca? The standing up for Abbie? Something else? Whatever it is, he doesn't sound happy.

I concentrate on the wrinkled skin right between his eyebrows so I don't have to meet his gaze. I have no idea what to say.

"I'm glad," Jem continues. "I mean, you should've said

something. I don't know why you even let it go on so long. You didn't…"

"Didn't what?"

"You didn't used to be like this."

Is that what happened to us—I mean, to them? Grace got popular and mean, and Jem stayed unpopular and…well, he isn't mean, but he hasn't exactly been nice to me, either. "If I were like this from now on, would you like me more?"

The words escape on an exhale and I can't believe I even said them. I'm looking at this Grace's twin and all I can think about is my twin. The emotions bled over. Jem and I could say anything to each other. We were always honest. We never held back—that's why you have a brother, that's why you have family, so you never have to hold back.

Kind of like he is now. Jem watches me and says nothing and I'm suddenly so tired I want to collapse.

"I'm sorry, Jem. For everything. I'm really sorry. Can we try again?"

His mouth opens, closes, opens. "Let's just go, okay?"

He sounds irritated as ever, and briefly, I think my apology was far too little, far too late, but then he unlocks my door, tugging it open before walking around the truck's hail-scarred hood.

I hesitate, then climb in, fastening my seat belt as he reverses out of the parking space. He's not talking, and I'm grateful for the silence. It gives me time to study the school, to search for Ander.

And for Finn.

My fingers clench around my knees and I force myself to loosen them. It's a new situation. The timeline no longer works. Finn found us early. Ander isn't Ander.

And I need a plan.

Cold sweat blooms between my shoulders. A plan. Like *what*? Throw myself between Finn and Ander? I thought I understood helplessness before—all these Falls, all this loss, I thought I understood how waiting for the inevitable chews you from the inside out. But this? This is worse. So much worse.

Jem makes a hard left out of the parking lot, and I lean against the door, taking an unsteady breath. I have two days. I have to do something.

"Hey." Jem nudges me and points to our left. "Your boyfriend."

I sit up. Sure enough, Finn's walking through the school's front doors with half a dozen other students. He's easy to spot. Honestly, Finn's always easy to spot. He's always a little taller, a little darker, and a little apart from everyone else.

"Are y'all not talking?" Jem asks.

As if on cue, Finn's eyes meet mine. I wave, and he smiles like I am his everything. "Nah, we're good."

We are *so* good at this stupid farce.

Jem drives on, and I slump deep into the bench seat as the back of my skull prickles again. The memory of Finn's fingers in my hair? Or something else? Why can't I remember…

Wait.

Earlier, Finn felt familiar. He felt like he really did belong to this Grace. What if it could work in reverse? If I'm feeling some of this Grace's emotions, what if *this* Ander could feel some of *my* Ander's emotions?

What if I could make him remember?


Both parents are gone when we get home. Jem goes upstairs, leaving me to take Visa out. I don't really mind. It gives me time to think. Visa wanders around and around our backyard, and I wander around and around behind him until we're both tired of it.

Visa circles back to me and lolls at my feet, showing me his fuzzy black tummy.

"Can you smell the difference on me?" I scratch him, and he thumps his tail. I can't tell if it's an affirmative thump or a just-keep-scratching thump. "I missed you."

Stupid, since he's not my dog any more than Jem is my brother. They *feel* like mine, though, like everything I've wanted.

Visa's tail wags harder. In my original life, I loved him. I enjoyed him. He was my friend, and I didn't realize how much I loved him until I Fell. Until he was gone.

I think it was our third or fourth Fall when I realized loss had taught me more about what I had than having it ever did. I didn't know how lucky I was until Visa was gone.

The reminder makes my stomach swoop low, and I hug Visa hard. He slurps my ear and rolls to his feet. Petting time is over. Now he wants dinner.

"Some things never change," I say, following him back to the house. I dig dog food out of the bin by the pantry and fill Visa's bowl. While waiting for him to finish, I try to search Ander's name on my cell, but the internet won't connect. Sighing, I help myself to the family computer, scrolling through all the same newspaper articles from before, but after a couple more minutes of surfing, I find his parents' names, and that leads me to their address.

I hesitate, hand hovering above the mouse. Is this crazy? It feels a little crazy. Actually, it feels desperate, and that's somehow way worse. This isn't a fairy tale. I can't kiss Ander and make him wake up.

I could try to talk to him again. Maybe something would surface? Maybe some instinct would call him back? We can't have gone through *this much* to lose it like this…right?

Right. I open another browser window and check the aerials to see if anything seems familiar. As far as I can tell, Ander lives on the other side of Boone, in the last house at the end of a long dirt road. Their front yard is a wide expanse of lawn. Their side and rear yards are mostly trees and wetlands—kinda like the swamp is creeping up on the house.

I zoom out until I find the main road, zoom out a bit more and see the two-lane highway that leads into Boone. Got it. I know where I'm going.

Now I just need a ride.

I print a copy of the directions and shout for Jem, but there's no answer. "Hey!" I go to the bottom of the stairs, tucking the printer-warm pages into my back pocket. "Jem? Could I borrow your truck?"

The pipes clunk twice, and the water cuts on. Jem must be showering. I don't blame him. My own shirt's clinging to my skin after waiting for him in the parking lot. Might be a good idea to change before I try again with Ander.

I run up the stairs and into Grace's room, peeling off my damp shirt. I grab another polo from the top dresser drawer and stop.

Something feels off. No. *Different.*

I tug on the new polo and turn in a small circle. There's still too much furniture, still a rag rug on the floor, still a pink comforter on the bed.

Wait a minute…*pink* comforter?

My skin goes cold as I run my palm over the pale pink stripes. I could've sworn that I—I mean, this Grace—had a *blue* striped comforter. Maybe I have sunstroke? Or maybe I'm remembering another lifetime?

I trace my fingers along the fabric. I must have forgotten. It's not like it matters. Part of me worries maybe it does, though. Think of the condom wrappers. Those disappeared, and I *know* they were there. Am I losing it?

Wouldn't exactly be surprising. After all, how many times can one person relive a nightmare before cracking?

In the bathroom, the pipes clunk again as the shower shuts off. Jem's done. It's now or never.

I wait by my bedroom door and listen for his footsteps. After a few minutes, he bangs out of the bathroom, tugging on a clean T-shirt.

"Hey," I say, my hands going from my pockets to my sides to my pockets again. "Could I borrow the truck?"

Jem's pause is so long I'm convinced he's going to say no and then, finally, "Why?"

"I have to run an errand."

He studies me and then shrugs. "Yeah. Fine."

"Thanks." I dash down the stairs before he can change his mind and swipe the truck keys from the counter. I'm in the driver's seat when the first chills creep up my spine.

I twist side to side, searching the poison-green trees. Nothing. I'm alone, but even after I put the truck in drive and rumble toward the street, I can't shake the feeling that I'm being watched.

# chapter nineteen

*then...*

There was something about the heat that made everyone want to party. Jem loved it. He never said no. Any excuse to hook up with girls and stay away from the house.

To stay away from me?

If that's what he wanted, it didn't work. Everywhere Jem went, Ander went, and everywhere Ander went, he wanted me to come, too. I'd gone from being Jem's Twin to being Ander's Girlfriend.

"Wasn't she always?" Amanda Allen asked, and people laughed and laughed.

I smiled like I found it just as funny, like my skin wasn't crawling from their stares.

"Buck up, Graceful," Jem said, and I tripped him, which made Jem swear and Finn laugh and the whole thing feel... worse.

My name was such a joke. I wasn't graceful. I would never be a whiskey laugh or a clear glass giggle. I was a rock in your shoe, a crack in the sidewalk. I was *apologies*. Always sorry because I was always wrong, always off-footed.

Maybe I was graceful on leap days that didn't happen, in the moments before I woke.

It wasn't just waiting for Alton's response that was getting to me. It was *everything*. Underneath my skin, I was a landslide. No matter how hard I smiled, I could still feel the cracking.

"You don't have to come tonight," Ander told me. We were on the red couch, listening to my mom shuffle bills in the kitchen and watching the afternoon sunlight turn gold. Jem wanted to go to some pasture party, and Ander had agreed to go with him.

"But if you *do* come," he continued, smiling a smile that twisted heat up my throat, "we could spend time together with Jem and then hang out later...alone."

I swallowed and dipped my eyes, noticing he had on the same T-shirt as yesterday. I recognized the smudge of white paint on the hem. "Did you go home last night?"

"No."

He leaned back and I almost followed. If Ander didn't go home, where had he gone? He hadn't stayed with us, and I wanted to know why. He was always welcome. He always stayed. Why hadn't he this time?

I opened my mouth...and closed it. My mom sometimes said we had to give her the space she needed. Maybe this was the same thing?

"Don't you want to be with me?" he asked, and it was so soft it almost didn't feel like an accusation.

Almost.

"You know parties aren't my thing."

"Maybe they could be *our* thing? I won't leave you alone."

I took a shaky breath. "Will there be a lot of people?"

He grimaced. "Yeah."

We studied each other. I didn't know what to say—actually, that was wrong. I did know. I was supposed to say, "I'd love to go." I was supposed to *want* to go.

*How are you going to go away to Alton when you can't even manage a party with your boyfriend?*

I gritted my teeth. Because I wasn't planning to.

Ander stroked the backs of my fingers. "Are you going to hide forever?"

*Could I?* The idea tasted like hope and want and everything I was not supposed to have.

He tilted his head, sun-streaked hair falling in his eyes. "You remember when Mr. Davis made us read *Doctor Faustus*?"

I straightened. "Yeah. I wrote my paper and most of Jem's on it for the final."

"Remember that part when the fallen angel said something like 'this is hell nor am I out of it'?"

I nodded.

"I think he's right. We're all living in hell," Ander continued, and he was so close the words curled against my cheek. "It's a matter of how you deal with it." He paused. "Sometimes, I have to block it out. Most of the time, you hide. How are you going to make it at Alton if you can't make it through a party here?"

My laugh sputtered. This was what ten years of friendship looked like: he knew all my flaws, my worries, my *thoughts*. I wished it also meant it didn't hurt as much. Ander made me feel like my ugly underbelly was being exposed to sunlight.

"Is this how you want to live?" he whispered.

I hesitated and finally shook my head.

"You want to be with me?"

No hesitation. "Yes."

"Then be with me."

• • •

*I*t was after nine when we finally turned off the main highway, taking the narrow lane toward the cemetery. We'd had to pick up Finn at Farley's and then go almost to the interstate to find a gas station that would take Ander's fake ID.

In the end, I didn't think the cashier actually believed Ander was twenty-one, he just didn't care. It irritated Ander. He sat in silence, staring out the open window at the summer-scorched fields beyond us.

I rode in the middle, as usual. Jem drove, as usual. Finn rode in the back, which was increasingly usual.

I shifted and shifted and still couldn't get comfortable. My nerves made the truck feel too small. Then again, maybe it was the storms rolling in. There was lightning on the horizon and pressure in my ears.

Jem turned off at the next right, eventually winding us closer to the river. He parked between an ancient Jeep and an equally ancient Ford truck. I hopped out behind Ander. Somewhere in the dark, people laughed—a lot of people—and my stomach turned sour.

"It's like the beginning of a horror movie," Finn said, pivoting in a small circle. Lightning bugs drifted past our heads, drawing closer and closer to the cemetery that lay beyond the fence line. "Who has pasture parties next to dead people?"

"We do." Ander's smile was a flash of white. "Hurry up."

He was already striding toward the bonfire and the others. I had to run to catch up. Jem and Ander hauled the cases of beer toward the coolers, leaving me to slide into the group.

Or not, because I hovered just outside the firelight like the world's most socially inept moron. The static in my ears turned into a roar.

Fingertips grazed the back of my arm. Ander.

No.

Finn.

The firelight turned his eyes to bullet holes. "You okay?"

*Not at all.* I buttoned on a smile. "Totally."

He studied me, and I smiled harder, wider.

Finn tilted close enough so his words were only for me. "You're never this shy around Jem and Ander."

"I don't have to worry with them."

Finn pulled back. "You're not shy around me."

"I guess you get lumped in—lucky you."

"Yeah. Lucky me. C'mon." He urged me toward the semicircle of guys in baseball hats and girls in cowboy boots, white plastic lawn chairs and dented coolers turned into benches. I hesitated and then followed him. It was kind of the perfect cover. The girls went motionless when Finn was around; no one else noticed me edge in next to him.

Well, no one noticed until Hannah Benson turned and saw me.

"Hey." Hannah had gorgeous blond-from-a-bottle hair and over-plucked eyebrows. It made her look surprised by everything, or maybe it was just that she was surprised by me. "I didn't expect you to come," she added.

*That makes two of us.* Finn watched me from the corner of his eye, and I pretended not to notice. I wouldn't screw this up. I wouldn't. I was trying to be better.

"Hi." I swallowed, everything I should say and couldn't say and couldn't think to say jamming up in my head. "What's up?"

"We're playing Best Day Worst Day."

"What?"

"You tell us your best day and then your worst day and then you take a drink."

"Oh." I took the closest spot on the grass, drawing my knees close when I realized I was crowding Hannah. She moved a little sideways, tugging her boots through the dirt like she couldn't be bothered—which she probably couldn't. These were Jem's friends, Ander's friends, not mine.

"You first." Hannah passed me the bottle, and I almost dropped it. I wasn't expecting the weight, and my hands were sweaty.

*They want me to* share *stuff with them?* To my left, someone shifted. Finn. Callie's sister, Tisha, was sitting next to him, and when he opened his mouth like he wanted to say something, she tilted closer.

"C'mon," Ander breathed. He dropped down next to my feet and leaned his shoulder against my legs. "Just play along."

But that was the point: I didn't want to.

Hannah looked at me like I was stupid, and maybe I was. I'd let Ander and Jem talk me into coming. I could barely hear anything past the humming in my head.

"My best day?" I shoved the words so hard, I sounded pissed, and that made me sweat even more. "Best day was when we checked out Vanderbilt." It had been so pretty and felt comfortable, like I was *supposed* to be there.

Next to me, Ander stiffened and someone snorted and my neck went even hotter. I studied the toes of my tennis shoes until Ander nudged me—nudged me again—and I forced myself to look up.

"That's too easy," Mark said, mashing the brim of his camouflage baseball hat so it curved even tighter over his eyes. "Come up with something better or you'll have to do two shots."

I shook my head. "My best day was walking around Vanderbilt. It's where I want to go to school."

There. I sounded better—still a bit pissy, but at least I wasn't backing down.

"Why?" Finn's voice was so soft and yet everyone heard

him. I could tell in the way they stiffened. "Just tell them why, and they'll understand."

They wouldn't, though, and Finn of all people should've caught how Jem was staring at me like he was searching for my lie and how Ander wouldn't look at me at all. He'd gone rigid. No one here wanted to leave Boone. It was enough for them, and it wasn't enough for me.

Finn knew that.

"God, you're such a Susie Sunshine." Hannah's mouth screwed into a knot. "Fine. Whatever. I don't want to hear your worst day. It's probably when you watched a kitten fall out of a tree."

"Two shots," Mark said, slapping a mosquito on his arm. I couldn't see his face, but I could hear how he rolled his eyes.

I unscrewed the cap and lifted the bottle. I probably should've pretended to drink, just let the alcohol hit my lips, but I caved under their focus, and the bourbon blazed a trail down my throat. I coughed and coughed and coughed some more. Someone—Hannah?—muttered something I missed, and I was glad I did.

Ander slid his palm up my spine and drew circles between my shoulder blades. Somehow it made everything slow. I passed him the bottle, and the firelight flashed the amber alcohol into slit-wrist red.

"Best day?" Ander took a swallow, which I supposed was cheating. No one said anything, though. He twirled the bottle neck in his fingers. "Best day was yesterday…when I told my old man to piss off because we didn't need him, and we all knew it was true."

Ander's eyes met mine, pinned me to the spot. He hadn't said anything.

We always told each other everything.

Mark made a grunting noise of approval and tipped his

baseball hat. There was a knowing in his expression I didn't share, would never share, because there are some things words can only describe and those words will always fall short. Ander's home life was a horror. Mine wasn't. I could sympathize, but I could never *know*.

"And your worst day?" Mark asked.

"Yesterday," Ander said. "When I told my old man to piss off because we didn't need him, and we all knew it was true."

Ander took a shot and then another, the skin along his neck sliding as he swallowed. He passed the bottle to Tisha. She grabbed it with both hands and wouldn't look him in the eyes.

No one would look him in the eyes.

Except for Finn. He studied Ander like he was seeing something I couldn't.

# chapter twenty

Freaking internet directions. The turnoff is two miles past where it's supposed to be and after almost twenty minutes of driving back and forth, I finally spot the dirt road cutoff. I slow down and check my crumpled directions again. The road looked different on the aerial, more…used. This turnoff is crowded with bright green kudzu and bushes on both sides. Weeds prick through the hard-packed dirt like no one's driven down there in forever.

It can't be the right turn. I glance at my directions again, knowing full well I don't have a better idea. Maybe it'll look better farther down?

I turn the truck off the main road, maneuvering it past the overgrown bushes, and there's a long, *long* fingernail-scrape against my door.

Crap. Jem's going to be furious.

It's no better farther in. The turnoff dead-ends into a clearing, and I pull to a stop under a drooping water oak. Somehow it's even hotter under the trees. The air's close, and it's only scraggly pine trees and thick underbrush as far as I can see.

Double crap.

Then again…I put the truck in park and hop out. My actual directions might be off, but the aerial still looks right. I worry my lower lip.

What are the chances of the online directions being this wrong? Pretty good…right? I mean, it can't matter that I'm in some weird parallel universe, because crappy internet directions are universal.

Surely I'm not having some weird…glitch again.

Surely.

I put my back to the road and face the tree line ahead. I need to go east. Ander's house should be just past this stretch of woods. If I hike straight, I should get there.

I think. I'm almost positive.

*Well, I'm going to find out.*

I stuff the useless directions back in my pocket and hike deeper into the woods, slapping at mosquitoes and gnats as I go. The trees are thick, but the brush is thicker, and everything smells like roses. I dash one hand across my nose. It's almost nauseating and makes my lungs feel filled with sand.

I shove through a tangle of blackberries, and branches snap to my right. I stop dead, listen. My eyes jump from tree to tree, searching and searching…and nothing. I'm alone.

I glance toward the truck again and realize I'm too far away. All I can see is woods, more woods, and shadows. They're gathering in pools.

I use the bottom of my shirt to wipe my face and swat at another mosquito. It's still another couple of hours to sunset, but the trees are so crowded, they're blocking the early-evening sun. I need to hurry.

And then I realize how quiet it's gotten.

No more snapping branches. No birds. Nothing. It's like

the whole world is holding its breath.

"Get going," I mutter and shove on, ignoring how I'm wheezing hard now.

Several hot and sticky moments later, something long and red slips past the trees ahead of me. It's a car.

I hustle forward, branches snatching at my hair. The ground slopes down, curves up, and as I struggle to the top, I see Ander's house just beyond a wall of kudzu.

In Fall 10, Ander's house was a trailer. In Fall 17, he lived in a three-story mansion with stairways that led to nowhere. This time, it's an old cottage, all faded yellows and curling trim. The tin roof is dented, rusty smears bleeding down the sloped sides. It kind of looks like somewhere Red Riding Hood's grandmother would live.

The car parks somewhere on the other side of the house. Doors open and slam. I hover next to an old oak, careful to avoid the fire ants marching along its trunk, and struggle to breathe. Hiking in humidity plus anxiety equals the feeling of a three-hundred-pound man sitting on my chest. I swallow and swallow again.

Somewhere deeper in the woods, a fox cries, and I tense. A woman's laugh rings across the yard, and I glimpse two figures before they disappear around the side of the house. I lean forward. Are those his parents? Siblings?

There's a moment of silence, and then taillights appear. A dark sedan backs out of the garage, bumps down the driveway, and disappears around the bend. Great. Will anyone even be home?

I tug my damp shirt away from my skin—so much for not smelling like a goat—and spot movement at the window. A pale curtain twitches. Someone *is* home.

A shadow passes another window, moving toward the back of the house. My feet stutter-step forward and I stop.

There is *zero* way to explain coming out of Ander's woods without looking like a total stalker.

Hell, I *am* a total stalker. I'm creeping around his house. If I get caught, there's no explanation in the world that'll sound believable. He could call the cops, my parents.

*He could die anyway.*

I bite my lip, considering my options. All around me, the woods are dipping into dark, shadows gathering around my feet. What if I just edged around the side? I could walk up to the front porch like a normal person and see if he's home.

I make it two steps and feel something brush my palm, squeezing my fingers like it's trying to take my hand.

I whip around, heartbeat in my teeth. Nothing. I'm alone.

That's when I hear the rustling.

I freeze and carefully—*carefully*—turn my head toward the sound. It's coming closer, moving in an uneven line that almost makes me think it's an animal.

Almost.

A figure slides into view. Finn.

He's maybe twenty feet away, and a whimper wedges in my throat. I drop to my knees, fingers stabbing into pine needles and dirt. Finn wavers next to a fallen tree, looking up at the house, looking around at the woods. It feels like ages before he turns and moves farther down the tree line, always keeping Ander's yard well within sight.

I push slowly to my feet and draw closer to the thicket of young pine trees on my right. I'm soundless, but Finn turns like he heard me, and I freeze.

Can he see me? I can't tell. He doesn't move and I don't move and we wait and we wait and I'm too far away to smell Finn's breath and yet somehow I do. It's tied to the scent of pine and dirt and water, just as I remember him whispering, "We all have to pay for what we did."

A door slams. I flinch, turning just in time to see Ander step onto the porch. Finn tenses as Ander leans against the railing and studies the darkening backyard.

*Stay on the porch.* I step forward. I can't help it. *Stay on the porch.*

But Ander doesn't. He drifts down the steps, his boots thunking hard against the painted wood. There's another sharp animal cry from deep in the woods, and Ander pauses, listening. Finn's listening, too. He's a shadow within the shadows, except he isn't listening for the fox. He's studying Ander.

My heart's thumping everywhere now, and my stupid lungs have never felt so small. It's only day three, but if Finn's here now and the timeline has already sped up…does that mean the Fall is tonight?

Ander shoves both his fists into his pockets and scuffs off toward the potting shed at the edge of the garden. Finn trails behind him.

And I follow like he yanked me.

# chapter twenty-one

## then...

They did three more rounds of Best Day Worst Day before Jem disappeared into the dark with Hannah, and another two rounds before Ander tugged me to my feet.

"It's a pasture party," he said, swaying a little. "Let's go look at the pasture."

Gladly. I had to jog to keep up, though. Ander had always been taller than me. Tonight, though, he seemed bigger in every way. The bonfire threw his shadow ahead of us. It stretched and stretched and I stumbled after him.

"Ander?" He didn't answer, but his hand tightened around mine. Grass whipped my bare legs, and I could feel welts rising. I was going to be itchy for days.

We walked the edge of the firelight, away from the others and away from the trucks. He kept going, pressing farther and farther into the tall grass, until I started to worry about snakes.

"Ander!"

He stopped, braced himself against the cemetery's falling-down fence, and turned his face to the sky. For a moment, I did, too. The air was still hot and overfull from the earlier afternoon rain. Everything smelled like wet grass and wetter dirt, and somewhere far off, thunder rolled.

"I'm sorry about your dad." I leaned one hip against the split-board fence, gripping the railing with both hands so I didn't reach for him. "Why didn't you tell us?"

He sighed, rubbing his forehead like it hurt. There was ink on his knuckles, the color so dark it looked like dried blood. "I don't know. I don't want to talk about it and it's kind of *all* I want to talk about."

"I get that."

The moon pushed through some clouds and turned his smile silvery, dipped his eyes into smudges. "I know you do. I'm scared shitless—that's why I need you."

*Need you.* I shivered and he stepped closer.

"Are you cold?"

"A little." Not at all. In the dark, Ander was a crooked slash. He leaned toward me, his breath boozy, and for a crazy second, I was convinced fear had a smell and this was it.

"Are you going to be okay?" I ask.

He shook his head. "Are you really going to go to Alton?"

I paused. That wasn't anywhere close to an answer. "I don't know. It's a super tough school to get into and I would need a major scholarship and—"

"And you want to go. Just say it."

I bit my lip. I'd known Ander for eleven years. I knew his moods, what would make him laugh, who he was when he showed up at our house with movies. I didn't know this tone, though. I'd never heard it before.

"Is it really that awful here?" he asked. It was softer this time, like he caught himself.

*Yes.* "No. It's just…everyone here knows me. I'm Jem's sister and my father's daughter and the Quiet Girl Who Sits in the Second Row. It's not awful. Sometimes, though…it's suffocating. It's not me."

"Why not?"

Because I wanted something more, and saying it would only make Ander feel worse.

He tugged the heads off the long grass, flicked them away. "I'm never getting out of here."

"You can do anything you want to."

His laugh was a bark. "You can *aspire* to anything you want to. Doing it? That's different."

I watched him, trying to decide what to say and realizing there was nothing. He was spinning apart, and I didn't know what to do. "Ander…"

"I'm dropping out of school, Grace."

I blinked. "What about art school? What about—"

"What about it?" He turned away from me, and briefly, I thought he was going back to the others—then I realized Ander couldn't keep his feet.

"I'll get my GED," he added, drifting sideways. "But I need a full-time job."

I tried to pull him back to me, to haul him upright. "Ander!"

He went to his knees and took me with him. We hit the ground in a tangled pile. I was barely up again before he vomited. It was all liquid.

Behind us, someone laughed.

"Well, you two were busy," Jem said, slouching toward us. He put one hand on the fence for balance and peered down at Ander. "Wow. You know you're having a good time when…"

"It's not funny!" I wrapped both hands around Ander's upper arm and tried to heave him upward. He slumped lower, settling on his back. "He's sick!"

"He's *drunk*. There's a difference."

"Jem…"

My twin made a disgusted noise. "Don't 'Jem' me. He's

fine. He just needs to sleep it off. Toss him in the back of the truck and come back to the party."

"Jem!"

"God, Grace, would you just calm—"

"If he vomits again like that, he'll choke." Finn strode out of the dark. In the moonlight, his face was made of shadows and hollows. Everything golden about him was gone. "I'll help you get him to the truck," he said quietly.

I swallowed, suddenly self-conscious. I wanted to tell him not worry about it, but Finn already had his shoulder under Ander's arm. He hoisted Ander to his feet, and briefly, they both staggered.

Jem sighed. "Just let him sleep it off, Finn. He'll be fine." Then his hand closed around my arm, and the next words were only for me: "He's okay, Grace. Don't make this into a thing, yeah? You'll just embarrass the hell out of him, and he's got enough going on."

"He's my best friend," I whispered, having to force the words past the tightness in my throat. "He's *your* best friend."

"And that's why I know he'll be fine. You'll make it worse if you make it a big deal."

I shook Jem off. It was already worse. Why didn't he see that? Out in the field, someone shrieked and laughed. A bottle broke. Jem leaned toward the sounds like they were beckoning him with long fingers.

I punched him in the arm. "I want to go home."

"Grace—"

"I want to go home. Please."

Jem swore under his breath. "I'll get my keys."

I followed Finn and Ander toward the cars. Farther in the woods, the crickets were at a fever pitch, and the whole world felt overstuffed. A storm was definitely coming. In the distance, lightning lit up the tree line, turning the tops into rows of broken teeth.

"Can you get the gate?" Finn asked, tilting Ander to one side so I could drop the truck gate. I brushed dead leaves out of the way, and Finn lowered Ander onto the rusted bed. "Turn him to his side."

I pushed and Finn pulled. Ander flopped over and moaned, his hand closing around mine.

"Does he do this a lot?" Finn asked.

"*No.*"

"I didn't mean it like that. I mean…" Finn sighed. "If this is a normal thing for him, there's a problem."

I almost smiled. How delicately put: not that Ander *had* a problem, but that there *was* a problem. Finn *had* been in a lot of therapy.

Or maybe he just had a lot of experience with this stuff. He maneuvered Ander with everyday ease. There would be a reason for that, or rather, there was a person behind that.

"Sorry," I managed at last. "I shouldn't snap at you." I wanted to look at Finn, and I couldn't. I wanted to say thank you and I wanted to die of embarrassment and I wanted…I wanted for this to have never happened. "How do you know what to do?"

Finn stiffened, and I realized I shouldn't have asked. His ease with Ander gave away a secret he never meant to give.

And now we both knew it.

"It's not my first time dealing with this stuff," Finn gritted and somewhere to our right, Jem was whistling, heading toward us.

I sagged with relief. We were going.

Finn hopped into the truck bed. "I'll ride back here. You stay up front with Jem."

"You don't have to do that. If he pukes again—"

"It's okay, Grace." Finn slid farther up the truck bed and

braced his back against the cab. Above us, a cloud slid over the moon, plunging us into shadows. He was just a voice in the dark now. "Really. It's okay."

And the way Finn spoke, it made the whole thing seem like it might be.

"Thank you for the help." I couldn't see his face, but I was sure I could feel his eyes on me. Heat trailed across my mouth and down my throat.

"I'm not doing it for him."

*now...*

*W*here's Finn now? Ander has disappeared into the potting shed and I'm still inside the tree line, chewing my lip until I taste blood. Lightning bugs are beginning to rise through the brush. I can't stand here all night, but I can't see where Finn went. It's like he just disappeared into the dark.

My pulse begins to thump in my hands and temples. I can't stay.

I can't leave.

So I guess I'm…walking up there? Sticking to the plan? My stomach threatens to heave into my mouth. Some plan. I wrench myself forward anyway, keep one eye on the trees as I push through the last brambles and into Ander's yard.

I pause, listening to nothing. Finn's not crashing through the trees behind me. There's no begging, no yelling, but somehow the silence is worse. Is he just standing in there, *watching* me?

I shudder. *Get going.*

I hurry across the wedge of lawn, heading for the shed.

I'm almost there when Ander passes the window again, and my hands go cold.

"Hey, Ander, sorry to barge in like this," I whisper. "Hey, Ander, I was wondering if we could talk? Hey, Ander I was wondering if you could stay put because I think there's a psychopath in your woods—yes, a psychopath that *isn't* me."

Ugh. The explanations sound just as stupid out loud as they do in my head. I edge along the shed wall until I reach the small windows by the door. I peek around the frame, peek again.

For two whole seconds, the world around me falls away.

It isn't a potting shed. It's an art studio. Canvases lean against the clapboard walls, and paint jars crowd metal shelves.

My Ander would have loved this.

I smile. This Ander's staring at one canvas, arms crossed. Whatever he's looking at irritates him. I can tell from the tension in his shoulders, the spread of his feet. What's so bad about the painting? I lean closer, gaze skittering past the other canvases. They're beautiful and so very Ander. The lines are slashes. The colors are muted. Some of the paintings are only half finished and some are dashed with white paint, half erased, but they're all beautiful.

He picks up the can of white paint by his boots. His shoulders and arms flex once, twice. He's stirring the paint up. Is he going to paint over the picture? Why?

Then he shifts and I can see. It's my drawing. My tattoo. He's going to erase it.

*He's erasing* me.

It's a stupid thought, and yet inside my head it's a shriek. Behind me, a twig cracks. Was that Finn?

I shrink down, pressing both knees into the grass. Inside the shed, there's a hard, metallic *thump*. A paint can being put down?

My hands roll into fists. *Is Ander coming out? Did he hear the snap?*

Another *thump* and I scuttle backward. If he comes through that door, he'll trip right over me.

I ease to my right, pulling deeper into the gathering dark as a shadow separates from the woods. It takes two steps toward me and stops.

*Finn.*

"Grace." He makes my name sound like a summons. "I see you."

"Ander's innocent," I whisper. "You cannot do this. He doesn't *know*."

There's another *thump* from inside and the shed door swings open; yellow light yawns across the grass.

Ander.

I rear back, holding my breath. If he walks toward the woods, he'll run right into me, and there is no explanation in the world that will ever sound legitimate. Ander won't understand. He'll call the cops. We'll never talk again.

He'll be vulnerable.

He takes another step, and my heart lurches. He's *already* vulnerable. I'm maybe ten feet away, hidden in the gloom, and Finn is maybe ten feet more.

Wait. Why isn't Finn already moving?

We stand and wait, and Ander stands and listens. He squints into the dark, the shed's overhead light creating a glare he can't see past. But I can.

Finn is an outline of shadows, and when Ander shuts the studio door, the rising moon catches Finn's face and coats his skin in silver.

"Please," I whisper. "Please stop this."

"I can't."

"You *can*." There's another scrape, and we both freeze.

Everything is silent, and then there's the crackle of a stereo speaker. Ander turns up the volume as a woman sings about lost love, and somewhere in the woods, the fox cries again. It sounds like someone sobbing.

"I can't walk away, Grace." Finn's voice lifts a tiny bit higher, like he's daring me.

He shouldn't. It actually gives me a little courage. I push away from the wall, fists at my side. "Whatever happened between us is between *us*. This Ander has no idea. He's innocent. You would be attacking an *innocent* person."

Finn's shoulders go tight. "Are you saying you aren't? You really think you're guilty?"

"I am so done with you and your stupid, cryptic—" I shake my head as a stagnant breeze threads through my hair, lifting it from my face with invisible fingers. "Leave now or I'll scream the place down."

Finn tenses. "You know how that will look. He'll never trust you again."

I nod, the weight of the idea shoving me a step toward him. "And if I do it right, we'll both spend the next two days in jail. You won't be able to touch him. Maybe *that* will stop the Falls."

Finn considers me. "Is that what you call them?"

I don't answer.

"Fitting," he says. "It really is like falling, isn't it?"

The song finishes, begins again, and Ander turns it up even higher. I have to clench both hands to keep from covering my ears.

I concentrate on Finn. "What could I have possibly ever done to make you hunt us?"

Finn pauses, and for a second, I think I'm supposed to say something, then I realize he isn't waiting for clarification. He isn't *here*. His eyes have gone vacant, glassy. Finn's somewhere else, seeing something that isn't there.

He frowns. "You're not the only person who lost someone."

The words tug something deep and nameless in me. I should know this. We were friends once. I *knew* this.

And it's like something flickers to life inside my head. A girl. In our original life, Finn had a girlfriend. Someone he loved. I remember that pasture party—the one where we played drinking games—and Finn walked out of the dark to help me with Ander.

There were so many girls at the party that night. I can't resurrect a specific face, but it feels…right? Maybe not right. It definitely feels closer, though.

"I'm caught in this loop, same as you," Finn continues, wonder and horror threading through his words. "I lost my life as I knew it, too."

Another hard tug and this time, it's not entirely nameless. Pity is beginning to chew my edges. At least I had Ander at my side. Finn was alone.

Ander passes the studio window, and the yellow light flashes like a broken headlight. I wait until his shadow goes still before asking, "Did I know her? The girl you lost?"

Finn flinches and looks back to the trees. His jaw clenches once, twice. When he finally faces me, his eyes have a liquid sheen. "I didn't lose some girl. I lost *you*."

# chapter twenty-three

## then...

*I*n the distance, lightning turned the cloud bottoms white. Jem drove five miles under the speed limit with both hands on the wheel. When we made the right onto our street and he actually used his turn signal, I knew he was buzzed.

"I can't believe you drank when you knew you were driving." I rolled down my window and could hear the swamp frogs, then Jem sped up and all I could hear was wind.

"Two drinks is not drinking, Miss Very Special Episode." The truck's turn signal wouldn't shut off, and Jem swatted it. "If I were drunk, how could I drive this well?"

I glared at him. "You're driving *well* because you're scared you're going to get pulled over."

"Why would I get pulled over? I'm not doing anything." Another flash of lightning illuminated Jem's face. He was pale. Angry.

Well, that made two of us. "You're an ass."

"And you're leaving."

"That's not an insult."

"You said you weren't. You *promised*."

The open windows hurled humid air through the cab. Jem downshifted to first. The truck lurched hard, and behind me, Ander swore.

At least he was awake. I leaned closer to the cracked window, trying to get as far away from Jem as possible. It was only a few inches, but it still managed to be stupid and satisfying.

Jem parked next to our mom's Corolla and flung open his door. I followed him, being careful to stay quiet. The house was dark except for the sole porch light. Both our parents were asleep because they trusted us and were exhausted and believed they had good kids.

And we were…sort of.

Jem had made me feel like I'd overreacted, like I was turning the whole thing into something it wasn't, and now I was wondering if maybe he was right.

Finn stood, heaving Ander up with him. They eased to the back of the truck and, somehow, managed to get to the ground without either of them face-planting. Jem hooked Ander's arm around his shoulders and shrugged away from Finn, staggering toward the house.

Funny step. Funny step. Ander found his stride. They disappeared into the dark, and one of them laughed.

"You okay?"

Finn. I turned and swallowed. He was close enough to touch.

"Yeah." I forked one hand through my wind-tangled hair. It did zero good. I was hot, sticky, and suddenly so tired I thought if I sat down I wouldn't ever get up again. "Yeah, I'm fine. It was a bad night."

"Are you always so hostile when people ask you to play drinking games?"

I stiffened and Finn grinned, and maybe it was the exhaustion, but it did seem a bit funny. "I'm not hostile," I said, smiling. "I'm just very, very awkward. Why did you ask me to explain?"

"I thought…I thought it would make it easier if you talked more."

"That's never easy for me."

"Easy when I'm around." Finn rubbed his thumb across his lips, and I caught myself staring. *Finn* caught me staring. "Interesting," he said.

My face went hot. "Not really."

"Why do you want to go to Vanderbilt?"

I picked at my fingernails. Jem had asked the same question and yet Finn's tone was so different, like he *wanted* to hear all the reasons. Jem hadn't.

"Maybe not Vanderbilt, but somewhere." The breeze grew stronger, lifting my hair until it writhed like Medusa's snakes. "If I get into Alton, I'm that much closer."

"Why's Jem mad about it?"

I shrugged. "We're twins."

He smiled again. He looked like he was biting down a laugh. "You shrug the same way as him."

"My point exactly."

"I think it's great that you're getting out."

Why did everyone say it like that? Getting out. Getting away. Maybe that was why Ander and Jem hated it. It made them sound like something I was running from, and they weren't. I was running from me. I didn't want to be here.

But I didn't know *where* I wanted to be, either.

"You make it sound like I'm running away."

"Nah. You're just running toward what you want."

I paused. Finn might've said "getting out" like everyone else, but he was the first to see me as running toward something

I wanted. Ander didn't. Jem didn't.

And Finn watched me like he knew.

"What do *you* want?" The question was sudden and unbidden, and I kind of couldn't believe I'd asked.

My entire body turned hot when he grinned like he couldn't believe it, either. "I want college. Maybe grad school. I want a BMW that moves so fast and smooth, it's like gliding. I want the big house and the fancy job."

"You want stuff?"

"I want a life."

"And yet you just cataloged *stuff*."

We studied each other and studied each other and the silence stretched and stretched and I didn't think I was going to get a response. Then quite suddenly Finn said, "I don't want anyone to know I'm from Boone."

"Is it really that awful?" A few leaves fell, drifting to the ground like dead angels' feathers.

"You'll understand once you get to Alton. Wait until you see how they look at you."

I swallowed. I'd be lying if I said I didn't already know exactly how they'd look at me. I saw it every year when they come to town. In a uniform, I'd blend better, but my accent would give me away. "I'm not ashamed of where I come from… and you shouldn't be, either."

He shook his head as thunder rumbled. "How long have you two been together or whatever?"

"Kind of forever and kind of since the beginning of summer. We've been friends since we were little." The explanation was so easy—another benefit to dating your best friend. There was no meet-cute unless you counted a six-year-old me following a six-year-old Ander into the dark.

Finn nodded. "Destiny. You were meant to be together." There was something amused living under his tone. It was just like earlier, when he'd teased me about being hostile, but this time I couldn't find it in me to laugh. "That's what everyone says."

"I know." He stretched both arms behind him, and his shoulders popped. He was leaner than Ander, harder somehow. "It's one of the first things you learn around here: the best parties are by the river, you can only get beer at the gas station out of town, and Ander Hale and Grace Freeman are the resident Romeo and Juliet—minus the warring families."

"And the suicide."

"And the four other deaths."

I laughed. "I thought I was the only one who was unimpressed that six people died over a three-day old relationship."

"It's the romantic in me."

I laughed again, and somehow, Finn's grin slipped wider.

"We aren't Romeo and Juliet," I said. "We didn't even start dating or whatever until recently."

"You've been friends forever."

"Yeah."

"Never apart, right?"

I hesitated. "Right."

His smile turned mocking. "You know no one actually calls you two Romeo and Juliet, right? Shakespeare's a little lost on folks around here."

"You're being an ass again." I crossed and recrossed my arms and realized Finn was studying every twitch.

Funny how we'd been hanging out together for almost a month now and I hadn't realized how much Finn wouldn't look at me—really look at me. Until now, his faded gold eyes always drifted, like they were searching for the edge of the world.

But now he wasn't looking away from me.

And I wasn't looking away from him.

*I'm not doing it for him*, he'd said after heaving Ander into the truck. I tried to swallow, my mouth suddenly dry. Which meant he did it for…me.

Did Finn want me to ask why? Possibly.

Definitely.

The smell of rain swept around us, and deep in the swamp, the crickets got louder.

He cleared his throat. "Storm's coming. I should get going."

"Okay."

Did his shoulders sag just a bit? Impossible—no, not impossible. Improbable. I'm not the kind of girl who inspires disappointment.

"I'll see you around," he said, and my stomach did a tiny swoop. Four little words. I used them all the time.

But when Finn said them, they felt like a promise I was never supposed to make.

*now...*

"The girl I lost was *you*," Finn repeats, and it hurtles my stomach into my feet.

"You didn't lose me." Inside the shed, the music keens higher. "We were never together."

"Is that what you remember?"

Not just what I remember. That's what *happened*. He's making zero sense, and yet suddenly I see an angle. I know how to save Ander.

I pull myself straight. "Ander for me," I say.

"*What?*"

The singer's voice wings higher. "You heard me. Him for me. You leave him alone. I'll go with you."

Even from here, even with the music climbing, I somehow hear Finn's gasp. Even more impossible, I can *feel* it, hot breath coasting against my skin.

But he still doesn't answer me.

"Leave Ander alone," I say slowly. "And we'll go talk."

"Where?"

"My truck. It's parked in a clearing beyond the woods,

near the road."

He steps to one side. "After you, then."

"No way." No *way* am I keeping him at my back. I point toward the trees, clenching my arm tight to hide my shaking. "You first."

A pause and then another nod. Finn spins toward the trees, silent on the grass. I suck in an unsteady breath and follow.

In the woods, Finn stays well ahead of me. He tries to move carefully through the underbrush and keeps getting caught in the brambles. I can hear him swearing.

Once, we would've both been swearing—and laughing.

*The girl I lost was you.*

Impossible. I was never his to lose. We were never together.

I grit my teeth. Briars keep catching my face, my clothes. It's ten times harder to do this in the dark. Or is it just ten times longer?

I don't remember leaving the truck this far away. I'm going to break an ankle for sure. The moon is a yellow smile in the distance, dribbling pale light through the leaves.

I wouldn't say it makes it easier, but it helps.

A little.

Odd how the lightning bugs are swarming. I've never seen so many. It would be almost pretty if the mosquitoes weren't so bad. I slap my neck, my arms, and Finn pauses, turns back to look at me. With the moon behind him, it turns him into shadows again.

"Don't make me change my mind," I say.

Finn hesitates and then pushes on. I follow, wrenching through the last of the underbrush. I must be tired. I really don't remember it being this thick before. I can see the truck now, though. The hood is almost black in the moonlight.

One last shove and I'm into the clearing. Finn retreats to the far side, and I pause. Now that we're here, my skin is vibrating.

I don't trust him.

"Need to grab something," I announce, heading for the truck. I open the driver door and lean into the cab, sweeping one hand under the bench seat. My fingertips connect with metal.

Chills coast up my skin, Jem's tire iron turning candy-sticky in my sweaty palm. I feel better, more in control. I turn back to Finn, keeping the length close to my leg, hoping he won't notice.

And the thing is…he might not, because he's staying about fifteen feet away from me right now. I don't get it. Our first time alone and he's deliberately keeping distance between us. His movements are so slow his sneakers slog in the dirt. It's almost reassuring.

Almost.

"You're going to hit me with a tire iron?"

"If you come after me." I pause, turning the words around and around. They still feel like they're made only of corners and edges. "I want this to stop. I want a truce."

He laughs. "How's that supposed to work?"

"Let us live. We'll make a new life in this Fall. We'll make this work."

"You can promise all that?"

"I can promise I'll try my best."

"That's not going to work." He sighs, rubbing the back of his head like it hurts. I get it. After my little jaunt through the woods, my whole body feels bruised. The skin around my tattoo is especially tender. I touch my fingertips to it, wince. It *burns*. Did I scrape something coming through the briars?

"How much do you remember?" he asks softly.

A cloud passes over the moon and for a second, I see a glimpse of the Finn that other girls see: still beautiful, still arrogant, now ruined. This Finn is a broken window in February, a single scream in the dark.

And yet I can still see the boy who stood in the boat for me, waiting in the dark. Every time the lightning bugs flare next to his face, I see the Finn who stood in Farley's barn with the dust turning to gold around him.

A mosquito stings the thin skin of my wrist, and I wince. How is that even possible? How could I see the original Finn inside this one? How can there be anything left of him?

"I don't remember a lot of things," I say. The rose smell is back, and it's *worse*. Every time I inhale, I feel like I'm in a funeral home. I'm suffocating. "I'm having…issues. I can't keep doing this. I'm tired. I need this to stop. I need *you* to stop."

"You think I don't want to?"

Another cloud trails past the moon, and everything vanishes, reappears.

And now Finn is closer. I hold my ground, watching him. "This Ander is innocent."

"He's never been innocent."

I try to swallow. Can't. "You're destroying yourself, too. You can't keep doing this and keep your humanity. You're becoming a monster."

He takes a single step forward and I take a single step back and we both stop. "This isn't *you*," I whisper. "I know you…or I did."

His pause stretches into forever. "I know you, too. Sad irony is I'm the only person left who knows who you *really* are."

*Isn't it, though?* I swallow around the sudden thickness in my throat.

"How can you love him?"

*Him. Ander.* I know exactly what Finn's talking about, and it still takes me a moment to find my words—any words. "How could I not? Once we started to Fall…our relationship was better than ever."

"Funny the things you can have in the Falls that you could never have in real life."

I go cold. "Not how I would put it, but I get what you mean."

"How could you not remember me? *Us?*"

"I remember you—of course I remember you—but there wasn't an 'us.'" My collarbone begins to sting again, and Finn starts toward me, two small steps. The hair on my arms stands up, but everything in me goes still, heavy. I place my free hand against the tattoo, and Finn's eyes follow the movement.

"Do you remember this?" he asks and *moves*. We are suddenly toe-to-toe. His hand cups my throat, his fingertips skim my jaw, and my heart turns like a key in a lock. We are breathing the same air.

Only we aren't, because Finn isn't breathing.

"Do you remember any of this?" he whispers.

I shiver, staring at my fist because it can't be my fist knotted into his T-shirt. Can't be. I shove him. Hard. He retreats a step and waits, watching.

"There could've been more," I add, because it's true and because it tastes like a lie and I can't tell the difference between them when he focuses on me. "But there *wasn't* more. I chose Ander."

Finn's features sharpen. In the woods, the crickets and frogs have started up, and we shouldn't be able to hear Ander's radio, but I swear I can hear that stupid song coming from so very far away.

"I can't give you a truce, Grace. This will never be over."

"I won't let you hurt him."

"Then take your shot."

Finn spins around, giving me the broad expanse of his back. It's not the first time he's walked away from me. This time it's different, though.

This time, he's giving me a target.

He strikes out toward the road, and my hand tightens around the tire iron. I could hurt him. Once upon a time, Ander would've begged me to hurt him. If the roles were reversed, would Finn have hurt me?

My stomach goes cold, oily. I don't know. He could have hurt me just now and he didn't. Because he was being humane?

I have no idea, but I do know this: I can't hurt him. Finn's a monster…and even monsters have souls.

"Finn?"

Too late. The gloom has swallowed him.

*then...*

The shadows had almost reached my armchair when Ander finally woke up and stumbled into the shower. Visa was snoring on the rug, and I was reading another paperback—I didn't remember anything about it, and yet I was almost done.

Jem had been sure Ander would be furious with me. Last night, I hadn't cared—well, I hadn't cared much. Now my mouth had gone dry.

Was he going to be mad?

"I think my head wants to explode." Ander appeared in the doorway. He braced his shoulder against the doorframe and rubbed the back of his neck with one hand. His hair was wet from a shower, and he smelled like my body wash. This had happened a thousand times before, but this afternoon felt different. *We* felt different.

"Did the shower help?"

"Yeah." We watched each other, and I wondered if being friends for so long allowed me to see Ander as he was right now and also as he used to be. I could see the kid I met at six years old still rattling around inside the nearly six-foot frame.

Was it the same when he looks at me?

Out in the kitchen, pots banged together, and he winced. "What time is it?"

"Almost four."

"Almost time for dinner." Mom ducked around Ander. She was already dressed for her shift at the diner: her dark hair was smoothed back, her uniform carefully washed. She'd worn it for so many years now the skirt was butterfly-wing thin at her knees.

No *are you eating with us?* No *do your parents know where you were last night?* She just accepted he was there. She took care of him—of all of us—like it was the most natural thing.

*It fills up the cracks in me*, she'd said.

Visa bounced to his feet as she passed my chair. Mom brushed one chapped hand through my curls. "Go wash up, Gracie."

"Okay." I smiled at her, and it felt good and true. She retreated to the kitchen and I faced Ander, my insides cramping. "What's going on?"

The dying sunlight tinged Ander's pale hair red, like he was burning from the inside out. "I had to blow off some steam."

"Some steam."

His chin jerked up. "Don't start. You don't have a clue what I'm dealing with."

He was right. I didn't have a clue, and I was suddenly embarrassed, like I should feel bad that my parents were my parents. I had as much control over mine as he had over his. We glared at each other.

"Sorry," he said at last. "I didn't mean to worry you."

"You remember me being worried?"

"I remember your voice. It was the only thing in the dark." His mouth screwed up like he'd tasted something sour.

"Actually, I remember Finn, too."

"He *helped* me."

"Is that all?"

I looked at him but could only see Finn's face, Finn's shadow. "He helped me because he felt sorry for me. I'm a little small to drag around someone your size. You can't keep drinking like that."

One brow arched. "It wasn't that bad."

"Ander…"

"It's not like that."

"Like what?" I refused to look away, even though staring him down made my teeth grind. "It's not like *what*?"

"It was just a mistake."

My stomach swooped into my feet. I wanted it to be a mistake.

"It won't happen again," he added.

"Won't it?" I needed him to *say* it. I needed the words. I wanted certainty, because right then…right then I didn't believe him, and I had *always* believed him.

"Of course it won't." Ander's lips flattened into something resembling a smile. "How many times can I lose Dan?"

Dan. His father. The man Ander knew they didn't need and was glad to see go, and yet…and yet…

"I guess it depends on if he comes back," I said.

"He won't." He shook his head once, then pressed his palms against his temples like his skull was trying to explode. It probably was. "He won't be back, which means I need to step up. Next few months are going to suck for me, okay, Grace? You have to understand it's going to suck and I'm going to blow off some steam, but I won't let it get that bad again, okay?"

"Okay."

"I'm sorry I scared you."

"I know." And yet the hard pit in my stomach grew.

"What can I do to make it right?" His hand skimmed my arm, my wrist. He touched me like I was as soft as a newborn's throat. Softer. "Can we try again?"

He leaned forward. His hand found my jaw. His thumb rubbed against my lower lip, trailing electricity across my skin, and when Ander kissed me, it didn't feel like trying again. It felt natural. Predictable? Maybe. As his mouth moved against mine, I felt like we were inching toward something as inevitable as the sun arcing across the sky.

# chapter twenty-six

## now...

*I* don't trust myself to drive. My legs feel like rubber, and there's an ache behind my eyes. I sit in the truck, listening until Finn's footsteps through the brush disappear into nothing, and then I sit some more.

*What am I going to do?*

*No idea. No idea. No idea.*

The cab still smells like gas. I roll down both windows. Useless. The air is humid and stagnant. I check my phone and promise myself I'll drive home in ten minutes. In ten minutes, I will be collected and calm.

In the meantime, I can freak out. I slump against the steering wheel and try to wrench my thoughts around.

This is what I know: Finn thinks we were together, Ander isn't my Ander, and Jem is back.

I thump my forehead against the steering wheel. *What do I do? What do I do? What do I do?*

The question is my heartbeat.

*Get going.* I crank the engine and back the truck around, hitting two potholes in the process. The truck's undercarriage scrapes hard against the ground, and I wince.

By the time I get back to the road, Finn is nowhere to be seen. I watch the woods to my left and right, wondering if he's ducking down to avoid me and then slam on my brakes when I catch sight of yellow eyes in the dark.

Not Finn. A coyote dashes across the road, vanishes.

*I lost you.*

What was Finn talking about? I squint into the dark, sifting through the days leading up to that first Fall. Yes, Ander and I had been fighting. Yes, I had been…interested in Finn.

And terrified of him.

He'd been brilliant and arrogant and pretty — a fairy-tale prince come to save all us rednecks from ourselves. But that's the thing about come-to-life Prince Charmings: there's no such thing. In the real world, villains make you laugh and have beautiful eyes and make promises they will never ever keep.

I wipe one hand across my face, exhaustion tugging at me. Looking back, everything's gone blurry, gummy. I had been so focused on Ander in those last weeks. We'd had to go through our own personal hell before we made it, and we'd been so close.

*Funny the things you can have in the Falls that you could never have in real life.*

My teeth grit. Finn was right. Sort of. Ander and I weren't… good before. But we were great now. Or we had been. The Falls had pushed us together, blotting everything else out. Yes, we'd had problems. I was leaving. Ander was drinking. But I'd still chosen him on the night of our first Fall. Ander said my name, and I took his hand.

And later, losing everything had a funny way of making none of our differences matter anymore. Or maybe we'd just put it behind us?

Or maybe…I lick my lips and taste dust. The hairs on the

back of my neck go rigid, and I can't shake the feeling that someone is breathing next to me.

"Impossible," I whisper, rubbing my eyes until they sting. I mash hard on the gas and retrace my route back to town. The truck's going at a good clip, but I still feel watched.

Hunted?

"I'maloneI'maloneI'malone," I whisper again and make a right at the square, clipping the curb with my back tire. "Stupid truck."

The streetlights flash past me. Light. Dark. Light. Dark. Light. *Everywhere*.

I take my foot off the gas, letting the truck roll so I can get a better look. There must be thousands of white lights strung through the town square trees. They've turned everything to twilight.

I pull to a stop, cold sweat sliding underneath my clothes. This is wrong. The first night of this Fall, after he picked me up from the party, Jem and I came through here and there weren't any lights. The square looked nothing like this.

Behind me, a car honks. I roll past two streets and then... my turnoff isn't there.

I lean across the bench seat, stomach down around my feet. A beauty salon is wedged into the space where my street should be.

I don't...I don't know where I am. I sit up, look right, then left. Not good. Everything's different. My turn should be *right there*. I'm sure of it.

Another honk, and I yank the steering wheel to the left, turning the truck into an empty parking space next to the beauty salon that shouldn't exist. I take a deep, deep breath and push it slowly out. Think. I have to think.

But all I can come up with is: Did I Fall again?

No. No, that's stupid. I'm still *here*. I'm still in Jem's truck.

My hands are still wrapped around the steering wheel. My clothes are the same. Nothing's changed.

But my surroundings? The town? The streets? They're different. Wrong.

*Or maybe it's me.*

The idea creeps to my surface, emerging in a cold, nasty, gleeful little voice. Maybe it's *me*. First the condoms, then the bedspread, then the woods, and now *this*.

What if I'm losing it? Am I going crazy?

In the very beginning, I thought I was. I couldn't take the Falls anymore. I couldn't stop crying.

And yet every Fall, Ander found me. We found *each other*.

Of course, Finn always found me, too, and now it feels… different, an ember glowing in the dark.

I shake myself. Details shifted, but the three of us always knew each other. I held on to who I was in every Fall by finding Ander. That's how I survived.

"And now?" I ask the empty truck cab. "Talking to yourself is a sign of crazy, too," I add, reversing the truck back onto the road.

I rumble around the square once more and take another road that goes in the general direction of my house.

*Will it still be my house? Will I even be able to find it?* I lean forward, watching closely as a road sign emerges from the dark. *That's* my turn.

There's no one behind me, and I slow to a stop, studying the reflective green road sign. It must be close to ten now, and the dark is heavy and damp. I should be burning up, but looking at that road sign, my teeth chatter.

*Did I just get confused?* I have to order each finger to unclench the steering wheel. I blow on my cold hands. I mean, it's possible…right?

Car headlights sweep over the hill behind me, coming up

fast. I can't sit here. I'll get rear-ended for sure. I force myself to breathe and press on, turning the truck down the lane and deeper into the dark.

Moments later, my mailbox emerges from the gloom. It's on the left just like I remembered. Maybe I missed the lights before? Maybe they were off?

Maybe I'm going nuts.

*First the condoms then the bedspread then the woods then the lights.*

"Get a grip, Grace," I whisper.

I park the truck under the trees and shuffle up the path to the house, nearly through the door before I realize there's a shape sitting on the swing, waiting for me.

"Grace?"

I jump, keys dropping from my hands.

"Honey? Are you okay?" My mom—this Grace's mom—steps under the porch light. "I thought I'd wait up for you."

"Oh," I manage, because all I think is "oh, that's nice" and "oh, you didn't have to," but most of all I think: "I'm so glad." The words tumble over each other until nothing comes out.

"Want to sit?"

I *do* want to sit, even though I'm a teensy bit scared if I do sit down, I won't get back up. I'm so tired my bones are mushy and my face is tingling.

And she watches me like she knows, like it worries her—and somehow that hurts even more because before I Fell, my mom had been worried about me, too.

"C'mon." She tugs me down to the swing. "I know I should bust you for coming in so late on a school night, but you've been so off lately. Is everything okay?"

"It's just…school stuff."

She sighs. "I'd like to tell you it gets better. Eventually, though, it's work stuff and coworker stuff and…ugh. I think

I just depressed myself."

"And me."

She rolls her eyes and hooks her arm around my shoulders. "It's still better than high school—*anything* is better than high school." She bumps her foot against the floorboards and sets the swing to swaying. "I think everyone's just scared and lashing out at each other. It takes so much courage to become who you are."

I laugh. "Is that supposed to be less depressing?"

"Yeah, yeah." She nudges me. This close, she smells like roses. It should aggravate my asthma, and it doesn't. This time, it feels kind of right. "Hang in there. We'll do something next weekend, okay? Something fun."

I smile because I should, but really I'm counting. It's the third day. Next weekend? That's after my timeline finishes. I won't be here. I'll be…wherever I go next, because Finn won't give up, and we all know how this ends.

"Don't stay up too late, okay?"

"I won't."

She smiles. I smile. For a beat, I'm not sitting on a porch swing with this Grace's mom, I'm sitting on a porch swing with *my* mom. It isn't a Fall or one of my creepy timeline glitches, it's just her.

"Night, sweetheart," she says, pulling me into a hug that feels so good I nearly sob.

Everything else is wrong, and yet this has never felt so right.

*then...*

The thin ribbon of road ran straight through the trees for almost two miles. On Friday nights, it was used for drag racing. On Sunday afternoons, Jem used it for drag racing practice. At the moment, he was using it for parking. The truck wouldn't stop backfiring—and then stalling—and we'd been messing with it for almost an hour.

Well, "we" was a bit of a generalization. Jem, Ander, and Finn were working on it. I sat in the grass and watched. Jem had offered me the blanket he kept in the truck for "emergencies" and I'd declined. The only "emergencies" that blanket ever saw was Jem trying to coax some girl into the truck bed. Even the stains had stains.

Finn pushed away from the truck and used the bottom edge of his T-shirt to wipe his face. He turned, and—

Busted.

I dropped my eyes to the open notebook on my lap, then the sun-ravaged grass under my hand. It was delicate as charred paper.

"Tired of supervising?" Finn asked, throwing himself down

beside me. He smelled like gasoline and grass clippings and boy.

"Something like that," I said. We weren't touching, but I could feel his warmth. Or maybe it was mine.

I cleared my throat and tilted my notebook toward him. "Did you finish that prep work for AP English?"

His smile was a narrow line. "The paper about how to improve social media?"

"Yeah."

"It was easy. I did it in less than an hour."

I blinked. "You did?"

"Yeah, I said Facebook needed to add another choice to their relationship status selections." He rolled to his back and shielded his eyes with a forearm. It rucked up the edge of his shirt again and this time, I didn't look. "I wrote four pages on how we need an 'In a Relationship with a Fictional Character' selection."

I stared, my mouth working up and down. Nothing came out. I couldn't think of anything.

His smile curved wider. "I can *so* see your face right now— seriously, though, people need to know about Hermione and me."

That made me laugh. He didn't move his arm from his eyes, but his knee slid sideways and touched mine. I pulled away.

"Why are you even worrying about it? Not like you'll be there this fall."

"We don't know that."

"I do."

Behind us, tires crunched across the gravel. I turned and saw Callie and her older sister driving up in Callie's hunter-green Jeep. Her on-again-off-again relationship with Jem must've returned to on.

"There!" Jem smacked one hand against the Ford's driver's

door. He leaned across the bench seat and fumbled with the keys. The engine ground...ground...turned over.

The truck belched to life, and Finn pushed up onto his elbows, watching Ander and Jem high-five each other.

"Losers," Finn muttered, but he was laughing. "Who high-fives anymore?"

Callie parked her Jeep alongside Jem's truck and got out, her sister, Tisha, following. The girls had long hair, longer legs, and said everything like it was a question.

Fitting since Callie always looked at Jem like he was the answer.

It would've been easy to say Jem had a type, and Callie (and Tisha) fit, only I thought it was really because Boone was a type. It was church on Sunday mornings and Wednesday nights. It was camouflaged baseball caps and cowboy boots with scuffed-up toes, straightened blond hair, and using "lovely" as an insult.

Ander disagreed. He swore Boone wasn't a type, it was inbreeding. I thought he was wrong. If you didn't look right, if you didn't fit, you didn't stay.

"Hey, you." Callie curled into Jem for a kiss, tossing a wrist-thick braid behind her.

Tisha's narrow shadow slipped over us. "Well, hey, Grace," she said. "Hey, Finn. We didn't know you'd be here."

Doubtful, but I smiled. Tisha didn't notice. Her attention stayed trained on Finn.

I scribbled tiny circles in my notebook while they chatted. Everything tasted like dust and smelled like exhaust.

"You know, I've never actually heard your sister talk," I heard Callie say to Jem, which was stupid because she had, and mortifying because we'd had four classes together in the past three years. I couldn't be *that* forgettable. Or maybe I could.

"She's shy," Jem explained. They were by the truck, and

it wasn't meant for me to hear, but I flinched anyway, and Finn noticed.

"Maybe you could ask to braid her hair," he whispered when Tisha returned to her sister's side. "That's how girls bond, right?"

I stared at him. He was making fun of me, wasn't he? Only there was something earnest and *open* in his expression. Was he trying to make me laugh?

"Not into hair braiding?" he asked. "What about nails? No? Huh. Let me think—"

"Don't strain yourself."

Finn's eyes brightened. "Maybe you could talk mathy to them?"

I laughed. "I so hate you right now. I didn't know I could hate someone so much."

"I'm good at helping people realize their potential. It's a gift."

And I might have hated him more, because he made me laugh again.

At the back of the truck, Ander tossed his wrench into Jem's toolbox and slammed the top down. The sunlight caught behind him, blurring his face, but he was looking at me and I was looking at him and suddenly it was too hot.

And Finn was sitting too close.

And I felt like I'd done something wrong and all I'd really done was laugh.

Except, of course, I hadn't. There was something underneath my laugh, and even though I didn't want it to be there, Ander had heard it anyway.

"Success?" I asked, lifting my voice so he could hear me over Callie's giggles. Jem picked her up, and she shrieked.

Ander shrugged. "Why don't you try it out?"

"No, thanks."

"Then I'll try it out. Hop in."

I shook my head. Maybe it was the heat or the schoolwork or just something I couldn't name, but I didn't feel like doing this anymore. I didn't want to drive around. I didn't want to spend the next few hours with Callie and Tisha. I wanted to go home.

No, that wasn't quite right. I wanted to be someplace else. Anywhere else. We were surrounded by woods and kudzu and *nothing* and I still felt smothered.

No, worse. I felt wrong. Off again. We used to fit. It used to be so easy. When did that stop?

Ander opened the passenger door. "C'mon. I want to try the shift from second to third. You're the one who said you wanted to be with me, remember?"

I stared at him, my skin suddenly too thin and the sunlight suddenly too bright. Tisha giggled, and what was left of me went up in flames.

"*Fine.*" I tossed my homework on the ground and stood, brushing off the seat of my shorts. Finn muttered something—the tone urgent and close—but he was so quiet, I never heard the words.

# chapter twenty-eight

*now...*

*T*hump. *Thump*.

I wake with a jerk, my heart in my throat and my whole body tingling.

*Thump. Thump.*

What... I blink. Can't focus. Blink some more. What's going on? What happened?

"Grace?"

I sit straighter. Door. It's morning. I'm in my bedroom. Someone's at my bedroom door.

*OhmyGodwhattimeisit?* I kick my legs free of the sheets.

I fork both hands through my hair as my room slides into focus. Daylight has turned my room dove gray and flesh pink. It's day four and I'm *late*. OhmyGod, I'm so late. "Uh...yeah?"

"Can we talk?"

For an entire second, I feel like the floor disappeared. *Jem* wants to talk?

"Yeah...yeah. Sorry." I swing my legs off the bed and tug a sweatshirt over my tank top, catching a glimpse of myself in the mirror.

Frizzy hair? Check.

Bloodshot eyes? Double check.

My transformation to full-on crazy-looking person is now complete. Ugh.

"You can come in," I say, scraping all my hair back into a ponytail. The door slides partway open, and Jem fills the gap. My Jem was taller than me, too, his shoulders way broader. It was inevitable that our differences would grow, and yet I still can't shake our memories. We were twins. We were never apart. People would see my face and look past me, already hunting for him. I liked recognizing myself in him.

Jem watches me, and I don't know what to say.

I don't think he does, either.

"Are you okay?" he asks at last.

No. Not at all. "I overslept. Can you give me two minutes?"

He leans his head against the doorframe, and I pause because even though this isn't my Jem, I can still read his body language. His face is relaxed, but his eyes are focused, slightly narrowed. He's thinking, weighing some unspoken thought that leaves me hovering one bare foot half into my tennis shoe.

"You want to skip?" he asks.

"*School?*" I can't skip school. It's day four and I should be doing…something. Except I have no idea what that something should be. The timeline is completely blown to pieces. Finn has his own agenda. Ander doesn't remember. And I'm…I don't know what I am.

"Yes," Jem says slowly. "Do you want to skip school with me?"

My chest funnels shut.

"Forget it." He backs away. "It was a stupid thought."

"No." I stumble forward, reaching for him with both hands. "Let's do it."

...

Just like yesterday, we leave our parents at the kitchen table. Mom smiles at us from above the rim of her coffee cup. Dad tells us to have a good day.

Jem laughs. "It's going to be a *great* day."

And our parents beam because apparently no matter the timeline, Jem is still a fantastic liar.

"Grace, honey?" Mom catches my sleeve. "Will you be home tonight? I'd love to talk again if you have time."

*I'll make the time.* The thought shouldn't be mine. I want more with her, though. I want another sit on the porch, another hug that feels like coming home. It's day four and I know how this ends and yet...

"I'll make the time," I tell her. Mom and Dad smile at me like I am everything they ever wanted in a daughter.

"Hurry up, Grace!" The screen door bangs shut behind Jem.

I grab more toast from the table and race after him. The morning is dew-soaked, and the truck tires squelch against the grass. Jem turns us onto the main road into Boone, and when we reach the square he goes left, taking us past rows of birthday-cake-colored shops.

I crane my head, studying the tree branches flashing above us. I can't see any type of lighting. Because the bulbs are too small?

Or because the bulbs aren't there?

The hairs on my arms go rigid.

"You're different," Jem says, steering us away from town and toward the river. He shifts into fourth and I straighten, focusing on him. "You're not yourself."

*Understatement of the year.* "Sorry."

He thumps his index finger against the steering wheel. "That's the thing. You never apologize."

"I don't want things to be like they have been."

"Me, either."

It's so sudden, like the words escaped him, but Jem doesn't seem weirded out and that makes him feel more like my real brother than ever. My Jem said what he meant, too. He never regretted being honest.

"I miss how things used to be," he says.

"Me, too." My hands tighten around my knees. Is it really going to be that easy? Can you really just start over? "So what do you want to do?"

He shrugs. "Fish? It's not like anything will be biting. It's something to do, though—and no chance of getting spotted."

I'm grinning like a total idiot. "I'd love that."

"'Love'?" There's a sputter of laughter in the word, and I realize I've made a misstep.

"I'd love anything that will get me out of class today," I say quickly. "I've had all the fun I can stand."

"Fair enough." Now he's grinning. "Honestly, I didn't think you'd ever go fishing again after I pushed you in."

"Yeah, well," I say, because what else is there? I tug a strand of hair behind my ear. Jem pushed me into the water? That's not so bad. Grace was angry enough to never go fishing again?

"I still feel bad about it," he continues. "What if you had lost a toe to the snapping turtles?"

"You would've owed me for *life*." I watch as the town falls away and the farms emerge. "Like, if I'm at a party and I want to go home, you'd have to take me because of the Toe Clause."

"I drive you around already."

"This way, you'd never be able to say no. I'd just hold up my four-toed foot and go, 'You were saying?' and then you would have to do whatever I wanted."

He laughs, slowing way down to navigate the potholes in the road. We've dipped toward the river, and the fields have disappeared into cypresses and cattails. This close, the swamp sounds are an anthem.

"We're lucky you survived childhood," he says. "Remember that time I dared you to jump off the tree house?"

I nod and smile and he goes on, walking me through a memory I wish were mine and praying he doesn't press me for details. Even though I want to press *him* for details. I want to know everything.

Jem has all these experiences I wish I shared.

*If I stay, we could have new memories.* The realization unfurls inside me, stretches like it's warming in the sun.

*I* want *to stay.*

"Hey," he says suddenly, eyes still watching the road ahead of us. "When did it stop being this easy?"

"I don't know. We grew apart, I guess."

Jem glances at me again, the skin around his eyes pleated and wrinkly. The squint is so familiar it's almost like looking at myself. "That's a sucky excuse."

"Yeah."

"Promise me we won't let it happen again."

I pause. That's a promise I have zero chance of keeping, but I want to make it. This Grace's parents are almost my parents. My brother is almost my brother again. It's a life worth fighting for.

"I promise," I say, and I mean it—I do—but there's a shake in my voice. Losing everyone once was bad enough, but to get them back and lose them again? It's infinitely worse, because now I know what's coming for me.

I will not give them up again.

# chapter
# twenty-nine

*then...*

Ander slammed the truck door after me, almost catching the edge of my sandal. I watched him walk around the front of the vehicle and climb in. He slammed his door just as hard.

"Ander—"

He popped the stick into reverse and floored us backward. I braced one hand on the dash, leaving fingerprints in the dust, and looked through the windshield for Jem. He was focused on Tisha and Callie. He hadn't noticed.

Finn had, though. He pushed to his feet as Ander shifted into first. We turned until the truck faced the opposite direction and Ander shifted again, hard. Gravel spit up as we jerked forward, picking up speed.

I smacked his arm. "What's your deal?"

"What are you talking about?" Another hard shift. The wind pushed under my hair like I was flying.

"Why are you driving like an ass? Slow down."

"I'm testing it." He downshifted and the engine revved. He held the steering wheel too loose and the gearshift too hard, and his knuckles stood out white. "C'mon, I want to drag race next weekend. We need to know how it does off the line."

Another shift and the truck leaped forward. My stomach tightened. "Ander!"

He didn't answer. The speedometer climbed and the trees on either side of us began to blur.

I hit him again. "Let me out!"

Ander stepped harder on the gas. The force pressed my stomach into my spine and my spine into the torn seatback.

"Stop it!"

"Stop making this into a big deal!"

"Let me out!" It emerged on a shriek and he jumped, hands jerking the steering wheel. The truck shuddered to the right.

Toward the drainage ditch.

He hit the brakes hard and we slung forward. The edge of my seat belt bit into my throat. The truck skidded, skidded, fishtailed, and I was crammed against the door. The world swung around, and we slid to a stop in an explosion of dust.

Under his tan, Ander was ashen. When he reached for me, his hands shook. "Grace—"

I tugged off my seat belt and shot out of the car on rubber legs. Deep in the woods, the cicadas were humming, and something twitched in the dead leaves. I turned in the direction we'd come, but we were too far to see the others. The horizon was smudgy with dust and heat.

Ander came around the front of the truck like someone shot him from a cannon. I rounded on him. "What was that about?" I yelled.

He grabbed me and I shoved him, his hands catching mine. I could feel his heartbeat under my palms. "Sorry."

I wrenched myself backward and he followed. "I'm sorry," he said.

"Let go."

"I'm *sorry*."

He was. That was the worst part. I knew he was sorry. I could see it in the way his mouth turned down and his eyes wrinkled up and how his voice got tight. I knew *him* and it wasn't enough to stuff my panic back down. "Let. Go."

For a long moment, we stared at each other, breathing hard.

"I'm only going to ask you this once: What's *wrong*?"

He shook his head, refusing to answer.

I tucked a knot of hair behind my ear and counted to five. "Is it about your dad?"

Ander studied the horizon, a muscle ticking in his jaw. "Yeah. Yeah, and my mom and the rent payment that's due and you."

I blinked. "Me?"

"You didn't think I'd notice? He stares at you *all the time*! What were you trying to do? Get me back for not spending enough time with you?"

"I'm not like that. You *know* I'm not like that. I've never done something mean to get back at you."

He shook his head. "You're always pulling the shy girl card, but you're not shy with him. What gives?"

I could feel the color drain from my face. "He's your friend!"

"So's Marcus, and I didn't see you chatting him up the other night!"

"It's not…we get along because we both know what it's like to be on the outside."

"What are you *talking* about? You're always with me."

I glared at him. I was mad and yet there was something else plucking at me with dirty little fingers: how it wasn't enough to always be with him.

How could I say that?

How could I want to be enough for him and know he wasn't enough for me?

Ander glared down at me. "I don't even know how to spend time with you anymore. You're always studying and when you're not studying, you're in your head. You never want to go *anywhere*."

I opened my mouth, closed it. What could I say? This was who I was around him, who I *really* was. This was *me* and knowing he hated it…stung.

"I've always been shy," I said slowly. "I've always studied, always wanted to make the best grades. You never minded."

He shrugged and it felt like a slap. I *thought* he never minded.

"It's gotten worse," he said. "It's like you only look at me when you have time and you *never* have time. You're on the verge of *leaving* and you don't care. Maybe I shouldn't, either. Think about it, Grace. What's the point?"

Tears pricked my eyes. "You mean, what's the point in staying together?"

"Yeah, even if we stay together…what do we have?" He glanced over his shoulder, down the road toward the others. "You're going to go off to save the world and I'll be here. Face it, you leave Boone, you're not coming home again. It doesn't work like that. Maybe we should break up."

*Argue with him*, I told myself, but I didn't—because I couldn't? Or because I agreed?

He glanced at the road again. "Every time I look at you, all I see is what I'll never have—what *we'll* never have."

"That's not…it's not…" I couldn't finish. I could barely breathe. Part of Ander blamed me for trying, and I hated that part of him. But a greater part of me knew how much he must be hurting, and that part, *that* part threatened to upend me. He was my best friend and he was imploding.

Ander straightened. "We're done, Grace."

I agreed.

"I'll drive you back."

I opened my mouth to say I didn't trust him to drive me anywhere and shut it. It would only make things worse, and even though it was kind of true, it was a lot of mean.

He stalked back to the truck, and I followed. Inside, he turned the keys, and the engine chugged to life.

"I'm sorry," he said at last.

I leaned out my window. "I'm sorry, too."

It only took a few minutes to return to the others. Ander parked in the shade and didn't get out when I did.

Jem trotted around the front of the truck, his grin slung wide. "How'd it drive? It looked great!"

Ander said something behind me. I didn't stop.

"Grace?" Jem raced after me, catching my arm so I had to face him. He still had his shirt off and there was a smudge of Callie's hot-pink lipstick on his throat. Gross. I shook him loose and kept walking.

"What's the matter?" Jem tried to duck in front of me so I'd stop.

"I'm going home."

"C'mon, Grace. We just got it going. Let me get some practice runs in and I'll drive—"

"Do what you want. I'll walk."

"It's, like, four miles."

"I'm going *home*." I shoved past him, feeling bad for snapping and not able to stop myself. I dropped to the grass and tugged my stuff together, jamming everything into my bag, not caring that I crushed my new paperback and my social media paper notes. I couldn't get away fast enough.

I slung my backpack over my shoulders and ignored how Tisha whispered something to Callie. They would tell everyone. Did that matter?

Yeah, it did—and that made me angrier.

I pushed by like it didn't, though. I stuck to the very edge of the road, where the grass met the gravel. My feet dragged in the dust, and I didn't have to look behind me to know Finn was following.

*now...*

*I* make it through day four with no glitches, no missteps. Jem and I aren't the same, and yet we're so close, I catch myself relaxing next to him.

We come home close to five, sunburned and laughing. I'm worried it'll be a dead giveaway that we weren't at school, but Jem laughs it off.

"Mom and Dad won't notice." He downshifts for our turn, and the truck jerks hard. "And if they do notice, they'll just be glad we're not mad at each other anymore."

I'm glad, too. This is the closest I've been to being me in…a long time.

Definitely since the Falls began.

Probably since *before* the Falls began.

I feel…happy. Complete.

The truck hits our gravel driveway in a puff of dust and crunch of undercarriage and Jem swears under his breath, grinding into a lower gear. Even so, we round the bend doing over thirty. Our slumped-roof house rises ahead of us, the edges a little blurry thanks to the late-afternoon light.

It really does feel like coming home. I brace one hand against the door. It feels like coming home, and that's worth fighting for—it's everything worth fighting for.

"You've got company," Jem says, angling the truck toward its usual parking spot.

*What?* I straighten, seeing the rusted motorcycle by the porch and then the boy by the rusted motorcycle.

Finn peels away from it, hands deep in his pockets. It's so familiar it feels like something that belongs to me, like this is our once-upon-a-time lives, not the one we have now. Maybe I really am getting better. When I landed in this timeline, I felt like I was starting to fill out Grace's body. Now I feel like it *is* my body. This is me.

"I'll meet you inside," I tell Jem as I hop out of the truck.

He nods, waving to Finn as he heads for the house.

"Jem," Finn says in greeting—then he flicks those pale eyes to me.

My mouth goes hot. Finn draws closer, his shoulders tight underneath his tee, and it feels like the swamp comes with him. The tree line feels closer somehow, the shadows heavier. The longer I watch, the more the dark seems to be rippling under the trees.

I shiver.

Finn scuffs to a stop next to me. His already lean face is narrower, sharper, like he hasn't been eating. There are pale blue smears under his eyes. They make his lashes stand out in black fringes.

I lick my dry lips. "You look like hell."

He laughs, eyes darkening to amber. "I wanted to see you. It's the fourth day."

"Yeah."

"Means tomorrow is the fifth."

We both go quiet. I can feel the heat glowing from his

skin. Is he waiting for a response? What am I supposed to say? Finn's so close; I can see how much the light loves his skin. It turns him half golden.

"I'm glad you came," I say at last.

"You are?"

"I want to stay."

"We can't."

"We *can*." I hesitate again. He really does look horrible—cheekbones that are more like pits, a gray tinge underneath his tan. "We could stay."

Finn flinches like I punched him. "You really believe that will work?"

"I don't know. You really think you can survive running down an innocent boy?"

Another flinch. He focuses on something in the distance, and a muscle in his jaw spasms. "You're never going to get over him, are you?"

"It's not like that."

"You're holding on."

"We could make a life for ourselves here. I could help you."

He shakes his head like my words are a bone stuck in his throat. "You really want to stay? This isn't your life, Grace."

"It's the closest thing I'm going to get."

Finn freezes. "You would take *this*? It isn't real."

"It's close enough." I swallow. "It's better than nothing."

He steps back, steps back again. He can't believe what I'm saying. Once, I might not have believed it, either. But the lie is the closest to the truth I'm going to get. We're never going home. We Fall again and again, and every time it's a little bit different, but it's never right.

"I have to go," he says at last.

"Finn? You trusted me once, right?"

His mouth opens on a silent laugh. "Don't do that."

"Don't do what?"

"Don't ask me favors based on what we were—what we used to be."

My breath shallows. "You were my friend."

"You know how this ends."

"Stop it!"

Finn freezes. He goes so still he could be prey.

Which would make me the wolf.

I advance a step, and those pale eyes widen. "Stop being so vague and freaking *say* what you mean. I don't know anything, but you? You seem to have a pretty good idea what's going on."

"Then open your eyes," he speaks slowly, clearly, like he's trying to summon something. It might even be working. My skin has started to sweat. "Think about what you remember. You were running after Ander. I was chasing you."

"And you *killed* Ander and we *Fell*. It happened every time."

Finn shivers. "And who controlled that?"

*He thinks I do*. Now I'm shivering. I wrap both arms around my torso, pressing tight because I feel like I'm going to rupture. "How could I control any of this? If I did, it would've stopped a long time ago. I would never want any of us to endure this hell—"

"What if that's because you know you're hiding from something that's worse?"

"What does *that* mean?"

"The truth is right in front of you." He spreads both hands, motioning to my house, Jem's truck, the swamp. "You control all of this."

My lungs burn and pinch and I'm wheezing through it. I want to say, *What are you talking about?* I want to demand, *What do you mean?*

And I can't. I can't say *anything*, and Finn nods like he knows.

"This is you, Grace. This is all you."

"How…why…" I grit my teeth until they hurt. "And you're just *now* telling me?"

"I couldn't get close to you before now. He always pulled you away. You wanted him to."

It's like being dropped from a very great height. For a long moment, I stare at him. He's right. Ander did pull me away, and I let him. "Why…why would I want to keep away from you?"

"Because you think I did something terrible."

My joints go liquid. "What?"

"You think I did something terrible." Finn's so quiet I shouldn't be able to hear him, but I feel every word climb into me. "Deep down, you blame me. You blame *us*. You think we have to pay for what we did. Every time, it's the same thing: I chase, Ander dies, you Fall."

"Then tell me what really happened."

Finn's mouth works side to side like he's looking for the words, like they're gathered behind his teeth. "I can't. It's your truth. I can't say something you don't want to hear. You won't let me."

"I give you permission, okay?" I roll both hands into fists and still feel my trembling. "Go ahead."

He shakes his head, stares at the ground. "It doesn't work like that."

"Of course it doesn't." My laugh is a snarl. "How convenient. Whatever. Be that way—but Finn?"

His gaze swings to mine. Sticks.

"I'm keeping this life," I say. "If I'm in charge, we're staying."

...

*I* go through all the motions that night, and I don't miss a single beat. I smile. I eat. I help Jem clean up. This is my new life. This is what I want. I'm in charge of everything? Fine. *Good.*

Hours later, I crawl into bed and wonder if I'll sleep. I'm afraid of what I'll dream, but the next time I roll over, it's the fifth day.

I lie on my back, study the hairline cracks in the ceiling. Sunlight blisters the white plaster silver. I push up, waiting for my stomach to try to twist into my throat and…it doesn't.

Day five.

I don't remember ever being this calm before. Maybe right after our first Fall? When I didn't know what was coming?

*You know how this ends.*

*Not anymore.* I swing my feet to the floor. In the mirror, my room looks exactly like I remember. No glitches. My face is mine. My body is mine.

This will be my new life.

This *is* my new life. I can't stop my smile. I grab clean clothes from the dresser, hopping from foot to foot as I pull on my tennis shoes. The hallway's empty, and Jem's door is still closed.

"Jem!" I call, retreating into the bathroom. There's no response. I brush my teeth, spit, rinse, and feel almost presentable. Nothing from Jem, though.

I tug my hair into a topknot and tap my shoe against his door. "Jem?"

Downstairs, Mom turns on some radio station, and music mixes with the sounds of pans banging together. I smell bacon. If we hurry, we'll have time for more than toast.

I knock on Jem's door again and wait. "Jem, c'mon. We're going to be late."

Still no answer, and my insides drop two inches. This feels...wrong.

It shouldn't. Everything's fine. It is. I'm being ridiculous. I turn the doorknob, revealing an empty room. The bed's blue plaid blanket is pulled tight against the mattress, and Jem's rock posters are down from the walls. The air smells like potpourri, and there are vacuum marks in the carpet.

No footprints.

No clothes on the floor.

Nothing personal on the dresser...or by the bed...or near the closet.

My hands go cold. Where's Jem?

I force one foot forward and then the other. I check the dresser. Empty. I check the closet. Nothing. Under the bed? Boxes of clothes.

But they're *girl* clothes—sweaters and jackets and scarves. No band T-shirts. No ratty jeans. Downstairs, the music swells.

"No, no, *no*. Not again." I kick to my feet and run down the hallway to the bathroom. I tear the shower curtain to one side. There's only my purple shampoo by the drain, my green soap in the dish. I spin around, fling open the cabinet under the sink. Girl deodorant. Girl razors.

Nausea crashes over me in an unending wave. It's like Jem's vanished. *Again*.

"Grace?"

Mom. I pop up, slamming the cabinet shut. I run down the steps. "Mom?"

"In here." Her voice floats in from the kitchen, and the music lowers. I follow the sound and find her at the sink, rinsing dishes under the faucet. Sunshine slants past the curtains, brightens the walls to petal green. This could be any other morning.

"Mom?" Only one word and my voice still cracks.

She turns to me, wiping off the dish in her hands, and the sunlight catches behind her. I have to squint to see her face. "What's the matter?"

"I can't find Jem."

Mom's hands slow. "What are you talking about?"

"Where's *Jem*?"

Even with the light in my eyes, I can still see how her shoulders straighten and relief makes me woozy. I know that gesture. She's going to tell me he's outside. He's waiting in the truck. I'm acting crazy.

I am crazy.

Except she doesn't say any of those things. Mom looks at me and says, "Who?"

# chapter thirty-one

*then...*

It took me almost twenty minutes before I could talk again, and by that point, it was awkward.

*What else is new?*

I kicked a rock, sending it flying into the grass on the side of the road. "You don't have to walk me home." I was still facing straight ahead, so it was basically like I'd announced it to the cicadas and the grass and dirt road stretched beyond us.

"I know."

I spun on him. "Really," I said using my best student-speaking-to-teacher voice, the one I'd had to practice in front of my mirror because it was so hard to talk to people. "I'm *fine*."

"I know."

And yet he didn't *go away* and I had no idea what to do about that—or about the fact that he eased closer.

"I had all the fun I could stand, too," he said. "C'mon. I have to walk past your place anyway."

Now he was ahead of me, striding along like he expected me to run along behind him. Which of course I had to if I wanted to ever get home.

"So." Finn knotted both hands behind his neck as I caught up to him. "Do you want to ask me about Hermione and all the things she taught me in middle school?"

I kept my attention on the road ahead. Guys from Boone didn't read Harry Potter, and if they did, they didn't admit it.

"Never go to the bathroom alone," Finn continued. "You'll get attacked by trolls—oh and ghosts sometimes live in the toilets, so you gotta be prepared."

I chewed down my laugh—stupid really, because swallowing it just made my insides hot.

Finn bumped into me. "It's okay. Three out of four girls find me charming."

I stared straight ahead, willing myself not to smile.

"It's true," he added. "According to the survey I just made up."

I laughed and then wondered if I should've. Ander said Finn was always staring at me—and wasn't I always staring at him? We were all supposed to be friends, and yet kissing Ander, *being* with Ander, had ruined it.

Finn scuffed one Converse into a dirt clump. It skipped ahead of us. "You want to talk about fighting with Ander?"

"No."

"You want to talk about Branson's paper?"

"No, I think you've got me beat on that one." I scowled and caught myself. "He'll probably award you bonus points for ingenuity."

Finn grinned. "Is it hard to admit that? Because you sound a little choked up. Jealous, Freeman?"

I rolled my eyes. Dark thunderclouds smudged the horizon. We'd have another round of storms tonight. It wouldn't do anything for the heat, just make everything feel closer and hotter, like we were breathing through wet towels.

I walked faster, and Finn strode along beside me. "Were you always the best student at your last school?" I asked.

"Yeah." For one small word, he could fit a lot of smug into it. "Have *you* always been the best student at your school?"

"Yeah." For some reason, I felt like he was going to argue with me, and he didn't. His eyes hunted across my face, and I sped up.

He chased after me. "Huh. How long do you think that'll last?"

"Long enough for me to graduate first in our class because you're too busy playing slacker." The road split. I went left, and Finn came along. Ahead of us, a faint cloud drifted above the rise. A car was coming.

"You can't take less than an hour to do Branson's homework," I said. "Good idea or not, he's supposed to be super tough."

"Challenge accepted."

"Your funeral."

He laughed. "I bet you don't talk to anyone at school like this."

*I don't talk to anyone like this, period.* There was a smile in his voice I was pretty sure I hated. "I'll make an exception for you because you're irritating."

"Good. It makes me hope you won't get into Alton so I can continue irritating you."

A red sedan came over the hill, the driver barely visible above the steering wheel. My mom. She must've been heading in early. Finn stepped aside as the car slowed, then stopped. Mom leaned across the seat and rolled down the window.

"Everything okay?" She was asking me but studying Finn.

"Fine. Are you going in?"

Mom nodded. "Talk later?"

She was still speaking to me and still staring down Finn.

I got it. He didn't look like the boys from Boone. He wasn't Ander.

And he smiled like he knew it.

"Finn's just walking me home," I said. She nodded again, and there was the briefest hesitation before she pulled away.

"Your mom is *so* going to have The Talk with you tonight," Finn said. He was trying for funny again and missing it. The words were flat. He was right, though. Her eyes kept checking the rearview mirror.

"It's not going to be *that* talk," I told him. It was going to be the one about how she was worried about Ander, how she was worried about me, how most boys weren't like Ander and I should remember that.

I wondered what she'd say if I told her most boys don't drink themselves comatose every weekend, too. Actually, there was no need to wonder. She'd call the school, ask for a counselor. Social Services would get involved, and if they saw how his dad left and he was dropping out of school…

"She a fan of Ander's?" Finn asked.

"Yeah. She loves him like a son. He's like family." Suddenly all the reasons kissing Ander had made so much sense felt like all the reasons I should never have kissed him in the first place. "We've known him…forever."

His nose wrinkled. "You make it sound like time is the only measurement for love."

"What are you talking about?"

"Time." He looked at me and for a single heartbeat, his eyes dropped to my mouth. "You can be with someone for a year and feel nothing. You can be with someone for a week and feel…everything. Time is not an accurate measurement for love."

He paused, waiting for me to say something, and when I don't, his ears begin to go a little pink. "I'm trying to say that just because your mom has known Ander forever—"

"Finn?"

"Yeah?"

"Shut up."

We walked the rest of the way in silence, and when we reached my front porch, I stomped up the steps without thinking, making it almost to the top before I realized Finn was following. Again.

I turned. He looked up.

And suddenly we were one step apart.

His head was just above mine. My mouth was inches from his throat. His hands went to the splintery railing on either side of me…and gripped.

His face went red, redder. "Whoa. Sorry. I guess I was following you inside?" He laughed and it was forced. "I wasn't thinking."

I wasn't thinking, either. Finn was irritating and smug and now that we were inches apart, there was a sudden rushing in my ears.

*He stares at you all the time.*

I licked my lips, and his eyes dropped to my mouth, lingered. It made heat roll up me. "Thanks for walking me home," I whispered.

"No prob."

Inside, Visa barked and jumped at the door. When that didn't work for him, he braced both front paws on the windowsill and peeked out, spotting Finn and me. The force of his barking sprayed the glass with white spittle.

"Holy shit, he's huge!" Finn gaped and leaned a little closer to the window. Visa scrabbled both paws against the sill. "I think he hates me even more than your mom."

"It's a total lie." I faced the window and Visa grinned. His whole body wagged. "Visa, hush!"

Visa kept barking.

"'Visa'?" Finn asked.

"He's everywhere I want to be."

He laughed, turned…and suddenly we were closer again.

"So." I swallowed. "See you around?" I knew my smile was cramped at the edges, forced, *wrong*. I was acting like a freak.

I always acted like a freak.

So maybe it was desperation or maybe it was a lightning bolt of stupidity, but whatever it was I wrapped one arm around his shoulders in a hug, in a thank-you I'd seen Tisha and Callie and so many other girls do before.

I pretended I was normal, and Finn went rigid.

Or maybe it was just the way he was made. His chest was hard, and his arms were hard. If I fell against him, I would bruise, break. And as soon as I realized it, I knew this was wrong. It was a mistake.

A mistake because I wasn't supposed to hug other guys after having just broken up with Ander. I wasn't supposed to feel how hard Finn's heart began to beat.

And he wasn't supposed to feel how mine answered.

*chapter*
*thirty-two*

*now...*

There is a rushing in my ears, a droning. I inhale hard, inhale again, and still can't shake it.

*Jem. Jem. Jem.*

"Grace…honey…?" Her shadow advances, and behind it trails Mom. My Mom.

This Mom?

She steps away from the sink, and her face slips into focus. "Who are you talking about?"

*Not again. Please. Please not again.* I press both hands to my temples. Did I Fall again? It's the fifth day. I could have Fallen…

But it was my ashen face in the mirror, my tattoo that's burning under my shirt. It's me. Or as close to me as I ever get.

*You know how this ends.*

I drop my hands, rolling them into fists. If I'm in charge, we're not falling. I refuse. I just need to stick to what I know: my face is still the same. It's still my tattoo along my collarbone. It's still my mom staring at me with white showing all around her eyes.

She's afraid of me. I have to fix this.

I swallow. "Where is my twin?"

"Your *twin*?"

Mom says the word like she's never heard it, and I have to fight down an animal howl.

*Not again. Not again!*

"Grace." Mom takes another step toward me, eyes still wide, and that's when I see it. Or maybe I feel it. My stomach contracts like I've just been punched.

"What's wrong with your eyes?" I whisper, edging back.

"What do you mean?"

I mean there's something wrong with her eyes. They're flat. They're…*wrong*. Beyond the windows, a humid breeze stirs the tree branches, making the sunlight wink against the petal-green walls.

Petal green.

Our kitchen is blue. *Was* blue.

"Honey!" Dad's voice floats through the screen door, and footsteps follow. Mom and I stiffen, tilt toward the sound. Not just one set of footsteps. Dad has someone else with him.

"In here!" Mom doesn't look away from me, and the footsteps get heavier as Dad rounds the corner.

My breath goes jagged. Ander's with him.

"Look who came to visit," Dad says.

"Morning, Ander!" Mom's face creases into a wide smile. She knows him. How could she know him? In this timeline, Ander and I are not friends. Has that changed, too?

"Hey." Ander's drawl makes the word glide.

I give him a tight smile. "Hey."

"How're your folks?" Mom asks, returning to the sink to grab two clean dishes. The china is so old and delicate the plates ring when she stacks them together. Mom passes me one and passes Ander the other. "Breakfast?"

He nods. "Yes, please. They're good. Great, actually. Dad's taken a supervisor position at the mill. We're all really excited."

I sit at the table because everyone else sits at the table, but all I can think about is how Ander had always wanted a family excited about life. Mostly, he'd only known dread.

Mom's hip brushes the table edge as she takes scrambled eggs and bacon from her frying pan and piles them onto our plates. Her eyes meet mine again, and it's the same flatness looking back at me. It's like this mom has the idea of eyes, like someone stitched matte-brown buttons underneath her lids, and the more I stare at her, the more the edges of my vision begin to haze.

These are not my parents.

Mom touches my arm, hands delicate as spiders. "Are you feeling okay, sweetheart?"

"Yes." The lie is immediate, and her not-eyes narrow like she sees it.

This isn't my kitchen.

These are not my parents.

Jem is *gone*. Ander is *here*. Everything has changed. Again.

But I'm supposed to be in charge. I pick up my fork, put it down. *Get oriented*.

"You weren't yourself when you came downstairs," she adds.

"Sorry. I was…" I was hallucinating? I was sleepwalking? I was teasing her? There aren't any explanations that will make me sound remotely normal, and I'm done trying. If this is another new life, I'm just rolling with it.

I'm also stuffing down a scream.

"Sorry," I repeat.

"Are you sure you don't need to go lie down?" Mom asks. "I could check on you later."

I shiver. The thought of staying in bed while Mom and

Dad circle the downstairs makes my skin crawl.

"I'm fine." I study the kitchen's petal-green walls and Mom's crooked smile and feel my tattoo throb once. Twice.

Everything in me wants to spin apart, and I hold on tighter. Everything *has* changed.

Only *I* haven't.

"I'm fine," I repeat. They watch me, concern wrinkling the skin between their brows.

"I have a favor to ask," Ander says. "It's why I stopped by. I was hoping I could catch a ride into town. If that's not too much trouble?"

I focus on him. From his sun-bleached hair to the smile that pulls only one corner of his mouth, I know him. In fact, Ander's the only thing I really do know anymore in this kitchen.

*You're my everything,* he'd said during one of our Falls— and he's almost *my* everything now. Nothing else is the same.

And there it is again: a creeping wrongness that seeps under my skin to storm. I am glass-smooth on the outside, but inside I can hear the thunder.

Ander laughs. "You going to make me beg, Grace?"

His sidelong look should conduct fire across my skin. Should. Doesn't. My brain is stuck on repeat: If everything else has changed, does Ander remember now?

If everything else has changed, what happens next?

"Grace?" Dad watches me, a piece of bacon halfway to his mouth. It glistens under the kitchen lights. "You can take Ander, right? The truck isn't too messy?" He switches his matte gaze to Ander and smiles. "She looks like she lives out of the damn thing."

I suck in a breath, hold it. Truck. Jem's truck. And now it's mine?

*I still won't be able to park it.* Ander grins like he's thinking the same thing.

"Sure thing. Happy to give you a ride."

"Good." Ander loads the slightest force into the word, and it makes my scar prickle. His focus is only for me. "We gotta go."

The prickle turns to a burn, and that's when I know: Ander is back. It's the fifth day.

And now we have to run.

# chapter
# thirty-three

*J*em didn't come home. I sat at our chipped kitchen table and tried to finish Branson's social media paper—not that it worked. I ended up staring out the windows until darkness returned my reflection to me.

A bit after nine, headlights traced across the wall. Mom was home.

"Hey," she said, shuffling into the kitchen in bare feet.

"Hey." I put my book down and summoned up a smile. It was a little hard, since we both knew what was coming. The lines between her eyes were always worse after work, and when she sat next to me, I could smell the diner's grease and smoke.

"Do you want any dinner?" she asked.

I shook my head.

"Good, because I'm tired of food." She took a silver tube of aqua-blue oil paint from her apron pocket and passed it to me.

I had so many blues, and yet she never got the same one twice. With anyone else, I would assume they were keeping a list, but somehow my mom just remembered.

"Thanks," I said, sliding it into the pocket of my book bag.

"Don't tell your father. He'll think I'm interfering with your precious education." She tapped two fingers against the water-stained paperbacks Dad had left on the tabletop. "Who was that boy you were with today?"

"Finn," I reminded her, trying hard to keep the edge of irritation out of my voice. "He lives here full time now with his grandparents. The Larkins."

Recognition lit Mom's eyes, and she nodded. "Mr. Larkin used to supervise your dad's shift, didn't he?"

"I think so." Actually, I had no idea. Finn and I talked about a lot of stuff, but not that—which was weird because who your parents were and where they worked were pretty much the first things you were supposed to know about someone in Boone.

"He's a nice guy, Mom. We'll probably have classes together in the fall. Might even apply to some of the same colleges."

Funny how she could nod like she understood even as her mouth went thin because she didn't. "Unless you go to Alton," she prompted.

"Right. Unless I go to Alton."

"Everything okay with you and Ander?"

And there it was. I drew tiny circles around a bird sketch Ander had left in my notebook.

"No," I said at last. "Not really. I don't think…dating is for us."

A sharp inhale. "Are you dating Finn now?"

I drew circles within my circles. If that was the first thing Mom thought, it would be the first thing everyone else thought, too. "No. We're not dating. I wanted to come home, do some homework for that AP class I told you about. Finn was going home, too, and he decided to walk with me."

"Ander was okay with that?"

I stiffened. This should've been the part where I told her we broke up, but then it would also be the part where she'd be even more disappointed in me. "Why wouldn't he be?"

Mom twisted her wedding ring back and forth. "I would've thought *Ander* would walk you home. He's such a nice boy, Grace. I was so happy when you two found each other. Ever since you were little, you were never apart."

I focused on my drawing, pretended it was someone else's heart banging against my ribs like a gorilla in a cage. "We're still friends, Mom."

She covered my hand with hers. "I really hope you two work it out. I think he's good for you. He brings you out of your shell. Jem can't always be there for you."

"I know."

"I met your dad in high school. Love finds you when it finds you, but you have to recognize it." Mom's sudden laugh is soap-bubble bright. "I wanted to think Ander would be the reason you'll come home after you go away to that fancy school—or maybe that you'll decide not to go at all. I don't understand why you can't get a job here. It's not like you know what you want to do with yourself."

It was true, and it still made my teeth grind. There was nothing I could say—no, nothing I knew how to say that would make this any better.

Her fingers *tap, tap, tap* again. "Do you really want to give up someone like him for something…something like school?"

"I'm not giving him up." Was I? I pressed the tip of my pen into my notebook page until it dug a tiny hole. Was I giving them up, too? My family?

Because it suddenly felt like it. Worse, that was how Mom and Jem saw it. I was deserting them.

"Are you scared you'll have regrets?" She squeezed my

hand, squeezed it again. "Did your dad scare you?"

"It's not like that. Dad didn't say anything I haven't thought about. He—" I snapped my mouth shut. By defending Dad, I made Mom feel worse. Her eyes wrinkled at their edges.

"Aren't you happy?" she whispered.

"No." And it sounds so simple when I put it like that. I put down my pencil. "I have no idea how to get back to being happy."

She was waiting for more explanation, and I didn't have any. How could I explain there was a shadow space inside me? A gap behind my soul? I felt like I was missing something important. It was like walking into my bedroom to get something and suddenly forgetting what it was.

You're supposed to stand there until the memory returns, except with this…it doesn't.

Mom sniffled. "Please don't throw us away because you don't know what you want. Your family will always be here, but Ander? He won't be. Please don't hurt him."

I didn't say anything. I couldn't.

"Love is hard, honey." Mom stared at the kitchen wall, and for a heartbeat, I was six again and she'd just found out her dad died. "You have to work at it."

"I'm *seventeen*, Mom. Don't you think it's a little early for marriage talk?"

"Who said anything about marriage?"

I faltered. She hadn't. She'd meant it, though. I knew she did. "You think just because you met Dad at seventeen, it'll be like that for everyone. It's not."

And I regretted even bringing it up, because now we were both thinking about how Dad regretted the way his life had turned out. Mom might have hurt me by always siding with Ander, but I had just wounded her far worse.

She pushed both hands into the tabletop and stood.

"Honey, you will give your life to become who you are, so make sure it's worth it. Make sure you don't look back and realize you became someone you thought you wanted to be rather than staying true to the person you are."

For a second, I hated her. I hated her because she was wrong. But I hated her more because she was also right.

*I* got up the next morning expecting to see Ander on our doorstep.

He wasn't.

I pushed the screen door wider, scanning the backyard for his blond head moving past the kudzu, his flash of red T-shirt, but there was nothing. Was this our new normal?

"He's going to give you some space for a bit."

I turned to Jem. I hadn't heard him come home last night, let alone get up that morning.

"Space?" I asked.

He nodded.

"Are you mad?" Ander was his friend, too. If he was giving me "space," Jem was also affected.

"Don't overthink it."

"I'm not overthinking anything." Except of course I was, and it only got worse as Jem talked about how Ander was going to start third shift at the mill on Monday. Then it got worse again as I realized we would be on opposite schedules, wouldn't see each other at all.

It shouldn't have felt like a gut punch.

"How long did you know about the third-shift job?" I finally asked, watching Jem pour cereal into a bowl.

"About a week."

My mouth hung open. Jem had known for a week and hadn't told me? *Ander* had known and hadn't told me? "We'll never see him! Why didn't you say anything?"

"Because he didn't want you to know!" Jem shrugged, keeping his attention trained on his breakfast. "What do you want me to say?"

That he was sorry. That he didn't mean to put Ander first. That I was his sister, his *twin*.

And that was when I realized, in this moment, being Jem's sister meant more to me than it did to him. Jem had put his best friend before me, and it hurt. But under the hurt was something worse because I was just as bad: I was going to put Alton before Jem.

Wasn't I?

"I have to pick up my soccer stuff from school," Jem said, still not looking up. From this angle, the part through his hair was a jagged lightning bolt. "Come with me?"

He said it like everything was normal, and if he could pretend, then so could I.

"Don't I always come?"

He grinned. I grinned. We drove to Boone High, talking about Jem's last year playing soccer and Callie's upcoming birthday, and it almost felt right.

Almost.

At school, Jem left me by the front entrance while he went to find Coach Daley. It wasn't even nine in the morning, and it was already crazy hot. The grass and trees were crispy. The cicadas had already begun to whine.

I lay on top of one of the splintery picnic tables, waiting and sweating, and somehow I felt him before I saw him. He took a whole minute before saying, "Hey."

Finn. I sat up. "Hey."

"What are you doing here?"

"Waiting on Jem. He had to pick up his soccer uniform. You?"

His mouth twisted. "Had to pick up the last of my enrollment paperwork. Want me to wait with you?"

I nodded and scooted over, making enough space for him, and yet when Finn sat down, our shoulders still brushed. Something I did not want to name cartwheeled through my stomach.

"I heard you and Ander called it quits," he said, shifting his file folder of paperwork from one hand to the other.

"Yeah."

"That's hard."

"Yeah." I concentrated on the tops of my tennis shoes, how a thin film of yellow pollen covered the white. "It ruined everything—us getting together."

"That's not what ruined it." Finn shifted quickly, and I looked over, startled. We studied each other, only inches apart. "You know he's imploding, right? You won't be able to stop it. People don't need water to drown."

The entrance doors *swooshed* open, and I turned away, unable to decide if my stupid, galloping heart meant I was grateful for the distraction.

Or if I agreed with Finn.

Tisha and Callie stepped into the sunshine. Callie had her cheerleading uniform under one arm and was leaning into her sister with a laugh that belonged to Jem. She must've seen him in the hallway. He always made her sound lighter, like the world was more than the world.

The pair made it about four feet before Tisha noticed Finn sitting next to me. Her smile turned liquid.

"Hey!"

He lifted his chin. "'Sup?"

"Nothing. You?"

He gestured toward me. "Talking to Grace."

Tisha blinked like she'd only just now noticed me. She probably had. When Finn was around, he was all girls saw.

*Remember that*, I told myself. *This is his effect. Don't be that girl.*

"Oh. Hey, Grace." She played with one of her dangly earrings. "Y'all coming tonight? It's going—"

"Of course they're coming," Callie said, tugging her sister away. "Let's go. I'm going to be late!"

Tisha wilted but followed her. "You have to come, Finn." She walked backward toward the parking lot. Humid wind swirled her ponytail. "You promised."

"Wouldn't miss it."

She beamed, completely missing how his tone was flat.

Or maybe she didn't. Because Tisha tucked close to her sister, whispering. They pulled out of the parking lot in a squat yellow Hyundai that trailed a ribbon of pale smoke.

I glanced at Finn. "You and Tisha, huh?"

"Tisha and me."

"She's nice."

He watched their blue smoke trail rise. "Is she? Y'all hang out that much?"

"Is Ass just your default setting or what?"

His ears went pink. "Sorry."

"No, you're not."

A pause. Finn's jaw clenched and unclenched. "I'm not actually *with* her. I'm just…" He took a shaky breath and then another, and when the words finally came they were only a blur: "Youwanttogooutsometime?"

"*What?*"

"Please don't make me spell it out."

I sounded like I was sucking air through a straw, and his expression turned agonized.

"Every time I talk to you, I want more. I want to know what you think about everything and that's insane because before you I didn't care about what any girl thought."

"That's because you're an ass."

"And when you say it…I actually hate that it's true."

"That's…that's not nearly as flattering as you think."

Finn swore and rubbed his face with both hands. "I know. I *know*, all right?"

*Leave*, I told myself. But I was cemented to the picnic table. I picked at a loose thread on my shorts so I wouldn't have to meet his eyes. "I can't."

Finn shifted, and the boards underneath us creaked. "Why?"

"I'm not going to be another groupie for you, and I'm *not* going to be the girl who kisses all her brother's friends."

"You won't go out with me because you're worried what people are going to say? Don't worry about them."

"It's different for you."

"Is it?"

I wouldn't look at him. If I looked at him, I didn't know what I would say. No, a lie. I was afraid of what I *would* say. We wanted each other, and we shouldn't.

"We're not good for each other," I whispered.

Another shift. Another creak. "Grace," Finn managed, turning my name rough. "I want to see where this could go."

I closed my eyes and saw Ander, Alton, my mom. I opened them. "I already know where it'll go."

"Grace?"

Finn and I turned. My brother pushed through the double doors, Ander right behind him. His gaze slid from Finn to me and back again.

"I thought you were finishing at Farley's," I said.

Ander shrugged. "I had to sign the final papers to withdraw.

Thought I'd say hi."

I climbed to my feet, brushing off my shorts because I needed something to do with my hands. When I looked up, Ander stood close enough to touch his boots to my sneakers.

"Hi," I whispered.

"Hi," he said.

Behind us, Jem's voice raised. He wanted Finn to come out tonight. I was catching words like "Callie" and "birthday," but there was something a little too bright to Jem's tone, a little too forced. Ander and I weren't the only ones who were miserable.

Ander winced like he knew it.

"I saw the *Psycho* remake last night," he said.

"Yeah?"

"Right after I finished it, I wanted to call you. I wanted to know what you thought about it." Ander's sudden laugh was more like a puff of air. "That's the problem with dating—and breaking up with—your best friend. I keep reaching for you… and you're not there."

"I get that." Another problem with dating—and breaking up with—your best friend: he knew exactly how you felt. Ander and Jem made me feel real in the world, like I actually existed.

Behind Ander, Finn strode off, dragging something inside me after him. He didn't look back, and I was suddenly and stupidly grateful. I focused on Ander, and I tried to swallow past the thickness in my throat.

He was my best friend, and we didn't fit anymore. When did that happen, anyway? In movies and books, there was always that moment you could point to and say, "That's where it went pear-shaped."

But we didn't have that.

Or maybe I didn't want to see it.

He gave me a halfway smile. He picked at one fingernail, and I couldn't stop noticing how there weren't paint stains on his hands anymore. We weren't the only thing that was over in Ander's life.

"Jem's mad as hell," he said. "He thinks I've ruined everything."

Hadn't he? I hesitated. We were ruined, but our friendship? No, I realized, and the realization settled somewhere underneath my bones. We weren't ruined if I said we weren't. I could do that for Jem, couldn't I? I could just look past what happened. The three of us could pretend it never happened.

We could go back to the way things were.

It was the right answer. I knew it as soon as I said it, as soon as Ander grinned. Right answers usually had a way of making me feel full, but this time I went hollow.

*now...*

*I* stumble after him, feeling Mom and Dad watching me. Ander strides into our front yard like he owns the place. Like he knows what's going on.

And I begin to shake.

The truck is parked beneath a drooping water oak, its limbs slender as ribs. Ander speeds up, almost breaking into a jog. "You coming?" he asks.

I am. Of course I am. It's the fifth day and we always run. Except...except...

I slow. Stop. "Ander?"

"Yeah?" He turns, and sunlight slices through his hair, turning the strands to silver.

"What day is it?"

His brows climb an inch. "Saturday."

Chills crawl across me. Not the fifth day. Not the day we Fall. Just...Saturday.

Wait.

I fumble with my cell, running my thumb over the keypad. Ander's right: it's Saturday. It should be Wednesday. I check the screen twice, a third time, and finally push it deep into my pocket.

"We good?" Ander walks around the truck and climbs in.

I hesitate. We are *so* not good. This isn't my Ander. He's close. Clos*er*. But he isn't mine. It's like I Fell again, and I didn't. The house is the same, but the colors are different. The truck looks right, but the bumper is smashed. My cell is exactly the same, but the date has changed.

And Jem is gone.

My brother is *gone*.

I can't breathe again. Behind me, the screen door *swish-creaks* and I stiffen. Mom or Dad or both of them must have stepped onto the porch to watch us.

*Get going.* I push one foot forward and then the other, concentrate on my tennis shoes until I'm at the truck door. I'm wheezy like I've been running, and all I can think is: *we have to get out of here.*

But it's blotted out by: *he'll never believe me.*

He'll *never* believe me. What do I do?

Ander doesn't say a word as I step myself slowly through climbing into the truck cab and fitting the key to the ignition. The ancient Ford had always been Jem's territory, and when I fit my hands to the steering wheel, my fingers look exactly like his fingers.

Tears flash into my eyes. Is this all that will be left of him? *You know how this ends.*

I suck in a breath and then another. Does that mean I made it happen? If I did, I could fix it. I *have* to fix it.

"Grace?" Ander shifts in his seat to face me. "Are you okay?"

I press my lips together, shake my head.

"What's wrong?" he asks.

More tears. *He doesn't know. He doesn't know. I lost Jem,*

*and Ander still doesn't remember and Finn is still coming…
right?* "What if I wanted to drive to Mexico right now?"

He laughs. "Would kind of interfere with my work
tonight—you're shaking."

I nod.

"C'mon." His tone turns low, reassuring, and it pulls
something so deep inside me, it might have reached back to
that first afternoon when we crawled into the dark. Except I'm
the only one who remembers that anymore. "Let's take a walk."

*What?* I blink, blink again. *Are we together again? Are we?*
I hold the thoughts under until they stop kicking. "A walk?"

"Yeah, it's this thing you do with your feet…"

I laugh. I almost can't believe it, but I do.

Ander grins. "I love that sound. Always have."

I force my fingers to loosen, just now realizing I'm white-
knuckling the steering wheel. Ander was the boy who loved
my laugh. Who made me feel like myself. Who trapped me in
this truck. I shake off the memory. It isn't about the mistakes
you made, right? It's about who stuck with you.

Something brushes my hand. I glance down, but there's
nothing. Ander's attention is pinned to the hazy horizon,
where vultures circle something only they can see. He didn't
touch me.

But someone did. It felt like fingertips.

"Walk where?" I finally ask.

There's a smile in his voice as he says, "The woods."


The woods around this house are weedy and sparse—a bunch
of juvenile pine trees that eventually creep into thicker, older
forest. Everything smells like wet earth and wetter leaves.

*Rotting* leaves. I brush one hand against my nose and smell mud. I stare at my skin. It's clean. No dirt. No mud. No blood.

To my left, someone gasps.

I spin sideways. The gasp sounded like *me*.

"What are you doing?" Ander has that half-assembled smile again. It makes me shake—or was that the gasp? It was so small, and yet it's swallowed me whole. "Did you hear something?"

"No." *Yes*. I turn, slowly scanning the trees, the sweeps of kudzu. Their leaves hang down in electric-green curtains. No one else is here. It's just us.

*It's just us*. It coats my arms in chills.

And then I smell blood.

The air goes close, humid. *You know how this ends*.

I pass a clammy hand across my face. Except…except what else had Finn said? Briefly, I can't resurrect it and then the memory surfaces, buries its face against my stomach and wraps both arms around my waist: *this is you. It's all you, Grace*.

I take two quick steps to Ander's side. He grins, slinging one arm around my shoulders. "Talk to me."

I do, and he talks to me, and it should be a verbal minefield, but in some ways, this is stupid easy. It's almost like picking up where we left off in our real lives.

This Ander loves my laugh.

This Ander paints in oils and works on cars.

This Ander is not my Ander. He doesn't remember me like I remember him, but he likes me. We're friends. We could start over. I know all the right things to say.

*I could make him love me*. Off in the trees, a bird cries twice and goes silent. The whole forest feels like its holding its breath.

"I miss you," Ander says. "Don't leave me again, okay?"

The hair along my arms stands up straight. Leave him

again? I've never left him. In my real life, I had never been the kind of girl who fell in love. I didn't have crushes. I didn't have my wedding planned. I mean, I might have sort of figured it would happen—and I might've smothered the worry that it *wouldn't* happen because weddings were a Big Deal to our mom—but I assumed forever love would be later. Much later.

Maybe that was why I didn't recognize that forever was standing right in front of me. I didn't recognize Ander for who he was. Everyone else knew. They recognized it.

But I didn't.

It was only after the Falls began that we reached for each other instead of everything else. The reminder settles me. If I'm in control, I can choose to stay. I can choose to make this work.

I haven't said a word, but Ander offers me his upturned hand like he can read my mind, like we are in our old lives before everything went wrong.

A branch snaps to my right.

"Grace!"

I jerk, wheel around in a small circle. There are only trees and bushes and spider webs, but that was *Finn* calling my name.

Ander gapes. "Are you okay?"

"*No!* Did you hear that?"

"Hear what?"

The footsteps are running through the woods now. I turn and turn and see nothing. Trees are all around us—closer than before? I can't tell. Their leaves make shivery sounds in the breeze, and the footsteps crash through the underbrush.

They sound like us. They sound like we did during the last Fall.

Oh God. We're Falling. Finn is close. He's coming for us.

Ander steps to me, and I lift my face to his because this

is us. My heart should stumble.

And it doesn't.

"I know you can hear me, Grace."

Finn again. I wheel around. Impossible. It's *impossible*. He's close enough he can hear me, but I can't see him?

"Grace?" Now it's Ander. I turn, and his eyes track my face, my body, my mouth. He smiles, and my smile falters. My Ander looked at me like we were in on the same joke. This Ander looks at me like he can see me naked.

He's not the same. The boy I loved is not the boy standing next to me. I could *make* him into the boy I loved, but it would be wrong. Manipulative.

I take a deep breath and it catches in my throat. We're not the same. Everything we had is gone. All those years… all those memories…

*Time is not an accurate measurement for love*. It's like Finn's sitting next to me and for less than a second, I'm not standing next to Ander. I'm on that road again, walking back to my house.

*You can be with someone for a year and feel nothing. You can be with someone for a week and feel everything. Time is not an accurate measurement for love.*

And when I open my eyes again, Ander's gone.

I spin, still watching the trees. The ground should be hard under my feet, but it feels like it's softening, turning to mud. Am I Falling? I can't Fall. I can't keep *doing* this. I can't be a thousand more Graces.

All around me the woods go quiet. Still. The breeze disappears. The leaves stop brushing against each other. The only thing left now is my breathing: uneven, shallow.

Then comes the crashing.

I tense. Finn? No. It's too heavy to be Finn, way heavier than the earlier footsteps. Far off, too. To my left? No. My right. I turn and hear roots rip up from the dirt. A tree slams to the ground in a crackle of breaking limbs.

I stumble backward. Whatever it is, it's coming fast.

Coming straight at me.

I turn back the way we came, running with everything I have, and it's still not fast enough. The branch snaps are closer. The footsteps are heavier. I'm being hunted.

I push myself harder, lifting my knees and ripping past the underbrush with my brain stuck on a loop: Jem is gone. Ander is gone. My life as I know it is gone. Forever. All that's left is…me.

All that's left is me.

Crooked beams of sunlight pierce the briars ahead of me, and I plunge through them, hitting my backyard's grass at a dead run. The lawn is bright, but the edge of my vision has gone gray. Black.

I can't get enough air. Everything smudges in and out of focus.

That's when I see Dad. He's coming up from the boat dock, and I know who's with him.

Even from here, I can see those cat-yellow eyes staring out of that beautiful face.

I was supposed to be running from Finn. Now I'm running straight to him.

# chapter thirty-five

*then...*

When we got home from school, the mail had come. I didn't know because I'd seen the white-and-blue Jeep trundle away from our mailbox. I knew it because there were fresh bills on the table. And I didn't know Alton had finally returned my application, because I saw the cream-colored envelope. I knew it because the school's answer was written on my mother's face. Her eyes skittered around and around the kitchen like she was searching for something that had vanished.

Ander hovered in the kitchen door as Jem dumped his uniform onto the table. "Mom?"

She ignored him, wordlessly passing Alton's letter to me. I'd gotten in. A full ride. An opportunity. My hands began to shake.

*You will be a charity case, a pet project.*
*An Alton grad.*

It will be just a plastic seal on a paper diploma, but it will mean so much more. No one will ever be able to take it.

My hands shook harder.

"You should call your father," Mom said, every word sounding pushed. "He'll want to know."

*Yeah. Yeah, definitely.* And yet I was pasted to the floor. I held my letter tighter. "Mom?"

"I'm happy for you. Truly." She smiled, and we both knew she was lying. "I just need a minute to get used to the idea."

"C'mon," Jem breathed, digging his fingers into my arm. He hauled me toward the living room, and Ander followed.

I tipped into the armchair by the door. I didn't trust my legs. I felt like I was going to shiver into a thousand pieces.

"Hold on." Jem ducked back into the kitchen—to her—and for several moments there was only the muffled *wah, wah, wah* of a conversation I wasn't supposed to hear and yet was all about me. It made my shaking worse.

Ander slumped into the chair next to me, and for a heartbeat, it wasn't today anymore. It was two months ago. Two years ago. It was so familiar it felt like something that belonged to me as closely as my bones and breath.

"Congrats, I guess," he said at last.

I nodded.

"We should celebrate."

"How?"

"Jem wants to go down to the Hollows tonight."

"Let him."

"He wants us to go *with* him."

"Too many people," I muttered. I was only half listening. I couldn't stop concentrating on how the water had turned on in the kitchen. My mom was trying to hide her crying.

Ander's fingertips found the curve of my hand, and we both froze. "It'll be good for you."

"Watching him make out with Callie is good for me?"

"You know how he is, Grace." He watched me, and I couldn't separate his steady stare from the best friend I'd known my whole life and the boy I'd kissed and the boy who'd scared me.

If I knew then what I knew now…would I still have wanted him? Kissed him? Because I had been wrong—I couldn't go back. *We* couldn't go back. I couldn't see him the same way. He wasn't a stranger, but he wasn't my Ander anymore, either. We had broken something that we didn't realize was even breakable until it was done.

"Just give him this one last party," Ander added, something bitter leaking into his tone. "You're going away. We all know this is over. You could at least pretend it bothers you."

"It *does* bother me. Stop acting like it—"

He jerked away. It left my side to cool, like his absence had a shape. Maybe it did. I was losing my best friend, my brother, my life. All my decisions led up to this.

"Just come hang with us trash for a while, okay?" His smile cracks his face open, exposes all his teeth.

I gaped. "Where do you get off? You're not *trash*. I've *never* said you're trash."

"And yet you're getting as far away from us as you can. Face it, Grace, we're not like you. Not with that big brain."

"My brain isn't that big." Only as soon as I said it, I felt stupid. Stupider. In the kitchen, the water poured on and on, and Jem's voice was still an indistinct murmur. "I work really hard for my grades. I'm not some genius. Remember when I screwed up that English project? I had to ask for a redo."

"And you got the only A in the whole class."

"After I spent almost sixteen hours on the stupid thing." Just remembering how I'd had to ask Mr. Ellison for another shot made my stomach turn cold and greasy. I never held myself up as some genius, and I *hated* listing my faults to make Ander feel better. He was hurting. I knew he was hurting. We were friends.

Had been friends?

The distinction almost didn't matter anymore. I glared at Ander, and he glared right back. Either way, we both knew how to wound each other.

He sighed, looked at the floor. "Sorry."

"Whatever." It was the only thing I trusted myself enough to say.

"He's like my brother, too."

In the kitchen, someone laughed, and my heart swung high. Mom. The water slowed…stopped. Jem had done that. The way he handled people was a little like magic. The way he handled *me* was a little like magic.

And I was leaving him.

Seconds later, Jem ducked through the doorway, dashing dark hair away from his forehead. "You're coming, right? To the Hollows?"

He looked at me and for the very first time ever, there was something awkward between us. Once upon a time, Jem would never have bothered to ask. He would've simply assumed, but now…

I nodded. "'Course."

*A*fter dinner, we waited for Jem by the truck. Somewhere in the swamp, honeysuckle bloomed, turning everything sticky sweet. In the shadows under the trees, something rustled through brittle leaves.

"Ready?" Jem asked, jumping down the stairs. He didn't stop for an answer. The three of us crammed into the truck and didn't talk about Alton. We didn't talk about anything. It could've been because Ander and I were mad at each other, but it also could've been because Jem was focused on Mom.

He kept his attention trained on the road, and his thoughts to himself. Honestly? It was a relief.

Until we swung past the turnoff for the Hollows.

We sped past two cars pulled to the roadside. Tourists stood in the long grass by the river, taking pictures. I didn't blame them. In the distance, the bridge was a skeleton spine curving for the lowering sun.

"I thought we were going to the Hollows," I said to Jem.

He shifted into third as we neared the bridge, and the truck stuttered. "Pregame at Amanda's."

Ander made some noise deep in his chest, and they exchanged a knowing look. Finn's cousin was one of Callie's best friends, a rising junior who lived at the edge of the river in a blinding white farmhouse her parents repainted every year. Her parties were legendary, and by the time we arrived, there must've been twenty cars parked on the lawn, most of them crowded too closely. Callie's Jeep was there. So was Finn's peeling Civic.

It made my chest loosen for a nanosecond before I remembered it shouldn't.

Jem parked us next to Tisha's Hyundai. Ander popped out first, and I followed him. The sky was everywhere, a vaulted ceiling of stars. We wandered up a lawn so thick it felt like carpet and smelled like clover. Some guy in a dirty white visor waited for Ander on the front porch. They managed to bro hug without touching more than each other's shoulders and went inside. Cheers went up, and my feet slowed.

Jem bumped into me. "Seriously?"

I couldn't answer.

He ran both hands through his hair. "Don't let it bother you so much. Grace…you could have all of this if you wanted it."

*But I don't want it.* The thought was clear and cold and entirely in my voice. *I don't want it.*

And something must've shifted in my face, because his expression sagged. The moonlight caught his grimace and turned it into an ugly slash of shadows.

"I can't believe you actually care what they think," he spat.

"It's not—"

"Why do they matter and I don't?"

I gaped. "What?"

"You didn't think anything of taking off on me, did you?"

I gasped and Jem swore again, looking away. He rubbed his eyes like they burned.

"I'm sorry," he said at last.

I studied my feet. "Sorry" was all we said these days, and it was always in that same tone, too, like we shoved the word off a cliff.

Jem thumped my arm. "I'm *sorry*. Forget I said that, okay? It's been a crappy night."

Because of me. I nodded, barely able to swallow around the tightness in my throat.

"Is this what you really want?"

"I want to try—you're always telling me to push myself. Maybe this is my chance."

Jem exhaled like I'd punched him. "I don't want…"

"Exactly."

"Because—"

"I know." And I did and he knew it and for the first time in so so *so* long, we really smiled at each other. "Everything feels so different now."

"Yeah."

"I don't want it to be."

Jem thought for a moment; a grin dragged slowly across his mouth. "I don't think we get a choice, but maybe we could choose to ignore the differences. I'll look at you and just… see you."

Hot tears pricked my eyes.

"And if you don't like it," he added, "I'll come get you."

More tears. The world went smeary. "I'm counting on it."

Jem searched my face. "Are you here because you want to be?"

I sniffled, almost laughed. I thought about telling him no, about asking Jem to take me home now. He would. But if he was trying to be the right brother for me, I could try to be the right sister for him. I lifted my chin. "I'm good. I'm okay."

Inside, there was more cheering, and Jem's expression screwed tight. "I don't know who I am without you."

"You'll do great," I said. "You won't have to drag me along behind you."

"I drag you along because I want you there."

Amazing how it made me feel illuminated, like I swallowed a star, like it really would be okay. "I don't know who I am without you either, Jem."

He shook his head. "Guess we're going to find out."

An hour later, I hovered in Amanda's white living room. It was looking less white and more spotted by the minute. There were bright orange handprints on the velvety couch. Cheetos?

The white lights threaded through the rafters kept blinking off and on, and the music was loud enough to make the floorboards vibrate. Callie and Hannah were dancing. Well, trying to dance. It was rap, and they were way off beat, but it seemed to make the whole thing funnier. They slumped against each other like folded-over pillows, their laughter silent against the deafening bass line.

Was this what I would feel like without Ander and Jem? I skirted the living room. Maybe I could find a bathroom to hide in. Maybe—

"I need you to fix this." Amanda planted both hands on her hips, stood there like Wonder Woman with straight-ironed hair.

My insides rocked to my feet. "Fix what?"

"Your boyfriend. He's puking everywhere. Get him out of my bathroom *now*."

"He's not—" I stopped and nodded. Ander wasn't my boyfriend. He was my friend, though, and even if we weren't going to be friends past tonight, we had history.

She stalked past me, and I wound my way back through the kitchen. People were throwing their empty beer cans into the oven, and briefly, I felt bad for Amanda, because even if she cleaned everywhere, I was pretty sure she wouldn't think to check inside the oven.

"Have you seen Ander?" I asked one of the guys.

He shrugged.

*These are the people who will care for him once you're gone.* I held the thought under until it drowned.

It took another minute of circling the downstairs before I found Ander. He was on his knees, forehead resting on his forearms, forearms resting on the toilet seat.

"Hey," I whispered, stepping inside and closing the bathroom door. "So we're both hiding in bathrooms now?"

Without looking up, he locked his fingers around mine and tugged me closer. For a heartbeat, I resisted. This was too much.

It was too sad and too familiar.

No, that wasn't right, because when I looked at Ander again, I didn't see how this was the second time in two weeks, I just saw *him*. We had always been together. I never learned how to love anyone else because he was there and I was there and we had the kind of history that predicted the future. I couldn't break him without breaking me.

Which also meant I knew what to do.

I hooked his arm over my shoulders, taking a deep breath of boy and booze and vomit. He shrugged me off so he could puke again and I sat down hard, legs buckling on the tile.

"Do you think you could make it to the truck? We could go home."

He shook his head. "I don't want to go home."

"Our house?"

His smile was tired. "I don't want to go there, either."

"Then…what do you want?"

He didn't answer, but his breathing hitched.

"Why do you do this to yourself?" I whispered.

"I need the click."

"The click?"

He nodded slowly, his forearm flexing against the toilet seat. "When the edge comes off—the click, you know?"

I didn't. Or maybe I did. Maybe we were all looking for that one thing that takes us out of being ourselves—even if it was just for a moment.

"It's like I'm not here anymore," he added.

"Is that what you want? To vanish?"

His expression turned into something that never used to belong to us. "Don't play therapist. You're no better. We're all running away from something."

"I'm not running away."

"You really believe that?"

The anger snaking through his tone kicked all the air right out of me. The question was ugly and quiet and…a little right.

My mom was right. I would give up my life becoming me. Whoever I ended up being, that version of me needed to be worth it. She was wrong, too, though. The only thing scarier than taking risks was not taking any at all.

I thought being with Ander was honest. I thought I was

myself around him.

But I never gave away anything I couldn't afford to lose.

Someone beat a fist against the door. "Hurry up!"

I flinched. I didn't recognize the voice—I half hoped it was Finn, but it wasn't. Whoever was outside was pissed. Maybe Amanda had sicced one of her cousins on us.

"Out"—I tugged Ander's arm—"out in a minute."

The guy grabbed the door handle. It rattled, and I froze. I couldn't get Ander up.

*What do I do?*

The door handle jerked once more, stopped. Ander heaved into the toilet again, spewed.

After seconds that felt closer to years, he tilted to his side and studied me. "I would do anything to be your everything," he whispered.

His fingers twitched. Was he going to reach for me?

He was.

Ander lifted one hand, palm upturned. "Grace…"

# chapter thirty-six

*now...*

Briefly, I think about taking off and driving as far as the truck will get. After that, I can run. After that, I can crawl.

I force myself to stand still instead. Finn and Dad stroll toward me like this is any other day.

*You know how this ends.* This time it isn't Finn's voice in my head. It's Ander's. His long-ago whisper breathes up from the grave.

Dad hesitates for a beat before veering toward the house. The screen door slaps closed behind him. We're alone.

This is how the Fall begins.

Finn moves closer, and it takes everything I have to stand my ground—and that's when I notice his expression. He doesn't look focused this time. He seems off. Wary.

Wrong.

*Well, everything else is, too.* I push up my chin. "Here to start the chase?"

"No." He circles me, his long shadow seeking mine.

I turn and turn to keep him in my sights. "Why not?"

"Because you don't want me to."

Chills. I keep turning. "Jem's gone. Again. And my parents aren't my parents. Ander's back. Was back. We're together again—almost like we used to be."

"Almost?"

"He reminds me of the way we used to be. Like coming home, only it's someone else's home. I'm done pretending. I'm done taking other people's lives. I'm *done*, Finn."

"Why do you think it's always us, Grace?" A cloud shifts against the sun, carving Finn into something made of orange-red sunlight and dusky shadows. "Why is it always the three of us Falling again and again?"

"We're just lucky."

He shakes his head and sighs. "Don't do that."

"What? You want me to explain why this is happening? News flash, genius, I don't know. It's not like there was a manual."

His smile is faint.

"*What?*"

"You called me 'genius.'"

"Well, you are, aren't you? I might have forgotten everything else, but in our real lives you were pretty adamant none of us would forget it."

He bites his lower lip, studying me with something that nudges dangerously close to hope in his eyes. "What else? What do you remember about the first night we Fell?"

"We were all at Amanda's. Ander drank too much, and she wanted me to take care of him."

"And?"

"He was sick." Funny how saying it out loud turns the words smooth. I sound like I'm practicing a school presentation in the bathroom. "But he reached for me…and I took his hand."

At first, I think Finn's holding himself still, and then I

realize he isn't still at all. He's vibrating. He looks as if he will shake into a thousand pieces.

"You took Ander's hand?" he echoes.

"I took his hand and we Fell. It was like a blink."

There's heat rolling off Finn now, like he's feverish.

Like I am burning him alive.

I force myself on. "When I woke up, I was in another bathroom. My dad had run off, and I lived in an apartment above the hardware store and you were gone until…"

*Until the fifth day.* I wait for Finn to respond. I wait and I wait and he says *nothing*.

"Look." I take a deep breath and still feel hollow. "Just tell me what I have to do to fix this."

He jerks left and I step back and suddenly we're pressed together. "Please," he begs. "*Remember.*"

*Begs? Finn doesn't beg.* I struggle and he follows me, holding my wrists harder—hard enough to edge into hurt.

"I'm right here, Grace. I'm not leaving, but you have to remember."

But I *do* remember. I do.

Finn puts his forehead to mine and I look into his eyes and quite suddenly…

# chapter thirty-seven

*then...*

Ander's fingers twitched. Was he going to reach for me?

He was.

Ander lifted one hand, palm upturned. "Grace..." he said, like my name was salvation.

Like I was *his* salvation.

"I'm not what you need. I'm not enough."

His mouth thinned. He didn't believe me, but I was right. He was my best friend, and I was going to have to watch him drown.

"I can't save you," I whispered, taking a step back. "I never could."

Another step back.

"*Grace.*"

"Good-bye, Ander." I tugged the door open, and it nearly smashes me in the face.

The boy on the other side stumbled into the bathroom. "What the—"

"Sorry!" I shoved past him and plunged down the hallway.

The music was even louder, and in the living room, someone shrieked. I tucked both arms around me and headed for the kitchen. Forget this. Forget *all* of it. I was done.

The hallway gave way to the open kitchen. The windows were dark squares, and two guys were setting up a keg on the marble-topped island. Pregaming was turning into a full-blown party.

No Jem.

I took a Solo cup of beer so I would have something to do with my hands and turned right, pressing past a couple making out against the fridge. I checked the sunroom. No Jem. I checked the living room. No Jem.

I swung back through the kitchen, and someone bumped into me.

"Hey, Grace." Finn grinned at me, and I realized I was beginning to recognize his smiles. He had one for every occasion: to charm you, to make you feel smaller, to promise you something was coming.

Tonight, though…tonight I couldn't read it.

"Hey," I managed, lifting my drink and turning away. I needed to leave. I needed to find Jem. I worked my way through the house again, past the keg and the couches and the guy trying desperately to DJ, and ended up on the porch. No Jem. Maybe he'd passed out somewhere?

Maybe he'd shacked up with Callie/Angie/Melody?

The thought cemented me to the spot. If he was caught up, I was stuck. Maybe I should just take the truck and let him find his own way home?

Beyond the porch railing, the grass ran on and on until it hit the river, and I should've been startled Finn joined me, but I wasn't. I knew his footsteps better than I knew my own.

Finn leaned both arms against the porch railing and waited.

I took a sip of beer. It was swamp-water warm, and I nearly gagged. I took a longer swallow, then three more in rapid succession.

There.

Better.

"Slow down, okay? Whatever happened…it'll blow over. You'll get back together."

My fingers tightened around the cup. "Why does everyone expect that?"

"Because you and Ander are like some predestined thing." He made "predestined" sound like another word for disgusting.

Or maybe just wrong.

I agreed.

"We aren't predestined." I swirled what was left of my beer. "We're done. Everyone thinks holding on makes you strong, but I think letting go makes you stronger, and I'm letting go of this."

Finn's breathing shallowed. "Why now? What changed?"

"Everything." I finished my beer, forcing it past everything in me that was hot and hard and furious. So furious. "What if you gave someone everything you are and it wasn't enough?"

Finn looked down at his Solo cup. "What if you gave someone everything you are and it isn't what she wants?"

There was a charge to his voice, a hair-raising hum that turned each word electric.

*Why are you still looking at him?* No, better question: *Why are you* always *looking at him?*

Finn was an ass. He was freaking Mr. Darcy from *Pride and Prejudice* down here to judge all us rednecks. And the worst part? I agreed with him and I *hated* that about myself.

"Why are you doing this?" I whispered. It might have been the bravest thing I'd ever asked anyone. I had to force it through my teeth. "People like me are just a joke to you."

He tensed. "You aren't. I swear you would never be." He ran one hand through his hair, then across his jaw. "When I met you…you were everything I didn't want—*shouldn't* want."

The back of my skull prickled. Not because I had thought the same thing. Not because I had repeated the same words. Not. Not. Not. We were not alike. This was not destiny.

"Is that supposed to be a *compliment*?"

"No—I—*no*, I'm trying to be honest. Grace, I never wanted to come to Boone, and then I met you and…" Finn stopped, started, stopped again. He looked like he was sifting through everything he wanted to say and couldn't find any words for it. "If I hadn't come to Boone, I would never have met you and I know I would've missed that—missed *you*. I would never have known your name or your face, but I would've known the absence of you, the gap that was left in me because you were never there."

Now I started and stopped, and when Finn grabbed the railing on either side of me, something inside me unraveled—no, not unraveled.

Something between my second and third rib *uncurled*.

And stretched toward him.

"I think I know what you mean," I whispered at last, and it was my hand but not my hand that put down my cup. It was my fist but not my fist that knotted into his T-shirt. I was spinning above us, and he exhaled like I'd struck him. The sound crashed into me, and I waited for him to push me away.

He leaned closer.

"Finn?"

"Yeah?"

I slid my other hand up his chest. I needed to steady myself, and his T-shirt was so worn I could feel the planes of his chest, the heat of his skin. I was convinced I would burn.

"I want…"

I kissed him and he froze. Then he kissed me back and he kissed me harder, hands going to my neck, jaw.

"I've wanted this," he breathed against my mouth. "I wanted you to want this…"

"I do want it." And saying it out loud made his hands still. He stared at me like he couldn't believe it. "I want it so much it scares me."

"Me, too."

"Again," I whispered, pulling his mouth to mine. Finn's fingers dragged over my cheeks, touching me like he was learning me, like he was desperate.

I understood. I felt it, too.

He crushed me against the wall, and I let him. His hips pressed into my stomach and his hands cradled my face and somehow it still wasn't close enough. I pushed against him, fingers digging into his shoulders because my legs were gone.

"*Grace…*" My name sounded painful in his mouth, and I knew I must be a horrible person because it made me smile. I could get used to that. He made me powerful.

Then the party trickled in again. I heard the music…and then the laughter…and somehow I heard a gasp.

I turned, smiling like I was drunk, and realized *he* was there, watching us.

Ander.

# chapter
# thirty-eight

*I* inhale, taste…mint. I'm tasting Finn like we just kissed.
"I didn't choose Ander, did I?"

Finn shakes his head. "No."

"I chose you."

The wind picks up, dashing dark hair into his eyes, but he doesn't notice. His hands curve around my face, fingers touching my skin like he is learning me all over again. "After we Fell, I lost you. I lost the person you were. You didn't remember."

"Ander saw us. We had just broken up and I was kissing you and…"

Oh God.

Dead leaves whip past our feet, and somewhere in the house my mom calls my name. I start to turn, and Finn's hands wrap around my arms. He tugs me closer.

"It was always you, but you didn't exist because you didn't remember. Just like this Ander is not your Ander, you were not my Grace. You were a variation. All these worlds, all these timelines, and you were there…only you weren't *you*."

He looks at me like I'm supposed to say something, and I have nothing.

No, that's not right. I have all these memories:

Finn laughing with the sun behind him.

Finn telling me I could be anything.

Finn seeing me for who I am.

And how I saw Finn for who he was—the boy who was screaming on the inside, who thought his background would bury him alive.

"Grace!" My mom is on the porch, a green dish towel in her hands. "Come inside!"

Finn squeezes me. "You were Grace, but you weren't *my* Grace, and every time we Fell again I kept hoping you'd come back."

A few miles off, the tornado sirens begin to wail.

"Are you crazy?" My mom slaps her palm against the porch railing. "Come inside! Can't you hear the sirens?"

I glare at Finn, hair whipping into my eyes. "You thought you could bring me back by terrorizing me?"

He studies me carefully. The moment stretches so long, the hair on my arms stands up. Or maybe that's just from the oncoming storm. Pink lightning splits the clouds above the river.

"Is that what you really remember?" he asks at last.

"You killed Ander in every timeline, and I had to watch." The wind swirls my hair off my sweat-sticky neck. "Finn, you *know* this. You *remember*. You've known what's been going on this entire time."

He shakes his head. His face has gone tight like he's bracing for a blow, like I'm hurting him over and over, and I don't understand. I don't understand any of this.

"Are you *sure* that's what's happening?" he asks. "You remember me killing Ander?"

"It's pretty freaking vivid."

Only as soon as I say it, I wonder if it is.

"I remember all the running," I say slowly. "I remember the fear. I remember Ander begging me to stay away from you and you always being able to find us and then…"

We Fall.

We run. Ander collapses. We Fall. We repeat.

Cold snakes down my spine and settles in my gut. Does Finn actually kill Ander? Is that what happens?

Or is it just what I *think* happens?

"Grace!" Dad has joined my mom on the porch. They cling to each other. "Come inside! There's a storm coming!"

He's right. All around us the sunlight is going green.

"You really believe I had that kind of choice?" Finn asks. "You're the one who's hiding!"

Hot wind hurls my ponytail into the air. "Stop with the effing riddles, okay? Tell me the truth for *once*. What is this? Why're we Falling? Why would I put us through this hell?" Only as soon as I say it, I think I know and I begin to shake. "Am I dead? I have to be, right? This is hell."

Finn's eyes are huge and haunted. Nausea surges through me. So *that's* what this is? I'm going to spend eternity Falling? This is my punishment?

But for what?

What did I do to deserve it? Break up with Ander? Kiss Finn? Maybe it's for all the things I left undone, the things I should've done and didn't.

"So that makes you, what?" I ask, studying Finn. Shingles rip off the house's roof, go spinning into the air. "You're a figment of my imagination? My hell or whatever? That means what we have right now isn't real. What I feel for you…doesn't exist anymore."

"You believe that? You think death can destroy love?"

"All this is me, right?" I pan both hands to our swirling surroundings, but Finn's eyes never leave mine.

"You can be anything you want to be." It sounds more like a plea than a promise. He's said that before—in our real lives—and now he's saying it again and I can't separate what's just repetition and what's for real and what's just a fairy-tale dream I'm telling myself.

"I can't do this anymore. I can't take the Falls."

"Then finish it."

I go cold. Without even explaining, we both know what Finn means. Slowly—so slowly—he pulls the blade from his back pocket and flips it open. He offers me the knife. "Finish me."

"Grace!" Mom is screaming now. She's held back by my dad. Her nails make scrabbling noises on the railing as she tries to shake him off.

*They're not stepping off the porch. Why aren't they stepping off the porch?*

*Because something's coming.*

And somehow I know it's true. There's a rushing in the distance. It sounds like a tornado.

It feels like something worse.

Finn presses the knife into my palm once more. "Killing me is the only thing we haven't done."

I test the weight in my hand, and it feels familiar—no, it's more than familiar. The knife feels like mine. The handle curves into my palm, and when I place the blade to Finn's throat, he shudders. And yet he doesn't move.

*He wants me to do this.* I can't stop staring at how the edge bites into his skin. The thinnest trickle of blood slides down his throat, rippling as he swallows. *Can I take his life to stop this?*

No.

"I can't."

Finn grabs my wrist. "Please, Grace. The past wants to be heard, and sometimes you have to wait until it's done with you."

I jerk, and his grip tightens. "How do you know that? My *dad* said that to me."

I jerk again and still can't get away. I want to drop the knife, and I can't. I can't stop staring at Finn's face. Something's wrong. His features have gone funny. Slack. It's Finn, but it's not Finn.

And when he opens his mouth, it's as if something's speaking through him, like he's suddenly a puppet.

"Because here's the thing." His grip on my wrist digs the knife in deeper, and I yank against him. "You're a better person than I am. If I had to do it all over again, I would have let Ander fall. If you hadn't asked me to save him... I would never have done it."

I swallow. He doesn't make any sense. His words sound like they're stretching across lifetimes. They're impossibly far away.

"Grace!" Dad hurls Mom to one side. She's crying.

They're both crying.

"*Grace!*"

Above us, a flock of blackbirds screams past, and the far-off rushing turns into an oncoming train roar. The storm isn't coming. It's already here.

Finn steps closer and I smell water.

Blood.

I look right, left. *Nothing*. There's *nothing*. There's only Finn, only me. I can smell it, though. It's everywhere.

"Please," he whispers. It's so soft I should miss it. I could pretend I missed it, but I don't.

I look at him as something inside me drops an inch, and

then once more. "In every Fall, I held on to who I was by finding Ander. I'm holding on to something that doesn't exist, aren't I?"

He nods.

"I have to choose, don't I?"

"Do you—" His voice breaks, and he clears his throat. "Do you remember...anything else from that first Fall?"

No...*yes*. I walked away from Ander. I kissed Finn and Ander saw and then...and then...

It's like voices coming from another room. Someone begging for a knife. Someone else screaming for help. "I remember the river," I say. "And the blood...someone died."

Finn stiffens, and I know I'm right.

"Someone *died*." The wind whips up around us, spiraling roof shingles into the air and branches into the sky. The mom-who-isn't-my-mom screams for me, but I hold on to Finn.

Until my feet sweep out from underneath me and we're plummeting.

We're *falling*. I can't summon even enough breath to scream.

"Someone died," I whisper to Finn. "It was me."

# chapter thirty-nine

*then...*

"Nice." Ander's word escaped on a hard exhale. People backed away from him, nudging each other. Ander noticed, and when his eyes slid back to me, he smiled like we were in on the same joke. "I guess I don't have to worry about apologizing to you."

"Ander—"

He spun around, stumbling down the porch steps and into the dark, and I was chasing after him before I even realized.

Finn caught my arm. "Grace!"

I tried to shake him off, and Finn's grip tightened. "Let go!"

"*Grace!*"

"*What?*" I spun around, meeting Finn's eyes even though I knew I shouldn't because it would make the whole thing feel worse.

And it did.

He looked at me like I was breaking him by going after Ander. I had done this. No matter what I chose to do, I was going to hurt one of them.

"Let him go," he breathed. Everyone was whispering and

watching us, but Finn just pulled me closer. "Stay with me?"

*Yes. No.* "I can't."

"You can. Just…let him go."

I backed up and Finn followed me and I understood what he was saying, but it wasn't that simple. How could he *think* it was that simple?

"Stay." It was a plea, a prayer, and my feet slowed… stopped.

"Please stay," he whispered, and the whisper rubbed something inside me. I froze on the top porch step and realized he was right. I could stay. I *wanted* to stay. I couldn't save Ander. I never could.

Then, out in the dark, Jem's truck rattled to life.

Finn and I both tensed. We turned as the truck veered past the other cars, two people in the cab.

My heart lurched. Ander was *driving* and Jem was *next* to him. Neither of them should be driving. They were too drunk. They were too—

"Shit," Finn hissed as headlights bounced across the lawn.

I whirled on him. "We have to stop them!"

"You can't save him!" Finn's fingers were tight on my arm again. "The most you can do is call the police."

"It'll only make things worse! Please, Finn. *Please!* Get your car!"

He jerked forward like the word was a summoning, a spell. We clattered down the steps and past people slumping up the lawn toward the party. I ran across the grass and he followed me, his fingers touching the bumps of my spine.

"Over there," he said, nudging me toward the cars parked along the lawn. I flung myself into the passenger seat of Finn's Civic as he fumbled his keys into the ignition. He floored the car backward and then put it into drive, skidding us around two more couples heading to the house. When turned onto the main road, we had to be half a mile behind Ander. He was flying.

"Jesus," Finn muttered. "How fast is he going?"

Too fast. Ander wasn't just driving to get away. He drove like we were hunting him. I pressed both fists into my stomach. The road straightened, and Finn picked up speed. Forty miles an hour. Fifty.

"Is he heading for town?" I asked, watching the truck drift left. An oncoming car illuminated the cab. Ander and Jem were smudges in the light then the car passed and they went dark again. "Is he looking for the turnoff?"

Finn punched the gas again. "They'll spin out if they take the turn this fast."

Ahead of us, the truck wavered. It bounced a little as it curved off the road, and Ander righted it with a jerk. They roared forward, dust billowing across the headlights, across the road in front of them.

"Finn…he's going for the turn. If he hits the bridge going this fast…"

The truck bounced hard on a pothole, and Ander straightened it.

"Hit the brakes," Finn muttered. "Hit the fucking brakes."

Ander didn't hit the brakes. They had to be doing almost sixty and were still gaining speed. The taillights flashed as Ander briefly slowed. The truck veered right, skidding… skidding…forward again. They were heading for the bridge.

"Finn!" His name was somewhere between a moan and a sob.

He swore, jerking us through the turn. I braced one hand on the dash. The truck disappeared from view as our car slid. My shoulder rammed against the door as Finn hauled us around. We spun hard and straightened—

Just in time to see the truck speed onto the bridge.

It bounced, hitting the uneven concrete, and the force briefly dipped the truck low before the speed sent it skidding again. Another hard bounce—pothole?—and the truck was airborne.

*Ander and Jem* were airborne. And for a single second, they looked like they were flying, and I had an irrational hope they'd make it.

Then came the fall.

The truck slammed down and slid. The front end slammed into the barrier with a metallic crunch, and the red taillights lifted up like eyes.

They were going over.

Finn swore, sliding us to a stop on the grassy slope by the bridge. I grabbed for the door handle. Missed. Missed. Found it.

"Grace—"

I hit the ground running. The truck's horn blared. It went on and on like something was wedged against it.

Ander. Had to be. I ran to the railing. The truck's front tires dangled over the side, but the barrier had somehow impaled the undercarriage, pinning it.

"Jem!" I screamed. "Ander!"

Nothing. The flickering headlights illuminated the swamp water underneath us, and smoke snaked up from under the smashed hood. Everything smelled like burning oil.

"I need an ambulance!" Finn was behind me, shouting into his phone. Somehow, I could hear his footsteps above the truck horn, hear how his breathing had gone ragged. He'd thought to call 911. I hadn't. I couldn't think past Jem and Ander. Their names were heartbeats in my ears.

The passenger door was closest. If I could get to it, I could get to them.

I hooked one leg over the railing, and Finn hooked his

forearm around my middle, dragging me back. "Are you crazy? It could fall!"

"Exactly! Help won't get here in time! We have to get them out!"

His eyes swung from me to the road to the truck.

"You know I'm right. I'm lightest. Let me get close, get the door open, and you can help me pull them out."

Finn's grip tugged tight…and then loosened. He let me go, and I swung my leg over the barrier again, wavered on a concrete ledge just big enough for me to shuffle sideways. I kept one hand tight around the railing, crept two steps to my left, and then another two.

"Grace…"

I ignored him. Another few feet and I could almost reach the passenger door handle. Another foot and I grabbed it. I wrapped one hand around the metal handle and tugged. Nothing.

Through the cracked window, I heard someone moan.

"Ander? Jem?" I tugged harder, linking my other arm around the mangled railing. The door suddenly gave. Jem was sagged against the dashboard, and across from him, Ander stirred, one palm pressed into the steering wheel. There were bits of glass in his hair. The windshield had completely shattered.

I leaned over, clinging to the doorframe as I eased into the cab. "Jem?"

Another moan. I braced my back against the dash and touched his face, his chest, his arms. It turned my hands black.

Blood. All over my palms. All over his shirt.

"Pull him to you, Grace." Finn leaned across the barrier, already reaching for my twin. Something improbably bright flashed in his hand. A knife. He hooked it under the seat belt strap above Jem's head and pulled. The nylon gave way with a *pop*.

"Okay, okay." Finn was barely breathing. "Now unhook his seat belt and get your shoulder under his arm."

I gritted my teeth, wedged myself underneath Jem, and lifted. Lifted again. Jem moaned. His eyelids fluttered up. "Grace?"

Finn seized him by the shoulders and hauled him closer. I followed, pushing with everything I had, and my sneakers slipped.

"Grace!"

"I'mokayI'mokayI'mokay." I wrapped both arms around the railing and watched Finn lower Jem to the ground.

Beside me, the truck groaned, and Ander said my name. I twisted, still holding on and knowing I needed to climb in again. There were sirens in the distance, and Ander said my name.

I forced one arm to loosen…and then the other. I braced both hands on the truck frame and eased myself closer…closer…I pressed myself across the bench seat and I ignored how close the swamp water seemed, how the fabric under my legs was sodden.

Bloody.

"Grace." His face was smashed and his breathing hitched, but it was Ander. He touched his fingers to my cheek like he'd been waiting.

"I'm going to get you out."

Ander smiled like he knew it all along.

"Can you get his seat belt off?" Finn called. "Do you need the knife?"

I pressed my hands to Ander, his chest under my palm, his T-shirt twisted in my fingers. No seat belt. Relief made my head go dizzy until I realized I'd still have to crawl across him to get leverage. I swallowed.

"Hold on. Just hold on. One second." Was I talking to him

or to me? I eased over Ander's legs, stuffed myself into the space between him and the door. Ander slumped sideways, toward Finn, and I gave him a shove. Nothing. I shoved him again and something deep in the truck creaked.

Finn's eyes went wide. "Push him!"

I rammed my shoulder into Ander's rib cage, kicked both feet against the driver's side door. He moved an inch and then another. The truck shuddered. It tilted forward, and I slipped.

But Finn caught Ander's arm…and Ander started to lift. Finn pulled and I pushed until Ander's sneakers disappeared and Finn reappeared. There was blood on his shirt. For a horrible second, I thought he was wounded.

"Grace!" Finn plunged his hand down again. His fingers wrapped tight around my forearm. "C'mon!"

I scrambled toward him, and something tugged at my shin, slid to my ankle, *gripped*. It felt like a hand, and my heart crammed into my throat.

It was Ander's seat belt.

"Finn—" I clawed at it, trying to work space between the strap and my ankle. No good. Blood made my fingers slick, clumsy. The strap pulled tighter. "I'm stuck!"

"What?"

"Your knife! Pass me your knife!"

"I can't!"

I twisted around.

Finn's face had gone pale. His shoulders flexed tight under his T-shirt. "I can't pass it to you without letting go!"

"Then let me go! I can't get loose! I have to cut it!"

Finn growled, tugged me harder, and the seat belt cut across my shin. I yelped. "You can't just yank me out of here!"

Finn swore. "Hold on. Do *not* let go of that seat edge."

A short laugh escaped me. Like that was going to happen. I had a death grip on the upholstery. "No worries."

Through the gaping windshield, I could smell the swamp below me, smell the boys' blood in the cab.

*I'm okay. I'm okay. I can do this.* Then the truck groaned again.

And shuddered another few inches lower.

My first two fingers slipped.

And then two more.

"Finn!" I thrashed, trying to kick myself higher, trying to get a better grip, any grip. "Finn, I'm—"

"No! Grace!"

Finn couldn't catch me as I fell.

# chapter forty

*I* wake up screaming in a voice that's mine, grabbing for a boy who's no longer there. I blink, blink again. My vision won't clear, and I shake my head. A mistake. My stomach heaves into my mouth, and I gag.

"Grace?"

I open my eyes, and his face slides slowly into focus. It's his dark hair...his faded gold eyes. It's him. It's *Finn* and I'm...

*Holding on to something that doesn't exist.* I shift, and everything *hurts*. No, I *was* holding on, and now I'm here.

Where's here?

Behind Finn, there are white walls and white tile and white...

I'm in a hospital room.

I don't understand. Everything I thought was real—it felt *so real*.

*I have to choose.*

I did choose. I take a shaky breath. I *did* choose, and now I'm here. This isn't a Fall, I'm *back*.

"Finn?"

There's beeping to the left and right. My cell? I turn, wincing as my back lights up with white-hot pain. Not my cell. It's…machines. Green lines bounce up and down on a screen by my head.

"Holy shit," Finn whispers. I glance back. His eyes widen until I can see the bloodshot red all around them. "Grace!"

I try to smile, and it *hurts*.

"Oh my God. Oh my God, you're awake. I knew you would wake up. I *knew* it!"

I stir, lightning bolts of pain forking down my legs, making me hiss.

"Easy." He's already scrambling up from his chair. "Easy. You have to stay put. I have to get help so just…stay put, okay?" He runs across the room in three long strides and hangs into the hallway, eyes still on me.

Always on me.

"Nurse! *Someone!*"

*The girl I lost was you*, he'd said. I try to sit up again, and black spots shimmer across my vision.

"No," Finn says, and I center. "You have to stay down, okay? You can't move. I'm not going anywhere."

*I kept hoping you'd come back*, he'd said.

There are footsteps in the hallway, and then the door swings open. A woman in pale blue scrubs rushes past Finn, waving him to the side.

"Grace?" She sounds like she's used my name a thousand times, like it belongs to her. "Welcome back, honey."

"Jem?" I lick my cracked lips and try to push onto my elbows. Pain starbursts behind my ribs. "Ander?"

"Don't talk, honey," the woman says, her hands moving lightly over me.

Tears scald my eyes, my cheeks. The woman murmurs encouragement, touching my arms and repeating my name.

"Is it the pain, sweetheart?"

It's everything. It's Jem and Ander and the Falls and Finn.

Two more nurses rush to my side. They check my vitals, my tubes—so many tubes. I'm more machine than girl. I look at Finn, and he looks at me like he's working through a mystery.

Like I am *his* mystery.

Then come more voices. I hear my mom before I see her. She's first through the door, nearly crumpling when our eyes meet. "GraceGraceGraceGraceGrace—"

I understand exactly what she means.

"We were so scared. I thought we lost you. Oh, honey. Oh, Grace." Her words lift like prayers.

"Jem?" I manage again. There's a roaring in my ears now. "Ander?"

The woman in pale blue moves between us. "I need you to give us some space. Your daughter is still in very bad shape. We *cannot* upset her."

Everyone starts talking at once, almost burying the hard *click* from across the room. The nurses and my parents don't notice, but I do. I look to my left, my right. Finn? He's gone. He *left*. That was the door shutting. That was him taking off.

The nurse—doctor?—in pale blue brushes her fingertips across my cheek. "Focus on me, sweetheart. It's going to be okay."

I nod like I believe her.

They check my vitals, my bandages. I stare at the white walls, smelling the roses someone put on the table next to my bed. Roses.

The roses in Ander's woods are here, on my bedside table.

The tattoo? A gouge in my skin the size of my fist. I smashed into…something in the water. We'll never know what.

The beeping I kept hearing? The hospital's machines.

And Finn's voice? Finn was in every timeline because he was here.

As soon as the doctors and nurses leave, my parents return. Mom takes the seat next to my bed, scoots it as close it will go. "I'm so sorry we weren't here when you woke up. I'm so sorry. I had to get something to eat—your father insisted."

Behind her, my dad is blinking back tears.

I give him my own watery smile and squeeze Mom's forearms with both hands. "I'm glad he took care of you."

Then I squeeze a little harder, because what I'm about to ask is going to take everything I have, and they both go still like they know.

"Jem?" I manage, and her breath strangles. "Where's Jem?"

Dad chokes and turns away. Mom doesn't move, but she's no longer here. Her eyes are looking for the ends of the world. They can't form words, and now neither can I. Because I know.

Jem is dead, and someone's screaming, and it takes my very own forever before I realize it's me.

# chapter forty-one

*now...*

W as in a coma for five days. Was dragged half drowned from the swamp. Broken ribs. Broken wrist. So many contusions.

Lucky to be alive.

All those Falls. All those Graces. Every single one of them was leading me back here.

Jem is dead.

The words rip right through me. I'm falling and falling and I don't move. Can't move. There is no word for losing a twin, but there is pain. I can't breathe around it. I can't move through it. It's wedged into my chest, exploring each heartbeat and rib.

And the scariest part? This is just a promise of what's to come.

All along, I think I knew. That's why Jem was never there and then, once he was, he disappeared again.

"I was afraid he was gone." My voice sounds like me, and there is almost enough left of the old Grace to find that impossibly strange—no, just impossible. How could I know this and still be whole?

The answer? I can't.

"I'm sorry," Mom whispers, tears leaking down her cheeks and past her chin. She leans closer, and the bed shifts, lighting up my side. "I'm so sorry, sweetheart. I'm so sorry."

I force myself to breathe and breathe again.

Jem is *gone*.

Every heartbeat is a battering ram. I am imploding and somehow still sitting up. Impossible-er and impossible-er.

"And Ander?" I manage, tears dripping off my chin.

Mom goes pale. "He's still alive."

"Mr. Freeman? Mrs. Freeman?" Dr. Ramirez again. She stands in the doorway to my room, clipboard in one hand. "Could I have another word?"

My dad shakes his head and presses my mom back into her seat. "I'll go. You stay."

And before either of us can argue, he's in the hallway with Dr. Ramirez, and Mom's hands are fever-hot on my cheeks.

"I don't know what to do," I tell her, and it's the truest thing I've ever spoken. "How…how do we go on?"

"I don't know." Her thumb brushes my temple, and I feel something stiff against my hairline. Stitches? "Grace…I don't know what happens next, but I swore I would tell you this again so I would *know* you heard me: I missed you. Before you were even born, I missed you. And when you were finally here…I couldn't stop thinking about all the things we were going to do together. Only the things I like to do and the things you would like to do…" Mom trails off, leaving me to fit in all the things she cannot bring herself to say.

Like how I would rather read than bake.

Like how she would rather have us than a career.

Like how I would always want more than Boone—no, not more. I want something different. I am not what my mom planned. I am not even what I planned.

Now we're both crying.

"I'm sorry," I whisper, tears smearing everything. "I'm so sorry."

"Don't be." The words ride an uneven exhale. "Don't apologize for figuring out who you want to be. I forgot that when I made all those plans…I forgot you had your own destiny, too, and maybe we aren't headed for the same places and maybe that's okay." Her smile wobbles, wobbles…spreads wider than her face. "In fact, it's better than okay. I love you, honey. It takes so much courage to become who you are."

Now I'm smiling.

And crying.

Because she said that before. Just like when Finn was here trying to pull me back, she was here, too. She was calling me back and urging me on.

"Wherever you go," my mom whispers, "I will be there. Whoever you become, I will be with you."

Because she always was. Even when my mind couldn't grasp the horror and hid, their words, their love, reached me. Finn was right: time is not an accurate measurement for love. Time can't constrain love, either. It can reach you anywhere, everywhere. Even when the person is gone, their love is still there.

I hug my mom as hard as I can, until colors burst behind my eyes because I am made of more pain than body right now. "Wherever I am," I manage, "I will hear you."

*now...*

Something brushes my cheek…my jaw. It curves under my chin, and then I hear my name: "Grace?"

I jerk awake. I can't see—and then suddenly I can. Shaggy hair, sharp cheekbones, and sunken eyes.

Ander.

The light from the hallway edges him in orange. He tries to touch me again and falters. "Grace?" he whispers. "They told me you were awake."

"Yeah," I manage. "Yeah." Light and quick, my breath sounds like an animal run to ground.

*Like before. Like when I was chased.* Images of Fall 41's ending come to me, and I try to focus on Ander instead. Fists wrapped around his walker, he eases into the chair by my bed. It's late, and he's half in the shadows. It's Ander and it isn't Ander.

Then again, I'm me and I'm not me.

I don't want to talk. I want to pretend Jem is going to stroll in any second now. If we stay quiet enough, it will happen.

"I'm so sorry, Graceful. I can't…I can't…I don't…"

*I know*. And that's the horrible thing. *He misses Jem like I do*.

And I hate it. I *hate* it. The feeling is hot, immediate, and mine.

"When I woke up after surgery," he continues, "it all came back to me…the bridge…the drinking…our fight. I knew I had ruined everything, and yet you were the person I wanted to reach for first and…and look where I put you."

His eyes sweep down my body, and I can't help but follow. My body feels like someone else's. It's some other girl's now-pointed hip bones, some other girl's now-smashed-up ribs. Her feet are fish-belly cold.

"I fucked up," Ander whispers. "I beyond fucked up. There's no going back. This is hell."

"Yes," I manage, and it's the truest thing I have ever known. Here's the next: I have lost them both. The Ander I loved died way before the night on that bridge, and the Ander in front of me now will try to die every day after.

I cannot watch him do that. We are inches apart and can no longer find each other. For the first time ever, I'm somewhere Ander can't reach, and I don't want him to.

"Can you ever forgive me?" he asks.

The room goes sleek and long, and I can't separate the Ander who drove Jem's truck from *my* Ander. I can't stop seeing the boy who *needs* forgiveness because he's killed the best things about himself.

About both of us.

"I'm not me without you." Ander puts his hand on my bed, uncurls the palm toward me.

It would take all my courage to take it.

It will take even more for me to refuse.

"Grace, I will make this up to you if it takes the rest of my life."

"You…can't."

And he knows. I see it in his eyes. We wear the same agony, the same despair. No one will ever understand losing Jem like Ander will, but it isn't enough.

"I can't save you," I whisper. "You have to leave."

Ander stands, curls his hand back into his side. He shuffles away so quietly I could pretend he'd never been there.

I could *try* to pretend.

"Grace?" Moments—years?—later, my dad pushes through the door. Even with the fresh vase of roses, I can still smell machine oil on him. It capsizes me.

"Hey," I whisper, tears coating my lips.

He rushes to my side. "Is it the pain? What can I do?"

"Nothing." Something else that's truer than true. I stare up at my dad and realize there is *nothing* he can do to fix this. "I saw Ander."

Dad shudders and goes still, and I watch his expression ripple as I try to explain: "I look at Ander and…" I have to suck in a breath, then suck it deeper. "I look at Ander, and I see…me."

Dad sits on the edge of the bed and pulls the roses' heads off. One by one, they patter to the floor, and he crushes them under his boot.

"You both…lost him. You're both…grieving," Dad says slowly, and with each word it's as if I've been dropped from a greater and greater height. I stare at my dad, and it's his dark hair and his overgrown whiskers, but it isn't him. Not anymore.

*That's because none of us is.* "You see yourself in Ander, too."

"Maybe seeing yourself in others is how it's supposed to be. Maybe when you stop, you're finished." More rose heads join the first, and I can't tell if Dad believes a single word he's saying. "Boone eats people alive, sweetheart. I know it better than anyone."

I take his hand before he can finish destroying the roses, and we sit in silence until sunlight seeps up the wall.

...

$\mathcal{I}$ am discharged after a week of observation. I have physical therapist appointments and follow-up appointments and an armful of booklets on exercises and depression and loss. The nurse actually looks a little embarrassed to give them to me. I wonder if she knows how useless they'll be.

Mom picks me up because Dad is working, but he's supposed to meet us at home.

If we ever actually make it there.

Mom's driving so slowly I'm beginning to think we might not. I push the sun-faded black buttons on the Corolla's dash, turning the air-conditioning as cold and high as I can get it.

Eventually, Mom makes a right onto our road, hitting a pothole with enough force that I feel it in my collarbone wound. It took ten stitches. I'll always have a scar. When Dr. Ramirez told me, I wondered if it would resemble the tattoo I dreamed about, and then I realized I couldn't remember what it looked like anymore.

"Sorry. Sorry." Mom touches one hand to my thigh.

"'S okay." And it really is, because everything I am is suddenly blotted out, and all I can see is the Hales' mailbox rising crookedly out of the swaying yellowed grass.

"I wish you had never met him," Mom whispers as we roll past. "I can't believe he's…"

Alive.

I lean my head against the window. Sometimes people come into your life and change everything. You become someone you would never have been without them. They crack you open, split you apart, let light into places that have only seen darkness, but it *always* comes with a price: you cannot go back to who you were before.

Mom slows, maneuvering around the last pothole before turning onto our driveway. The air-conditioning suddenly smells like water and earth and home. "It's going to be hell walking around town and seeing the Hales," she says. "A very special kind of hell."

"For them, too."

She shakes her head. "Ander *chose*. Sooner or later, we all sit down to a banquet of consequences. This is his—and ours."

*We all have to pay for what we did.* Mom goes quiet, and I watch the trees rush past. Ander and Mom are right. Hell isn't an eternity of burning. It can be what we do to ourselves. We live in a life of our own making, for better or worse.

Mom slows as we wind up the driveway. Dad's truck is already there, parked next to the space where Jem's truck used to be.

I sit up, and for a single second I think I see Finn standing by the porch, waiting for me. He's not, of course. I haven't seen him since waking up, and I don't know what that means. Are we over? Is there enough between us to be over?

"Welcome home, honey," Mom says. She stares straight ahead, jaw tight like she's trying to keep it together. I know the feeling.

Welcome to our new normal—boxes that will need to be filled, his laundry that will need to be done, his fishing rods that will never be touched again. I have to go in there.

*How* am I going to go in there? "I love you," I tell Mom.

"I love you, too," she answers. We're using the words as lifelines, as lightning rods against the coming storm.

I put one hand on the door handle, and briefly, I'm in Jem's truck again. We're waiting at Farley's. We're going to school. Everything is layered together...and that's when I realize I can't change the past, but it's never too late to change the future.

It's never too late to be brave.

# chapter
# forty-three

*now...*

Two days later, when Mom falls asleep and the evening shadows are long and narrow across the floor, I pull on one of Jem's still-dirty shirts. It smells like him—like bonfires and gasoline. I take her car to Farley's, park under the water oak, and lean against the steering wheel for a few minutes. The air-conditioning is icy, and yet I'm still sweating. After a long moment, I hoist myself out of the car and shuffle toward the barn.

"Hello?" I linger by the doorway, listening to the birds cram themselves into the corners of their cages. "Finn?"

Nothing. No one's here.

I turn to leave and spot a flash of movement to my right—a shadow against the trees, liquid dark churning past the branches.

It's Finn.

I push away from the barn doors, heading straight for the woods, straight for him. These were the things I used to know:

It was always the three of us.

No matter what we looked like, we always found each other.

No matter how far Ander and I ran, Finn always followed.

And now I'm following him, stumbling along, half expecting to smell swamp and rain. Instead, I get pine and heat and wet earth. "Finn?"

His shadow wavers…stops.

He turns, and my heart swings like a pendant on a string. "Grace?"

I take a step closer, and then one more. The shadows separate, and Finn appears.

I see a boy barely past seventeen who once had Ander's and Jem's blood on his shirt.

He sees a girl barely past seventeen who once had Ander's and Jem's blood on her hands.

"You look like hell," he whispers.

I almost laugh. I'd dreamed saying that to him. We really are alike. "I feel worse. What are you doing?"

"Night hunt. Had to…" Finn wipes both hands against his jeans, shaking his head like explanations shouldn't matter. "How're you?"

"I want to burn the world down."

"Some days you'll be glad it's still here."

"When?"

"Let me know when you find out." Briefly, those faded gold eyes darken. "Everyone thinks grief is this thing you can get away from, and it isn't. One minute you're fine, then you'll hear a laugh like theirs and"—he shakes his head—"grief isn't a thing you live with. It's a thing that lives in you."

This is the part where I should agree—because I do, I *so* do—but I can't speak. Finn looks at me like he hears me anyway. Because he lost his mom. Because he sees loss in me.

He takes a shuddery breath. "You'll have to live around the hole he left in you."

"The hole they both left."

His face clouds. I know what Finn's thinking—that I'm

not over Ander, that I'll never be over Ander—and in some ways he's right. I'll never be over losing my best friend and my brother, but Finn thinks I'll never get past loving Ander, and it's not that kind of love.

The reminder makes me take a deep, deep breath. "Why didn't you come see me again? Why did you take off?"

"You have enough going on." Finn studies me for a long moment. Above us, the pinkening sky is turning sooty gray. "I mean, you have family stuff; Alton. You're still going…right?"

I nod. "I have to delay starting until my doctors release me, but they've already sent classwork so I can stay on track." The study guides were thicker than Mom's Bible, not only filled with material we *never* covered at Boone High, but stuff I didn't even know existed. "It's going to be hard. I'm scared."

"You can do it."

"I know." I pause, placing one hand against a rotting tree trunk and tasting the mint of my gum when I swallow. "You stayed with me, didn't you? At the hospital. You talked to me."

Finn's breath hitches. "Did you hear me?"

"Yes. Again and again."

"I guess you agreed with me about coming back, then?" His smile is a flash of white in the gathering dark. "You should know by now, I'm always right."

He's trying for funny and failing. Another thing I've learned over this summer about Finn: when he's dying on the inside, he's flippant on the outside. He pushes people away before they can push him.

Finn forks one hand through his hair, turning the long dark strands spiky. "I can't believe you actually heard me."

I shrug. One day I'll have to explain—try to explain— about how I heard him and what I thought was real. Right now, though, it can wait.

"Do you remember telling me that time wasn't an accurate

measurement for love?" I ask.

The corner of his mouth pulls up and lingers. "You told me to shut up."

I nod and limp another step toward him—one little step—and he leans toward me, like I am his sun.

"And you actually did shut up," I continue. "I remember being a little shocked."

"I'm very good at shocking you. It's a talent. What did I say again about time? I don't really remember the whole thing."

He's lying, and it makes me smile. "You just like hearing people say your words back to you."

Now he's smiling, too, and even though I can't really see them, I know his ears are turning red.

"You *said*," I begin, "that you can be with someone for a year and feel nothing, but you can be with someone for a week and feel everything. You said time is not an accurate measurement for love."

"That does sound like something I would say."

He cocks his head, and ever so briefly I see Finn as he is now and the Finn he was before the accident and the Finn he was in my dreams. They're all tied up in the same person. We are prisms, always showing what we are and what we were and what we might be.

"Are you in love with me, Freeman?" A single muscle ticks in his jaw. "Because it kinda sounds like you're in love with me."

"And that kinda sounds like something you want."

"More than anything." His voice is hoarse, barely above a whisper. "I want to see who you're going to be. I want…I want to see where this could go, Grace."

My fingers twitch. I offer him my hand. "Then let's find out."

# Bonus Content

*Keep reading for exclusive scenes
from Finn's and Ander's points of view!*

# Finn

*Y*ou see that dirt-stained farmhand over there? The one hauling hay bales in 100-degree heat? The one sweating so hard he should have cartoon stink waves above his head? Yeah, that one.

You can't tell that one day he'll be so successful, he'll never have to do work like this again, but I can. I *am* that guy.

I heave the last of the hay bales to the fence line and wipe a forearm across my dripping face. My grandparents think newspaper clippings of teenagers arrested for meth or church sermons about the evils of drink will keep me from dropping out of school, but they're wrong because working for Farley? Best motivation ever.

The old guy runs a hunting preserve about twenty minutes outside of Boone, catering almost exclusively to out-of-towners. Technically, "out-of-towner" is almost as much of a stretch as "catering." Boone isn't big enough to be considered a town—if you blink, you miss it—and Farley's too gruff to cater to anyone, but for some reason, the preserve still thrives.

Probably because rich guys like the two sitting on the truck tailgate pay a ton of money to come down here and shoot.

Or sit and wait to shoot, which is pretty much all they're doing right now.

Now that the hay bales are done, I concentrate on moving the hunting gear into the truck bed while Mr. Bates and Mr. Shaw fidget with their rifles. They've been ready to leave for ten minutes, and Farley's...I don't know. Wherever Farley goes.

"How much longer is he going to be?" Bates grinds through clenched teeth. He's tall and trim and always has one hand on his rifle butt like he's scared I'm going to take it. "He's late."

"Sorry, I'm sure Farley will be here soon."

"You local, son?"

I pause. For the first time, Bates is actually looking *at* me rather than the air around me. "Not really," I say at last. "My dad's on deployment. I'm staying with my grandparents."

Bates nods, sniffs once like I've stepped in something. "So I was almost right. It's your accent. Makes you sound local."

Bates and his knife-faced friend, Shaw, laugh like he's hilarious, and considering how much I want a tip at the end of the weekend, I should laugh, too. I pretend to check the equipment bags instead.

I've been stuck in Boone, Georgia, for two weeks, four days, and eleven—no, make that thirteen hours. If I have an accent, I picked it up from my dad, but if I stick around Boone much longer, I'll have an accent because this place has a way of seeping into you.

Across the sunburned field, an ancient Ford pickup truck floors it down Farley's drive, dust billowing out behind it. All three of us pause, watching, as the driver skids to a stop next to the barn's massive water oak.

"Is that Farley?" Bates asks me.

"No." I think it's Jem Freeman. He's probably here to pick up Ander, another guy who works the preserve with me.

"This is utterly unprofessional," Shaw says, switching his rifle to his other arm and jamming a finger in my direction. "It's *ridiculous* to keep us waiting in this kind of heat. Get us a drink."

I consider him for a beat because you know what else is ridiculous? Using that tone of voice to talk down to someone while you're covered in deer piss. It might mask your scent, but it's still a golden shower.

"Didn't you hear me?" Shaw snaps his fingers at me. "A drink. Now."

"'Course." I grit my teeth and walk around to the truck cab. Farley always keeps ice-filled coolers on the bench seat. They have everything from champagne to beer to soda. None of it is for staff, and I don't let myself look at my long-empty water bottle lying on the floorboards.

I grab two imported beers and hand them over. Neither man says thank you. Maybe that's something you pick up when you're rich. Shaw and Bates certainly seem to have everything else. They flew down in a private plane, showed up to shoot with silver-trimmed rifles, and even though it's ball *sweatingly* hot, both men are still in tall boots and leather vests.

Honestly, they look pretentious, but it's what's behind the pretentious that interests me. Shaw owns a *plane*, their rifles are close to thirteen thousand apiece, and while I don't know what brand the clothing is, it looks expensive. What kind of job must they have to afford this? What's that like?

I have no idea, but I seriously want to find out.

I toss the last gear bag into the back of the truck and wipe my face again. My hands smell like dirt.

*Could be worse, though*, I think, watching the two men sip their beer. *I could smell like you two.*

"Finally," Shaw says, tossing his beer bottle to the ground and shoving away from the truck. "It's about time."

I turn, spotting my boss hoofing it across the field. Or *trying* to hoof it across the field. Farley's knees aren't in the best shape, and whether that's due to age or accident, I've never been told. He has the weathered face and permanently bent body of most men around here. Boone has a way of breaking you.

"Take the cages in for me?" Farley asks when he finally reaches us.

I nod, and my boss limps away, apologizing to Bates and Shaw. It only seems to piss the two men off even more. Whatever. With any luck, they'll be out for hours, and I can finish my chores in peace.

I grab the two large quail cages Ander left to dry by the fence and damn near burn my fingertips off on the sunshine-heated metal. For the right price, you can hunt anything, any time, on Farley's property: deer, quail, ducks, squirrels... Supposedly he once brought in mountain lions for some New York guy to shoot.

I reposition the cages so they scald my hands slightly less, and then head for the barn. I'm almost through the doors when I hear someone talking. *Ander*, I think. *He's muttering to the damn quails again.*

"Do y'all ever wash this place out? I think this is how you catch bird flu."

*Not Ander.* I hesitate, the metal bars biting into my fingers. That's a girl's voice. Freaking great. Now I have to go in and make small talk or be stuck hovering out here like a stalker and melt.

I sigh and shove through the doors, no doubt ruining Ander's moment because he's inches from the girl and she's staring up at him like he's made of magic.

Ander stiffens, eyes flicking to me. "Hey, man," he says, and then smiles at the girl. "Grace, this is Finn. Farley just hired him. Finn, this is Grace."

"Nice to meet you," she says, and I pause. I can't help myself. So this is Grace, or more appropriately, this is The Grace. Ander talks about her all the time, and I can't figure out if she's his best friend or his girlfriend.

Not that I care.

According to Ander, Grace is smart, sarcastic, and a sure thing for valedictorian at the local high school.

"If she's that smart, why's she still here?" I'd asked Ander. We were cleaning the quail cages, and I was irritable, but it was an honest question.

Even so, Ander looked like I'd kicked him. "Because it's her home," he'd said at last, scrubbing the metal bars harder.

*Like that explains anything*, I'd thought. Thanks to the army, I've made fourteen different places "home." In fact, anywhere can be "home," so why not pick somewhere that doesn't suck?

"So why are you staying?" I'd asked him. "Farley says you're an artist or something?"

His expression had never changed, but he paused mid-scrubbing. "Because you can't make a living being an artist."

He'd sounded like he was reciting someone else's words.

Ander had gone on to tell me all about how, in addition to being scary smart and happy to be stuck in Boone, Grace was also the only person who could handle her pain-in-the-ass twin brother, Jem.

Smart, sarcastic, and capable? If it were true, it'd be sexy as hell, but looking at Grace now, I'm pretty sure Ander's oversold it. She holds herself tight, a little apart from me, even though she offers me her hand.

"Hey." I shake it once, and briefly, the skin between her eyes wrinkles.

"You were on the boat last week, right? You were with

Amanda and Callie?"

I nod. "Amanda's my cousin."

Ander messes with his work gloves, tugging at the wristbands. "He'll be a senior with us."

"That's great!" Grace's whole face brightens, and maybe it's because of the earlier comments about *my* accent, but I notice hers. Grace's vowels are liquid. They rub against me.

*She's pretty*, I think, and immediately I'm annoyed. Or more annoyed. At this point, I'm not even sure. Anyway, I get what he sees in her.

"It's a nice school," Grace continues. "I hope you like it."

*I can pretty much assure you I* won't, I think, smiling.

She falters, something unreadable behind her eyes. No, almost like she's trying to read *me*, and I damn sure don't need that.

Then Ander asks if he can have ten more minutes, and Grace is all his again, staring up at him like he's all kinds of amazing. To her, he probably is. I can't imagine meeting the love of my life in high school. Don't want to imagine meeting the love of my life in high school. It won't push you on. It'll hold you back.

Ander glances at me. "We're going down to the hollow for a swim. You want to come?"

And get fish piss in my eyes and ears? No thanks. "Not really my thing," I tell him. "I only went because Amanda asked."

"Trust me," Ander says, slinging hay bales onto the stack. More dust explodes into the air, and the birds flutter frantically in their cages. "Swimming is everyone's thing around here. It's the only way to cool down."

*You know what's another way of cooling down?* I think. *Air conditioning. Not that anyone in this godforsaken town has any.* I flex my hand once, twice. For some reason, I can still feel Grace's skin.

I snatch another glance at her, and it should be impossible, but the barn actually feels hotter. Her eyes cut to mine. Busted. I look away.

"Maybe next time," I say finally. "That big hunt's coming through, and Farley's riding my ass." Not exactly the truth but close enough. "I'll see y'all around."

Unless I can avoid it.

I go back to the heat and sunshine, and minutes later, I watch them head for Jem's truck. Ander's walking backward, facing Grace and grinning like a jackass.

See that guy standing in the shadows glad he doesn't have a girl like that tying him down? Yeah, that one. I'm so freaking glad it's me. Ander isn't interested in a world beyond Boone, and it's because of her. As long as she stays, he stays. She's everything he sees.

"Ander still here?" Farley shuffles to my side, and briefly, I consider asking him why Ander isn't babysitting Rich and Richer. Then I remind myself I don't actually care.

"Leaving now." I nod toward Jem's truck. Ander's dicking around on the passenger side, but Grace is talking to her brother. As she leans into the truck's open window, she trails one toe in the gravel, calf flexing.

Farley whistles low. "You look like you've finally seen something you want, boy. Never thought that would happen."

*No kidding.*

I shake the thought away. No. Grace doesn't affect me. She can't. I'm immune to Boone girls who look at guys like they're magical.

*Immune.*

Yeah, hold that thought.

# Finn

*I*'m sure you're thinking: *What the hell happened to him?* Last time we saw that future CEO, he was hauling hunting equipment for rich people and smelled like a dead goat, but he had dignity.

So what *did* happen? Honestly, I'd like to know, too, because right now, I'm looking for distraction and I can't find it. Stupid, isn't it? Amanda's party is in full swing, Tisha will be here any minute now, and even if Tisha never makes it, there are plenty of other girls I could mess around with.

Except any time I look at them, I think of her. It's like every girl is doused in Grace.

Someone switches the party's hip-hop music to techno, and the crowd cheers. Tonight the crowd has cheered everything. Maybe if I have enough beer, I'll cheer, too.

I turn for the kitchen and knock into someone. My brain briefly registers dark hair, darker eyes, and nervous energy before I realize it's Grace.

I nearly laugh. Is this some cosmic joke? Everywhere I go, I find her. I should keep moving, but I don't. She's holding a Solo cup like it's a lifeline, and it tugs something inside me.

"Hey, Grace." I grin like I don't care, and her eyes linger

on my face. She's upset. Something's happened.

*It's not your problem*, I remind myself.

"Hey," she whispers, lifting her drink and turning away. She threads through the party, taking a piece of me with her.

*Do not follow*, I tell myself. *Do not follow. Do not—* Shit. I follow. Grace weaves her way through the living room and out onto the porch, and for a couple of seconds, I find what dignity I have left and hesitate at the doors. She's not interested in me. I should take a hint.

But the way Grace is gulping that beer? I can't look away. I join her at the railing, and even though we don't say a word, I already know everything. Whatever's wrong involves Ander.

Why do girls like her fall for guys like that?

"Slow down, okay?" I say at last, watching her take a third swallow. In the distance, the cicadas whine. "Whatever happened…it'll blow over. You'll get back together."

"Why does everyone expect that?"

"Because you and Ander are like some predestined thing." Oops, I might have let a little honesty seep through on that one. It's true, though. Grace's love for Ander makes him bulletproof.

When I glance in Grace's direction, I know it hit home. Her teeth are clenched, and that just kills me.

*What happened to me?* Grace happened. She didn't take anything from me. She broke me. There's a difference, and I will never be the same.

"We aren't predestined," she says at last, playing with her cup. The beer swirls around and around in it. "We're done. Everyone thinks holding on makes you strong, but I think letting go makes you stronger, and I'm letting go of this."

My heart thumps. "Why now? What changed?"

"Everything." She finishes her beer in one final swallow, and when she looks at me, her dark eyes are huge and shining.

"What if you gave someone everything you are and it wasn't enough?"

Gut punch. I can't breathe. She wasn't enough for him? I need to say something, and I have *nothing*. Every word I know is suddenly too small, and yet I can't stop myself from saying, "What if you gave someone everything you are and it isn't what she wants?"

A humid wind stirs. Grace backs up, and I'm following because I always follow. When it comes to this girl, I can't seem to help it.

"Why are you doing this?" she whispers. "People like me are just a joke to you."

I stiffen. Can't really fault her observation. I hate Boone. I hate how the accent sticks to me, how I've picked up little mannerisms that will eventually give me away for the redneck I am—and yet without Boone, I wouldn't have met Grace.

And that's the really scary part because it could have easily *not* happened. We might not have met. We might not have talked. We might've passed each other by. We're all living in individual universes, layered on top of one another, and yet light-years away.

"You aren't," I manage at last. "I swear you would never be." I fork one hand through my hair then scrub my hand across my jaw. "When I met you...you were everything I didn't want—*shouldn't* want."

"Is that supposed to be a *compliment*?"

Oh God, I'm an idiot. I shake myself. "No—I—*no*, I'm trying to be honest. Grace, I never wanted to come to Boone, and then I met you and..." I stop.

*Tell her the truth.* The idea grabs my breath as the humid breeze picks up again, swirling around us with even more force. "If I hadn't come to Boone, I would never have met you, and I know I would've missed that—missed *you*. I would never have known your name or your face, but I would've known the absence of you, the gap that was left in me because you were never there."

I'm breathing and not breathing and we're so close, I can't help myself. As she stares at me, I brush my fingertip against her knuckles, feel her skin's heat. It's like discovering something no one has ever named.

"I think I know what you mean," she whispers at last, putting down the Solo cup.

Grabbing my T-shirt.

I exhale —*hard*— and lean closer.

"Finn?"

"Yeah?" My heartbeat is deafening as her other hand climbs my chest.

"I want…"

Then she kisses me, and I'm frozen. I've kissed dozens of girls. But this kiss? I can't move. I can't *think*. She feels— Oh my God, this is what the first jolt of espresso feels like, what the first rush of whiskey *tastes* like. She's warm, but I'm *burning*.

My hands go for her neck, her jaw, her cheeks. She kisses me like she needs something, but I kiss her like she's everything.

"I've wanted this," I whisper against her lips. She's snowfall soft. "I wanted you to want this…"

"I do want it."

I pull back. Grace's lips are swollen and her eyes are wide. She looks like she just woke up, and it knocks the air from my lungs.

"I want it so much it scares me," she says.

I cradle her face in both hands. "Me, too."

Then she drags me down to her again, and I'm lost. My fingers in her hair, my hands along her cheeks, my thumbs bracketing her mouth. I can't get enough.

I'll never get enough.

I push her against the wall, and she pulls me closer. My hips grind into her stomach and she digs her fingers into my shoulders.

"*Grace…*" Her name rides my groan, and she smiles. Inside, the music climbs and people laugh and someone gasps. I shouldn't be able to hear it, but I do.

So does Grace. She goes still. I look up.

Ander.

He's drunk. Swaying a little. *Furious.*

Is this the part where he fights for her? Where she takes him back? My hands tighten around Grace, but she doesn't notice. She's turning for him. She's *going* to him.

Or is she?

Grace falters, and in the distance, heat lightning splits the blackened sky. A storm's coming.

Then Ander's eyes meet mine, and I know it's already here.

# Ander

*I*'m not that thrilled to work on Jem's POS truck, but the alternative means staying home and listening to my mom cry, so here I am. Or, rather, here we all are. Jem's so close, he's almost sweating on me, and Finn's nearly as bad. He's holding metal clamps against the water hose like I asked, but his eyes are everywhere else.

"Glad you're good at this," Jem says when I finally finish. He leans closer to study my work. "No wonder they wanted you to come work down at the garage."

I shrug. "When you have crappy cars, you pick up a few things."

Jem laughs. "No doubt. You should take that job."

I shrug again. He's probably right, but I don't like working on cars. Yeah, I'm good at it—I've had to be—but it's not what I want. I've known that for years, too. Even as I crawled under my mom's car to duct-tape some hose or scrubbed battery terminals on my dad's work van, I always treated it as a reminder that this stuff is so not what I want.

But right now it feels like I might've been ignoring my destiny.

Finn and Jem push away from the truck as I swap to a

socket wrench and go back to work. Maybe being a mechanic wouldn't be so bad. After all, people born and raised in Boone, Georgia, don't grow up to be artists.

*But I wanted more*, I think, and as soon as I do, my eyes stray to Grace. I can't help it. Whether it's "more" or "here" or "end up," it always finishes with Grace.

She's under the trees, taking advantage of the shade. If I still painted, I'd paint her like this: notebook open on her lap, mouth tight with concentration, wavy dark hair turning to frizz in the humidity. Reminds me of thunderclouds.

For three or four seconds, I can't get enough of how the shadows coat her cheek, and then Finn flings himself down next to her.

*Like they do this all the time*, I think, the realization sliding down my spine.

"Supervising?" he asks her.

"Something like that." They're close enough to touch, and then she makes it worse by tilting her notebook toward him. The shadows shift, lacing her skin in darkness and light. I would need charcoal for that, not paint. It's a stupid observation, and yet my fingers still curl. "Did you finish that paper for Mr. Branson?"

"The one about how to improve social media?" Finn asks, grinning like a jackass. I try to focus on the truck again. Normally, it doesn't bother me that Grace is a genius and Finn is pretty damn close. Normally. I guess today isn't normal, or maybe it's just the fight I had with my mom this morning.

Or maybe it's Jem's compliment. Everything sets me off these days.

I miss a screw bolt, striking my hand against the chassis instead. I wince and swear under my breath.

"Dude," Jem says, peering into the engine's depths. "You're shaking like a damn tweaker. How much have you been drinking?"

Too much and not nearly enough. "Like you can talk."

"Whatever. At least I can pay attention."

I wipe blood from my thumb, watching Finn and Grace. They're farther apart now. It should make me relax, but my hands are shaking all over again. This time, it isn't the drink. It's her.

Tires squelch the gravel behind us, and I look up, spotting Callie and her older sister driving up in Callie's ancient green Jeep.

"You can run, but you can't hide," I mutter to Jem. He grins, keeps yanking at the exhaust hose, refusing to look at Callie or the POS Jeep. Making her work for his attention is part of their game.

"There!" Jem pushes away again and heads around the truck's front. He gives the old Ford a smack and leans across the bench seat, fumbling with the keys. The engine grinds and grinds and *finally* turns over. Black smoke erupts from the tailpipe, and Jem high-fives me. I grin. Feels good to finally win at something.

Callie and Tisha angle out of the Jeep, Callie making a beeline for Jem and Tisha wandering closer to Finn. I wipe my oil-stained hands on the bottom of my T-shirt as Callie practically tackles Jem.

"Hey, you." Callie leans into him for a kiss, playing with her braid.

Extra guests don't bother me, but I know they're going to stress Grace. I glance over, checking on her, and sure enough, she's gone spooked-rabbit still. Tisha's saying something to her—or more likely to Finn—and Grace is smiling her I'm-pretending smile. Her hands are clenched so tight, the knuckles have gone gray.

My chest twists, and then suddenly, I'm annoyed. What the hell? She can talk to Finn but not Tisha?

"You know, I've never actually heard your sister talk," Callie says to Jem.

*Oh, please*, I think. *Y'all have had classes together*.

"She's shy," Jem explains, and I roll my eyes, looking to see if Grace is rolling her eyes, too. She isn't. Finn's whispering to her like they're in their own little world again.

Still? My stomach churns like I've been kicked. Then he makes her laugh. He makes her *laugh*. When's the last time I did that? I suddenly can't remember.

I hurl my wrench into Jem's toolbox and slam the lid shut. Grace's eyes meet mine. Forget earlier. If I still painted, I'd paint her like *this*: sunlight in her hair, feet curved into sandals, T-shirt askew just enough to show the line of her collarbone, eyes on me again. She looks at me like she gets it, gets everything.

Only that's when I realize she isn't looking at me like she used to, and she's damn sure not looking at me the same way she looks at Finn.

"Success?" Grace asks, lifting her voice so I can hear her. Callie and Jem are at it again. He picks her up, and she screams.

"Why don't you try it out?" I ask Grace.

"No thanks."

I stiffen. "Then I'll try it out. Hop in."

She shakes her head, and I feel like the world just slid out from under me. It isn't just the blowing-me-off bit. It's the wary way she's studying me. Like I might bite. It turns the back of my neck icy.

I open the passenger door. "C'mon. I want to try the shift from second to third. You're the one who said you wanted to hang out more."

A seriously nasty dig, and when Grace stiffens, I know it hit hard. We both know that's not what she meant when she asked if we could hang out more.

It also wasn't something she wanted announced in front of everyone. I'm an asshole for doing it, but I'm also an asshole who can't seem to stop. I glare at her, and she glares back, and suddenly we're six and we're still seventeen and we're something else.

I'm not sure what that something else is, but I don't like it at all.

*Choose me*, I pray. *Choose me even though* I *wouldn't choose me.*

"Fine." Grace throws her homework down next to Finn and stands, brushing off her shorts. She comes to me, but my chest doesn't heat like it used to and she doesn't smile like she used to and I'm shaking and shaking and I can't separate what's withdrawal from what's us.

*I've lost her*, I think and then realize: no, I haven't.

She's already gone.

Grace slides into the truck and I slam the door after her—harder than I mean to, and it just pisses me off even more. I stalk around to my side and slam my door even harder.

"Ander—"

I shift into reverse and gun us backward. Truck's responding well. It should be a relief. Should be. When I glance through the windshield, I spot Finn standing up, watching us like we're in trouble.

Like *I'm* trouble, and for a second, I'm not next to Grace, I'm in my mom's kitchen and we're fighting again.

"She doesn't love you," Mom said, swaying. It wasn't even eight a.m., and she smelled of stale sweat and staler vodka. "Once she's off to that fancy school, she won't even remember you."

"We've been friends since we were little. I'd be a bit hard to forget." I remember being pleased at my response. Even plastered, she recognized the logic.

Something feral gleamed in her eyes. "Maybe so, but

people who love you don't *leave*." She paused, studying me like she was seeing me for the first time. "You really are my son, you know that? Neither of us do the leaving. We get left."

Next to me, Grace makes a small sound, and it brings me back. All I can see is Finn through that windshield, and all I can think of is how Alton Prep isn't the only thing that's taking Grace away. I pop the stick into first and angle the truck toward the empty stretch of road. Under the engine's rumble, I can still hear Mom's voice say, "People who love you don't *leave*."

My hands clench. It shouldn't have bothered me then, and it shouldn't bother me now. It's not like it's the first time she'd said it. Every family has little bits of personal wisdom. *People who love you don't leave* is my mother's. *Blood always tells* is my father's.

I shift hard into second, third. Grace thumps my arm. "What's your deal?"

"What are you talking about?" I shift again, the truck jerking to keep up. Hot wind billows through the truck cab. It feels good—*great*—and suddenly I need more. We can't go fast enough.

"Why are you driving like an ass? Slow down."

"I'm testing it." I downshift, and the engine revs—almost loud enough to erase my mom's laugh. I try to keep my voice light. "C'mon, I want to drag race next weekend. We need to know how it does off the line."

I shift again, and the truck leaps forward.

"Ander!"

I kept my foot on the gas, pushing pushing pushing until the trees on either side of the road turn hazy and the horizon seems like something we can almost touch.

Grace hits my arm again. "Let me out!"

*People who love you don't leave*. I gun it again. *Shut-*

*upshutupshutup!*

"Stop it!"

"Stop making this into a big deal!" Only as soon as I yell at her, I wonder if I'm yelling at Grace or myself.

"Let me out!" she screams and I jump, jerking the steering wheel. The truck slings right.

Toward the drainage ditch.

I stomp both feet on the brake and we skid, spinning around until we stop in a halo of dust. I'm shaking even harder, and when I reach for Grace, my hands fumble. "Grace—"

She's already half out the door, staggering onto the dirt road to catch her breath. I fling off my seat belt and follow, rounding the truck at a dead run.

Grace spins on me. "What was that about?"

She shoves me, and I catch her hands against my chest, holding her like I'm falling. "Sorry."

She rears backward, and I don't let go. Deep in the woods, the cicadas whine. "I'm sorry," I say.

"Let go."

"I'm *sorry*." I barely sound like myself. My voice has gone thick, pinched, and I realize far, far too late that Grace has gone utterly still beneath my grip. She looks at me like my mom looks at my dad. She's afraid.

"Let. Go."

I do, and for the longest moment of my life, we stare at each other, breathing hard. I can't believe I scared her. I used to *protect* her.

Used to?

Her eyes narrow. "I'm only going to ask you this once: What's *wrong*?"

I shake my head. To clear it? To refuse? I'm not even sure. For the first time ever, I'm looking at the one person who has always understood me, and I'm afraid to tell her.

Except…is that really what it is? Because looking at Grace now—her tight shoulders and wary eyes—I realize I might be my mother's son, but I'm also my father's.

Grace hooks a strand of hair behind her ear, hand trembling a little. "Is it about your dad?"

All the hair on my arms stands up. Yeah—and my mom, and how Mom's right. We get left, but we also hit first. The words swell up before I even realize they're coming. "Yeah. Yeah, and my mom and the rent payment that's due and you."

"Me?"

"You didn't think I'd notice? He stares at you *all the time*! What were you trying to do? Get me back for not spending enough time with you?"

"I'm not like that. You *know* I'm not like that. I've never done something mean to get back at you."

I shake my head. "You're always pulling the shy-girl card, but you're not shy with him. What gives?"

She gapes. "He's your friend!"

"So's Marcus, and I didn't see you chatting him up the other night!"

"It's not… We get along because we both know what it's like to be on the outside."

Blood thumps in my ears. "What are you *talking* about? You're always with me."

She glares at me, and I glare right back.

"I don't even know how to spend time with you anymore," I say. "You're always studying, and when you're not studying, you're in your head. You never want to go *anywhere*."

Her mouth opens…and closes. She knows I'm right. It should have some satisfaction to it, too, but it doesn't. The "right" just reinforces everything else—I'm right that she's leaving. I'm right that she's already gone.

I'm right that this is already done.

"I've always been shy," Grace says at last. "I've always studied, always wanted to make the best grades. You never minded."

I shrug. "It's gotten worse. It's like you only look at me when you have time, and you *never* have time. You're on the verge of *leaving*, and you don't care. Maybe I shouldn't, either. Think about it, Grace. What's the point?"

"You mean, what's the point in staying together?"

"Yeah, even if we stay together...what do we have?" I glance down the road. The air is thick with dust and humidity. "You're going to go off to save the world, and I'll be here. Face it, you leave Boone, you're not coming home again. It doesn't work like that."

*Hit first.* The words breathe up from somewhere deep inside me. *No,* leave *first.*

"Maybe we should break up," I say, staring down the road again. "Every time I look at you, all I see is what I'll never have—what *we'll* never have."

The first truth I'd told her all day. It should've left me weightless.

"That's not... It's not..."

"We're done, Grace. I'll drive you back," I say, turning for the truck because I can't look at her. A second or two later, she slides onto the bench seat next to me, saying nothing as I turn the key in the ignition.

"I'm sorry," I repeat.

She leans out her window, forearms braced against the frame. "I'm sorry, too."

Minutes later, we drive back into the others and the shade. Grace hops out, and I don't have the energy to follow.

"How'd it drive?" Jem appears at my window, grin overreaching his face. "It looked great!"

"Good. It was good." But he doesn't hear me because he's

already chasing after his sister. Grace grabs her stuff in quick bursts and jerks. Everything in me screams to run after her, but everything in me also chased her away.

*Blood always tells*. And maybe it does. Maybe *this* is my family's prophecy.

My stomach heaves like I might be sick, and I shove myself out of the driver's seat, turning my face to a dazzle of afternoon sunshine so bright it turns the darkness behind my eyelids into a rosy Monet pink.

"What the hell?" Jem asks, returning to my side and scrubbing at the lipstick on his throat. "You two fight?"

I shrug.

"Don't worry about it. She'll come around. She's just under a lot of pressure. You know how she feels about you. Can't make it without you."

I shrug again, not trusting myself to say a word. Jem thinks Grace looks at me like I can save her, but he's wrong. When Grace looks at me, I know she's the only one who could have saved *me*.

I never should have let myself think she would.

# Acknowledgments

No one ever gets a book to publication without loads of help, and I'm crazy lucky that the best of the best always help me.

First off, thank you to my editor, Heather Howland, who saw what *Never Apart* was, but more importantly what it could be and helped me get there.

Thank you to Sarah Davies for everything and always.

Inexpressible thanks to Natalie Richards for reading…and re-reading…and re-reading *Never*. It amazes me you never lost your enthusiasm for the book (and me) even though you had to critique it 246,271,342 times. Love you beyond words. I am so *lucky* to have you.

Equally inexpressible thanks to Megan Miranda who still takes my calls even though I inevitably ask her the most random plot questions ever. I will forever remember us figuring out what the Falls really were—and then how we laughed hysterically because we enjoy being mean to characters.

There will never be enough thank yous for my husband, Boy Genius, and my parents. I literally could not do this without your help.

And, last but not least, a huge thank you to all the bloggers, readers, and librarians who have been so passionate about the Find Me and Munchem Academy series. I so hope you enjoy *Never Apart*.

# Grab the Entangled Teen releases readers are talking about!

## 27 Hours
### by Tristina Wright

Rumor Mora fears two things: hellhounds too strong for him to kill, and failure. Jude Welton has two dreams: for humans to stop killing monsters, and for his strange abilities to vanish.

But in no reality should a boy raised to love monsters fall for a boy raised to kill them.

During one twenty-seven-hour night, if they can't stop the war between the colonies and the monsters from becoming a war of extinction, the things they wish for will never come true, and the things they fear will be all that's left.

## Hide From Me
### by Mary Lindsey

*We all hold a beast inside. The only difference is what form it takes when freed.*

Something's not right about Rain Ryland's new hometown. On the surface, it's a friendly, tight-knit community, but something deadly lurks underneath the small-town charm. Everyone he meets is hiding something—especially Friederike Burkhart, the hottest girl he's ever laid eyes on. Rain's determined to find out her secret, even if it kills him...and it just might.

## entangled teen

an imprint of Entangled Publishing LLC